Between the Lines

ALSO BY JODI PICOULT

Lone Wolf

Sing You Home

House Rules

Handle with Care

Change of Heart

Nineteen Minutes

The Tenth Circle

Vanishing Acts

My Sister's Keeper

Second Glance

Perfect Match

Salem Falls

Plain Truth

Keeping Faith

The Pact

Mercy

Picture Perfect

Harvesting the Heart

Songs of the Humpback Whale

AND FOR THE STAGE

Over the Moon: An Original Musical for Teens

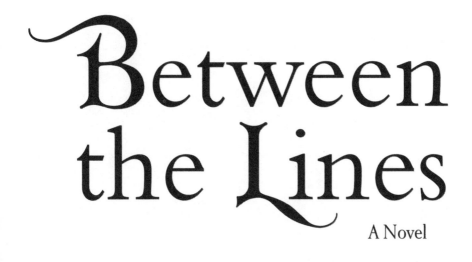

Between the Lines

A Novel

JODI PIC&ULT
SAMANTHA VAN LEER

ILLUSTRATIONS BY YVONNE GILBERT & SCOTT M. FISCHER

Simon Pulse/Emily Bestler Books/Atria

NEW YORK   LONDON   TORONTO   SYDNEY   NEW DELHI

Divisions of Simon & Schuster, Inc.

1230 Avenue of the Americas, New York, NY 10020

First Simon Pulse/Emily Bestler Books/Atria Books hardcover edition June 2012

Copyright © 2012 by Jodi Picoult and Samantha van Leer

Full-color interior illustrations copyright © 2012 by Yvonne Gilbert

Black-and-white interior illustrations copyright © 2012 by Scott M. Fischer

All rights reserved, including the right to reproduce this book or portions thereof in any form whatsoever. For information address the Atria Books Subsidiary Rights Department, 1230 Avenue of the Americas, New York, NY 10020

SIMON PULSE and colophon are registered trademarks of Simon & Schuster, Inc.

EMILY BESTLER BOOKS/ATRIA BOOKS and colophon are trademarks of Simon & Schuster, Inc.

For information about special discounts for bulk purchases, please contact Simon & Schuster Special Sales at 1-866-506-1949 or business@simonandschuster.com.

The Simon & Schuster Speakers Bureau can bring authors to your live event. For more information or to book an event contact the Simon & Schuster Speakers Bureau at 1-866-248-3049 or visit our website at www.simonspeakers.com.

Designed by Jessica Handelman and Mike Rosamilia

The text of this book was set in Adobe Caslon Pro.

Manufactured in the United States of America

2 4 6 8 10 9 7 5 3 1

Library of Congress Cataloging-in-Publication Data

Picoult, Jodi, 1966-

Between the lines / by Jodi Picoult & Samantha van Leer.—1st Simon Pulse hardcover ed.

p. cm.   Summary: Told in their separate voices, sixteen-year-old Prince Oliver, who wants to break free of his fairy-tale existence, and fifteen-year-old Delilah, a loner obsessed with Prince Oliver and the book in which he exists, work together to seek his freedom.

[1. Books and reading—Fiction. 2. Fairy tales—Fiction. 3. Princes—Fiction. 4. High schools—Fiction. 5. Schools—Fiction. 6. Mothers and daughters—Fiction.]

I. Leer, Samantha van. II. Title.

PZ7.P5557Bet 2012   [Fic]—dc23   2011039108

ISBN 978-1-4516-3575-1   ISBN 978-1-4516-3582-9 (eBook)

To Ema,
Who will always be
the hero in my story.
Love,
Sammy

To Tim,
Because sometimes
fairy tales *do* come true.
Love,
Jodi

A Note from Jodi Picoult

I was on a book tour in Los Angeles when my telephone rang. "Mom," my daughter, Sammy, said. "I think I have a pretty good idea for a book."

This was not extraordinary. Of my three children, Sammy has always been the one with an imagination that is unparalleled. When other kids were playing "stuffed animals," Sammy would scatter her toys around the house and create elaborate scenarios— this teddy bear is wounded and stuck on top of Mt. Everest and needs a rescue dog to climb to the top and save him. In second grade, her teacher called me to ask if I'd type up Sammy's short story. Apparently, it was forty pages long. He sent it home with my daughter, and I fully expected a rambling stream of words— instead, I wound up reading a very cohesive story about a duck and a fish that meet on a pond and become best friends. The duck invites the fish to dinner and the fish says he'd love to come. But then the fish has second thoughts: *What if I am dinner?*

That, ladies and gentlemen, is called CONFLICT, and it's the one thing you can't teach. You are either born a storyteller or not, and my daughter—at age seven—seemed to have an intrinsic sense of how to craft literary tension. Sammy's creativity continued to blossom as she grew up. Her nightmares are so vivid they'd give Stephen King a run for his money. As a teenager, she has written poetry that made me hunt down my own poetry journals from way back when—only to realize she is a much better writer than I ever was at that age.

So . . . when Sammy told me she had an interesting idea for a YA book, I listened carefully.

And you know what? She was right.

What if the characters in a book had lives of their own after the cover was closed? What if the act of reading was just these characters performing a play, over and over . . . but those characters still had dreams, hopes, wishes, and aspirations beyond the roles they acted out on a daily basis for the reader? And what if one of those characters desperately wanted to get out of his book?

Better yet, what if one of his readers fell in love with him and decided to help?

"Mom," Sammy said as I languished in Los Angeles traffic. "What if we wrote the book together?"

"Okay," I told her, "but that means *we're* writing it. Not me."

What ensued were two years of weekends, school vacations, and evenings spent side by side at my computer, diligently crafting a story together. I think Sammy was surprised by how much hard work it is to sit and imagine for hours at a time; for my part, I learned that if you think it's hard to get your daughter to clean her room, it's even harder to get her to stay focused on finishing a chapter when it's nice outside. We took turns typing, and literally spoke every sentence out loud. I would say one line, then Sammy would jump in with the next. The coolest moments were when we tripped over each other's sentences and discovered we were thinking the same thing—it was sort of like we were having the same dream, so that in the act of writing, we were telepathic.

Sometimes when I'm reading a great book, I think, "Wow, I wish I'd been the one to think up that story line." It has been an honor to have that same reaction when the story line was conceived by my own daughter. When Sammy first called me with her idea, I thought it was a great one. I hope, as you read *Between the Lines*, you think so too.

THE BEGINNING

nce upon a time in a land far, far away there lived a brave king and a beautiful queen, who were so much in love that wherever they went, people stopped what they were doing just to watch them pass. Peasant wives who were fighting with their husbands suddenly forgot the reason for the argument; little boys who had been putting spiders in the braids of little girls tried to steal a kiss instead; artists wept because nothing they could create on canvas came close to approximating the purity of the love between King Maurice and Queen Maureen. On the day they learned that they were going to have a child, it is said that a rainbow brighter and grander than anything ever seen before arched across the kingdom, as if the sky itself was waving a banner of joy.

But not everyone was happy for the king and queen. In a cave at the far edge of the kingdom lived a man who had sworn off love. When you have been burned by fire once, you don't leap into the flames again. Once upon a time, Rapscullio had expected to be living his own fairy tale, with his own happy ending, with a girl who had looked past his scarred face and gnarled limbs and had shown kindness to him when the rest of the world didn't. In his mind, he replayed the day he had been shoved roughly into the mud by schoolmates—only to find the most slender white hand reaching out to help him up. How he had grabbed on to her, this angel, imagining her as his lifeline! He'd spent days composing poetry in her honor and painting portraits that never did her beauty justice, waiting for just the right moment to confess his love—only to find her in the arms of a man he could never be: someone tall, strong, and destined for greatness. Rapscullio had then grown darker and more twisted by his own hate every day. His portraits of his beloved had given way to intricate plans for revenge against the man who had single-handedly ruined his life: King Maurice.

One night, a roar rose from outside the gates of the kingdom, unlike any other sound heard before. The ground shook and a streak of fire shot through the sky, burning the thatched roofs of the village. King Maurice and Queen Maureen ran out of the castle to see a monstrous black beast with scaled wings the size of a ship's sails, its eyes as red as embers. It stormed through the night sky, hissing sulfurous breath and spitting flames. Rapscullio had painted a dragon onto a magical canvas, and the demon had come to life.

The king looked at the panicked faces of his subjects and turned to his wife, but she had fallen to her knees in pain. "The baby," she whispered. "It's coming."

Torn between love and duty, the king knew what he had to do. He kissed his beloved wife where she lay in bed with her maids attending her, and promised to be back in time to meet his son. Then, with a hundred knights armored in glinting silver, he raised his sword high and rode out across the castle drawbridge on a wave of bravery and passion.

But it is no easy feat to best a dragon. As he watched his loyal soldiers being torn from their mounts and flung to their deaths by the fiery beast, King Maurice knew that he had to take matters into his own hands. He grabbed the sword of a fallen knight in his left hand and, holding his own sword in his right, stepped forward to challenge the dragon.

As the night grew deeper, and the battle raged outside the castle walls, the queen struggled to bring her son into the world. As was the tradition for royal babies, the kingdom's fairies arrived bearing gifts just as the newborn was delivered. They hovered, incandescent, above the queen, who was out of her mind with pain and worry for her husband.

The first fairy sent a spray of light over the bed, so bright that the queen had to turn away. "I give this child wisdom," the fairy said.

The second fairy sprinkled a flash of heat that surrounded the queen where she lay. "I give this child loyalty," she promised.

The third fairy had been planning to gift the royal child with courage, because every royal child needs a healthy dose of bravery. But before she could offer her gift, Queen Maureen suddenly sat up in bed, her eyes wide with a vision of her husband on the battlefield, in the fierce clutches of the dragon. "Please," she cried. "Save him!"

The fairies looked at each other, confused. The baby lay on the mattress, silent and still. They had attended plenty of births where the baby never drew its first breath. The third fairy tossed aside the courage she had been planning to give the child. "I give him life," she said, the word swirling yellow from her lips into her palm. With a kiss, she blew it into the mouth of the newborn.

It was said in the kingdom that at the very moment Prince Oliver cried for the first time, his father, King Maurice, cried out for the last.

It's not easy to grow up without a father. At age sixteen, Prince Oliver had never really been given the chance to just be a kid. Instead of playing tag, he had to learn seventeen languages. Instead of reading bedtime stories, he had to memorize the laws of the kingdom. He loved his mother, but it seemed to Oliver that no matter who he was, he would never be the person she wanted him to be. Sometimes he would hear her in her chambers, talking to someone, and when he entered there would be nobody with her. When she looked at his black hair and blue eyes, and remarked on how tall he was getting and how much he resembled his father, she always seemed to be on the verge of tears. As far as he could see, there was one critical difference between himself and his heroic late father: courage. Oliver was smart and loyal, but he was a complete disappointment when it came to bravery. In an effort to make his mother happy, Oliver overcompensated, spending his teenage years trying to do everything else right. On Mondays, he held court so that the peasants could bring him their disputes. He conceived of a way to rotate crops in the kingdom so that the storerooms were always full, even in the harshest of winters. He worked with Orville, the kingdom wizard, to create heat-resistant armor just in case there was ever another dragon attack (although he nearly passed out with anxiety when he had to test the armor by walking through a bonfire). He was sixteen, fully old enough to take over the throne, yet neither his mother nor his subjects were in any hurry to make that happen. And how could he blame them? Kings protected their countries. And Oliver was in absolutely no rush to go into battle.

He knew why, of course. His own father had died wielding a sword; Oliver preferred to stay alive, and swords didn't figure into that plan. It would have all been different if his dad had been there to teach him *how* to fight. But his mother wouldn't even let him pick up a kitchen knife. Oliver's only recollection of mock violence was at age ten with a friend named Figgins, the son of the royal baker, who would pretend to fight dragons and pirates with him in the courtyard, but one day Figgins vanished. (Oliver, in fact, had always wondered if his mother might have been behind this disappearance, in an effort to keep him from even *playing* at battle.) The only friend Oliver had ever had after that, really, was a stray dog that appeared the very afternoon Figgins disappeared. And although Frump the hound was a fine pal, he couldn't help Oliver practice his fencing skills. Thus Oliver grew up nursing a colossal secret: he was thrilled that he hadn't ridden off into battle or jousted in a tournament, or even punched someone during an argument . . . because deep down, he was terrified.

This secret, however, could last only as long as peace reigned. The fact that the dragon that had killed his father had slunk over the mountains and lain dormant for sixteen years didn't mean he wasn't planning a return visit. And when that happened, all the law Oliver had memorized and the languages he spoke wouldn't do any good without the sharp blade of a sword to back them up.

One day, as dispute court was winding to a close, Frump started barking. Oliver peered down the length of the Great Hall to see a lone figure, wrapped in a black cloak from head to toe. The man fell to his knees in front of Oliver's throne. "Your Highness," he begged, "save her."

"Save who?" Oliver asked. Frump, who had always been a good judge of character, bared his teeth and growled. "Down, boy," Oliver muttered, and he held out his hand to the man to help him to his feet. For a moment, the man hesitated, and then he grabbed on as if he were drowning. "Your grievance, good sir?" Oliver asked.

"My daughter and I live in a kingdom far from here. She was kidnapped," he whispered. "I need someone who can rescue her."

This was very different from what Oliver normally heard—that a neighbor had stolen another's chicken, or that the vegetables in the south corner of the kingdom weren't growing as fast as the ones in the north. Oliver had a flash of a vision—himself riding out in armor to save a damsel in distress—and immediately felt like he was going to lose his lunch. This poor man couldn't have known that of all the princes in the world, he'd picked the biggest coward. "Surely there's another prince who's better suited to this," Oliver said. "After all, I'm sort of a novice."

"The first prince I asked was too busy with a civil war in his kingdom. The second prince was leaving on a journey to meet his bride. You are the only one who was even willing to hear me out."

Oliver's mind was racing. It was bad enough that *he* knew he was timid, but what if news of his cowardice spread beyond the kingdom? What if this man went back to his village and told everyone that Prince Oliver could barely fight a cold . . . much less an enemy?

The man mistook Oliver's silence for hesitation and pulled a small oval portrait out of his cloak. "This is Seraphima," he said.

Oliver had never seen a girl so lovely. Her hair was so pale it shimmered like silver; her eyes were the violet of royal robes. Her skin glowed like moonlight, colored only by the faintest blush on her cheeks and lips.

Oliver and Seraphima. Seraphima and Oliver. It sort of had a nice ring to it.

"I'll find her," Oliver promised.

Frump looked up at him and whined.

"I'll worry about it later," Oliver murmured to him.

The man fell backward with gratitude, and for just the briefest of moments, his cloak opened enough for Oliver to see a twisted, scarred face, and for Frump to start barking again. As the girl's father backed out of the hall, Oliver sank back down in his throne, his head in his hands, wondering what on earth he'd just agreed to do.

"Absolutely not," said Queen Maureen. "Oliver, it's a dangerous world out there."

"There's a dangerous world in here too," Oliver pointed out. "I could fall down the castle stairs. I could get food poisoning from tonight's dinner."

The queen's eyes filled with tears. "This isn't funny, Oliver. You could die."

"I'm not Father."

The minute Oliver said it, he regretted it. His mother bent her head and wiped her eyes. "I've done everything I can do to keep you safe," she murmured. "And you're willing to throw that away for a girl you don't even know?"

"What if I'm *supposed* to know her?" Oliver said. "What if I fall in love with her the way you fell in love with my father? Isn't it worth taking a risk for love?"

The queen lifted her face and gazed at her son. "There's something I need to tell you," she said.

For the next hour, Oliver sat transfixed as his mother told him about a boy named Rapscullio and the evil man he'd become; about a dragon and three fairies; about the gifts that had been bestowed upon him at his birth, and the one gift that wasn't. "For years I've worried that Rapscullio would return one day," she confessed. "That he'd take away from me the last bit of proof I have of your father's love."

"Proof?"

"Yes, proof, Oliver," the queen explained. *You.*

Oliver shook his head. "This has nothing to do with Rapscullio. Just a girl named Seraphima."

Queen Maureen reached for her son's hand. "Promise me you won't fight. Anyone or anything."

"Even if I wanted to, I probably wouldn't know how." He shook his head, smiling. "I haven't exactly worked out a plan for success."

"Oliver, you were blessed with many other talents. If anyone can succeed, it's going to be you." His mother stood up, reaching for a leather cord tied around her neck. "But just in case, you should have this with you."

From the bodice of her dress, she pulled out a tiny circular disk that hung on the end of the necklace and handed it to Oliver.

"It's a compass," he said.

Queen Maureen nodded. "It was your father's," she said. "And I was the one who gave it to him. It's been passed down in my family for many generations." She looked at her son. "Instead of pointing north, it points you home." She smiled, lost in her memories. "Your father used to call it his good-luck charm."

Oliver thought of his bold and daring father, riding off to fight a dragon with this looped around his neck. Yes, it had brought him home, but not alive. He swallowed, wondering how on earth he could rescue this girl without even a sword by his side. "I guess Father never got scared," he muttered.

"Your father used to say that being scared just meant you had something worth coming back to," Queen Maureen said. "And he used to tell me he was scared all the time."

Oliver kissed his mother's cheek and slipped the compass around his neck. As he walked out of the Great Hall, he resigned himself to the fact that his life was about to get very, very complicated.

when we're done, or else someone might assume that there is more to the story than what they know.

I can't remember when I first realized that life, as I knew it, wasn't real. That this role I performed over and over was just that—a role. And that in order for me to play it, there had to be another party involved—namely one of those large, round, flat faces that blurred the sky above us every time the story began. The relationships you see on the page aren't always as they seem. When we're not acting our parts, we're all just free to go about our business. It's quite complicated, really. I'm Prince Oliver, but I'm *not* Prince Oliver. When the book is closed, I can stop pretending that I'm interested in Seraphima or that I'm fighting a dragon, and instead I can hang out with Frump or taste the concoctions Queen Maureen likes to dream up in the kitchen or take a dip in the ocean with the pirates, who are actually quite nice fellows. In other words, we all have lives outside the lives that we play when a Reader opens the book. For everyone else here, that knowledge is enough. They're happy repeating the story endlessly, and staying trapped onstage even when the Readers are gone. But me, I've always wondered. It stands to reason that if I have a life outside of this story, so do the Readers whose faces float above us. And *they're* not trapped inside the book. So where exactly *are* they? And what do *they* do when the book is closed?

Once, a Reader—a very young one—knocked the book over and it fell open on a page that has no one but me written into it. For a full hour, I watched the Other-world go by. These giants stacked bricks made of wood, with letters written on their sides, creating monstrous buildings. They dug their hands into a deep table filled with the same sort of sand we have on Everafter Beach. They stood in front of easels, like the one Rapscullio likes to use when he paints, but these artists used a unique style—dipping their hands into the paint and smear-ing it across the paper in swirls of color. Finally, one of the Others, who looked to be as old as Queen Maureen, leaned forward and frowned. "Children! This is not how we treat books," she said, before shutting me out.

When I told the others what I had seen, they just shrugged. Queen Maureen suggested I see Orville about my strange dreams and ask for a sleeping potion. Frump, who is my best friend both inside the story and out, believed me. "What difference does it make, Oliver?" he asked. "Why waste time and energy thinking about a place or a person you'll never be?" Immediately I regret-ted bringing it up. Frump wasn't always a dog—he was written into the story as Figgins, my best buddy from childhood, who was transformed by Rapscullio into a common hound. Because it's only a flashback of text, the only time he's ever read he's seen as a dog — which is why he stays in that form even when we're offstage.

Frump captures my queen. "Checkmate," he says.

"Why do you always beat me?" I sigh.

"Why do you always let me?" Frump says, and he scratches behind his ear. "Stupid fleas."

When we're working, Frump doesn't speak — he just barks. He follows me around like, well, a faithful pup. You'd never guess, when he's acting, that in real life he's always bossing the rest of us around.

"I think I saw a tear at the top of page forty-seven," I say as casually as I can, although I've been thinking of nothing but getting back there to investigate since first spotting it. "Want to come check it out?"

"Honestly, Oliver. Not that again." Frump rolls his eyes. "You're like a one-trick pony."

"Did you call me?" Socks trots closer. He's my trusty steed, and again, a shining example of how what you see isn't always what's true. Although he snorts and stamps with the confidence of a stallion on the pages of our world, when the book is closed he's a nervous mess with the self-confidence of a gnat.

I smile at him, because if I don't, he's going to think I'm angry at him. He's *that* sensitive. "No, we didn't . . ."

"I distinctly heard the word *pony* . . ."

"It was just an expression," Frump says.

"Well, now that I'm here, tell me the truth," Socks says, turning in a half circle. "This saddle totally makes my butt look fat, doesn't it?"

"No," I say immediately, as Frump vigorously shakes his head.

"You're all muscle," Frump says. "In fact, I was going to ask if you'd been working out."

"You're just saying that to make me feel better." Socks sniffles. "I *knew* I shouldn't have had that last carrot at breakfast."

"You look great, Socks," I insist. "Honestly." But he tosses his mane and sulks back toward the other side of the beach.

Frump rolls onto his back. "If I have to listen to that stupid horse whine one more time—"

"That's exactly what I'm talking about," I interrupt. "What if you didn't have to? What if you could be anywhere—*anything*—you wanted to be?"

I have this dream. It's kind of silly, but I see myself walking down a street I've never seen before, in a village I can't identify. A girl hurries past me, her dark hair whipping behind her like a flag, and in her haste she crashes into me. When I reach out to help her up, I feel a spark ignite between us. Her eyes are the color of honey, and I cannot turn away from them. *Finally*, I say, and when I kiss her, she tastes of mint and winter and nothing like Seraphima—

"Yeah, right," Frump says, interrupting me. "How many career opportunities are there for a basset hound?"

"You're only a dog because you were written that way," I say. "What if you could change that?"

He laughs. "Change it. Change the story. Yeah, that's a good one, Ollie. While you're at it, why don't you turn the ocean into grape juice and make the mermaids fly?"

Maybe he's right, maybe it *is* just me. Everyone else in this book seems to be perfectly happy with the fact that they are part of a story; that they are enslaved into doing and saying the same things over and over, like in a play that gets performed for eternity. They probably think that the people in the Otherworld have the same sorts of lives we do. I guess I find it hard to believe that Readers get up at the same hour every morning and eat the same breakfast every day and go sit in the same chair for hours and have the same conversations with their parents and go to bed and wake up and do it all over again. I think more likely they lead the most incredible lives—and by incredible, I mean: with free will. I wonder all the time what that would be like: to feel the book opening yet *not* beg the queen to let me go on a quest. To avoid getting trapped by fairies and run ragged by a villain. To fall in love with a girl whose eyes are the color of honey. To see someone

I don't recognize, and whose name I don't know. I'm not fussy, really. I wouldn't mind being a butcher instead of a prince. Or swimming across the ocean to be hailed as a legendary athlete. Or picking a fight with someone who cuts in front of me. I wouldn't mind doing *anything* other than the same old things I have done for as long as I can remember. I guess I just have to believe there's more to the world than what's inside these pages. Or maybe it's just that I desperately *want* to believe that.

I glance around at the others. Between readings, our real personalities show. One of the trolls is working out a melody on a flute he has carved from a piece of bamboo. The fairies are doing crossword puzzles that Captain Crabbe creates for them, but they keep cheating by looking into the wizard's crystal ball. And Seraphima . . .

She blows me a kiss, and I force a smile.

She's pretty, I suppose, with her silver hair and eyes the color of violets in the meadow near the castle. But her shoe size is bigger than her IQ. For example, she honestly believes that just because I save her over and over again as part of my job, I must truly have feelings for her.

I'll be honest, it's not a hard day's work to kiss a beautiful girl repeatedly. But it all starts feeling same old, same old after a while. I certainly don't love Seraphima, but that little detail seems to have escaped her. Which makes me feel guilty every time I kiss her, because I know she wants more from me than I'm ever going to give her when the storybook's closed.

Beside me, Frump lets out a long, mournful howl. That's the second reason I feel so guilty kissing Seraphima. He's had a crush on her for as long as I can remember, and that makes it even worse. What must it be like, watching me pretend to fall in love with the girl he's crazy about, day after day? "I'm sorry, buddy," I say to him. "I wish she knew it was just for show."

"Not your fault," he replies tightly. "Just doing what you have to do."

As if he's conjured it, there is suddenly a blinding light, and our sky cracks open along a seam. "Places!" Frump cries, frantic. "Everyone! Into your positions!" He runs off to help the trolls dismantle the bridge, only so that they can rebuild it again.

I grab my tunic and my dagger. The fairies who were our chess pieces rise like sparks and write the words SEE YOU LATER in the air before me, a trail of light as they zoom into the woods. "Yes, and thanks again," I say politely, intent on hurrying to the castle for my first scene.

What would happen, I wonder, *if I was late? If I dawdled or stopped to smell the lilacs at the castle gate, so that I wasn't in place when the book was opened? Would it stay sealed shut? Or would the story start without me?*

Experimentally, I slow my pace, dragging my heels. But suddenly I feel a magnetic tug on the front of my tunic, propelling me through the pages. They rustle as I leap through them, my legs moving in double time while I stare down, amazed. I can hear Socks whinnying in his stall at the royal stables, and the splash of the mermaids as they dive back into the sea, and suddenly, I am standing where I am supposed to be, before the royal throne in the Great Hall, at dispute court. "It's about time," Frump mutters. At the last moment there is a brilliant slice of light that opens above us, and instead of looking away like we usually do, this time I glance up.

I can see the Reader's face—a little fuzzy at the edges, sort of how the sun looks from the ocean floor. And just like when one stares at the sun, I can't make myself turn away.

"Oliver!" Frump hisses. "Focus!"

So I turn away from those eyes, the exact color of honey; from that mouth, its lips parted just the tiniest bit, as if she might be about to speak my name. I turn away, and clear my throat, and for the hundred billionth time in my life, I speak my first line of the story.

Save who?

I did not write the lines I speak; they were given to me long before I remember. I mouth the words, but the actual sound is in the Reader's mind, not coming from my throat. Similarly, all the moves that we make as if we're performing a play somehow unravel across someone else's imagination. It is as if the action and sound on our tiny, remote stage are being broadcast in the thoughts of the Reader. I'm not sure that I ever really learned this information—it's just something I've known forever, the same way I know that when I look at the grass and associate it with a color, I know that color is green.

I let Rapscullio convince me that he is a nobleman from afar whose beloved daughter has been kidnapped— a speech I've heard so often that occasionally, I murmur the words along with him. In the story, of course, he has no daughter. He's just setting a trap for me. But I'm not supposed to know that yet, even though I've played this scene a thousand times. So while he is going on and on about the other princes who won't rescue Seraphima, I think about the girl who is reading us.

I've seen her before. She's different from our usual Readers—they're either motherly, like Queen Maureen, or young enough to be captivated by tales of princesses in peril. But this Reader looks—well, she looks to be about my age. It doesn't make any sense. Surely she knows—like I do—that fairy tales are just stories. That happy endings aren't real.

Frump waddles across the polished black-and-white

marble floor, his tail wagging vigorously as he skids to a halt beside me.

Suddenly I hear a voice—distant, through a tunnel, but clear enough: "Delilah, I told you *twice* already . . . we're going to be late!"

From time to time, I've heard Readers talking. They don't usually read out loud, but every now and then, a conversation occurs when a book is open. I've learned quite a lot from being a good listener. Like, for example, *Don't let the bedbugs bite* is apparently a common way to say good night, even in rooms that do not appear to be infested with insects. I've learned about things the Otherworld has that we don't: television (which is something parents do not like as much as books); Happy Meals (apparently not all meals bring joy. Just the ones that come in a paper bag with a small toy); and showers (something you take before bedtime that leaves you drenched).

"Just let me finish," the girl says.

"You've read that book a thousand times—you know how it ends. *Now* means *now*!"

I have heard this Reader speaking to the older woman before. From their conversations, I'm guessing it's her mother. She is always telling Delilah to put the book away and go outside. To take a walk and get some fresh air. To call a friend (though how many could be within earshot?) and go to a movie (whatever that is). Repeatedly, I wait for her to heed her mother's directions—but most of the time she finds an excuse to keep reading. Sometimes she does go outside, but opens the book and starts reading again. I cannot tell you how frustrating this is for me. Here I am, wasting away inside a book I wish I could escape, and all she wants to do is stay in the story.

If I could talk to this girl Delilah, I'd ask her why on earth she would ever trade a single second of the world she's in for the one in which I'm stuck.

But I've tried talking out loud to other Readers. Believe me, it was the very first thing I attempted when I started to actively dream about life in the Otherworld. If I could just get one of those people holding the book to notice me, maybe I'd have a chance at escaping. However, the people holding the book see me only when the story is playing, and when the story is playing, I am compelled to stick to the script. Even when I try to say something like "Please! Listen to me!" I wind up announcing, instead, "I'm on my way to rescue a princess!" like some sort of puppet. If I ever had reason to believe that a Reader could see me for who I really am—not who I play in the story—I'd do, well, anything. I'd scream at the top of my lungs. I'd run in circles. I'd light myself on fire. Anything, to keep her seeing me.

Can you imagine what it would be like to know that

your life was just going to be a series of days that were all the same, that were do-overs? As Prince Oliver, I may have been given the gift of life . . . but I have never been given the chance to *live*.

"Coming," Delilah says over her shoulder, and I exhale heavily, a breath I hadn't even realized I was holding. The thought of not having to go through the motions again—it's a gift, an absolute gift.

There is a dizzying whirl of gravity as the book starts to close, something we've all gotten used to. We grab on to details—candelabra and table legs and in some desperate cases, the hanging tail of a letter like *g* or *y*, until the pages are completely closed.

"Well," I say, letting go of the drapery I was clutching. "Guess we got off lucky this—"

Before I can finish, however, I find myself flying head over heels as the pages are riffled through, and our world reopens on the very last bit of the story. As if by magic, and Seraphima is glittering beside me in her shimmering gown. Frump has a wedding band tied to a silver ribbon around his neck. The trolls are holding the pillars of a bridal bower; the pixies have spun silken ribbons that wrap around them and blow in the sea breeze. The mermaids gather in the shallows of the ocean, watching us bitterly as we wed.

I glance down, and suddenly panic.

 The chessboard. It's still there. The pixie chess pieces are gone, certainly, but the squares I drew with a stick—the proof that there is life in this book when no one is reading it—are still carved onto the beach.

I don't know why the book hasn't reset itself. It never makes mistakes like this; every time we are flipped to a new page we will find ourselves ready, in costume, with any necessary set in place. Maybe, for all I know, this *has* happened before and I never noticed it. But it stands to reason that if I noticed, someone else might too.

Like a Reader.

Delilah.

Deep breaths, Oliver, I tell myself. "Frump," I hiss.

He growls, but I can understand him clearly: *Not now.*

Okay, Oliver, I tell myself. *This is not a disaster. People read a fairy tale for the happy ending, not to hunt for a faintly visible chessboard scratched into the sand on the final page.* Still, I try to pull Seraphima toward me in an attempt to hide the chessboard beneath the fabric of her billowing dress. Seraphima, however, misinterprets this to mean that I might actually want to get closer to her. She tilts up her chin and her eyes flutter closed, waiting for her kiss.

Everyone's waiting. The trolls, the fairies, the mermaids. The pirates with their anchor lines tightly wrapped around Pyro the dragon to keep him subdued.

The Reader is waiting too. And if I give her what she wants, she'll close the book and that will be that.

Oh, *fine*.

I lean forward and give Seraphima a kiss, winding my hands in her hair and pulling the length of her body along mine. I can feel her melt beneath my touch, leaning into me. She may not be my type, but there's no reason I shouldn't enjoy myself at work, after all.

"Delilah!"

As the girl leans closer, the sky darkens above us. "How strange," she murmurs.

Her finger comes down, pushing at the edges of our world, bending the scenery even as we stand in it. I draw in my breath, thinking she is going to trap me, but instead, she touches the very spot where the chessboard is etched onto the sand.

"That," she says, "was never here before."

Delilah

I'M WEIRD.

Everyone says so. I suppose it's because while other fifteen-year-olds are talking about the best lip gloss and which movie star is hotter, I would rather be curled up with a book. Seriously—have you *been* to a high school lately? Why would anyone sane want to interact with Cro-Magnon hockey players, or run the gauntlet of mean girls who lounge against the lockers like the fashion police, passing judgment on my faded high-top sneakers and thrift-store sweaters? No thanks; I'd much rather pretend I'm somewhere else, and any time I open the pages of a book, that happens.

My mom worries about me because I'm a loner. But that's not entirely true. My best friend, Jules, totally gets me. It's my mom's fault that she can't see past the safety pins Jules sticks through her ears and her pink Mohawk. The cool thing about hanging around with Jules, though, is that when I'm with her, nobody even looks twice at me.

Jules understands my fixation on books. She feels the same way about B-movie horror films. She knows every single line of dialogue in *The Blob*. She refers to the popular girls in our school as Pod People.

Jules and I are not popular. In fact, I am pretty much banned from ever being popular or, for that matter, within a hundred feet of anyone popular. Last year when we were playing softball in gym, I swung the bat and broke the left knee of Allie McAndrews, the head cheerleader. Allie had to stay off the top of the pyramid for six weeks and accepted her prom queen crown on crutches.

The worst part was I completely missed the ball. Anyone who didn't hate me before the Injury suddenly had a reason to ignore me or sneer at me or slam me against a locker when we passed in the halls. Except Jules, who moved here a week after it happened. When I told her why I was a social pariah, she laughed. "Too bad you didn't break them both," she said.

Jules and I have no secrets. I know that she is addicted to soap operas, and she knows that my mother is a cleaning lady. There's only one thing I haven't told Jules, and that's the fact that for the past week, the reason I've avoided her is that I'm embarrassed by my choice of reading material.

A fairy tale written for elementary school kids.

If you think it's social suicide to literally bring the head cheerleader to her knees, you should try reading a children's book in plain sight in a high school. If you read Dostoyevsky, you're weird but smart. If you read comic books, you're weird but hip. If you read a fairy tale, you're just a dork.

I discovered this story a month ago, when I was eating lunch quietly in the school library. There I sat, chewing on a peanut butter and Fluff sandwich, when I noticed that one book on the shelf was upside down and backwards, as if it had been jammed in. Figuring I could help Ms. Winx, the librarian, I went to fix it, and got an enormous electric shock to the tips of my fingers.

The book was tattered and the spine was shaky—I would have thought that by now it would have made its way to the annual sale, where you could buy old novels for a dime each. It was illustrated—clearly a fairy tale—but it was shelved with nonfiction books about World War I. And strangest of all, it didn't have a bar code to be checked out.

"Ms. Winx," I asked, "have you ever read this one?"

"Oh, a long time ago," she told me. "But it's actually quite special. The author hand-painted the pictures and had it bound."

"It must be worth a fortune!"

"Not so much," Ms. Winx said. "The writer was known for her murder mysteries. This was more of an experiment for her. A prototype that never evolved. In fact, she never wrote another book after this one. I was a big fan of her other novels, and couldn't pass this up when I found it at a rummage sale. So for a nickel, it became the property of the school."

I looked down at the cover—*Between the Lines,* by Jessamyn Jacobs.

I checked it out that first day, and while I was in Earth Science class, I hid the fairy tale inside my textbook and read it from cover to cover. It's about a prince, Oliver, who goes on a quest to rescue a princess, who's been taken hostage by the evil Rapscullio. The problem is that Oliver, unlike most fairy-tale princes, isn't a big fan of taking risks. His father died in battle, and as far as he's concerned, it's far better to be safe than sorry.

I think that's what made me keep reading. The very first thing you learn about Oliver is that it wasn't easy growing up without a dad. It was as if the words had been taken straight from my mouth. My father had not died in battle, but he'd left my mother when I was ten years old and found himself a new, improved family. She cried every night that year. I was a straight-A student—not because I loved school but because I didn't want to be one more person who disappointed my mother. We had to move to a small house and my mom had to work hard cleaning the homes of the girls who treated me like pond scum.

True confessions time: Oliver is cuter than any guy in my school. Granted, he is two-dimensional and illustrated. Don't judge me—go take a look at Wolverine in an X-Men comic and tell me he isn't hot. With his jet-black hair and pale eyes, it seems that Oliver is smiling up from the page directly at me. Clearly, any normal girl would take this as a sign that she needs to get out more. But me, I don't have too many places to get to.

Plus, he is smart. He conquers one obstacle after another—not with his sword but with his cleverness. For example, when he is held captive by a trio of creepy, boy-crazy mermaids, he promises to get them dates in return for a pack of supplies—flotsam and jetsam that had washed into the ocean after shipwrecks. He uses that junk—other people's garbage—to rescue himself from the snares of the fiery dragon that had killed his own father. He's not your typical prince, more like a square peg in a round hole, kind of like me. He's the sort of guy who wouldn't mind reading side by side on a date. And he knows how to kiss, unlike Leonard Uberhardt, who practically tried to swallow me whole behind the jungle gym in seventh grade.

That first week, I read the book so often that I memorized the words; I knew the layout of the pictures on the pages. I dreamed that I was being chased by Rapscullio or forced by Captain Crabbe to walk the plank. Each week, I'd bring the book back to the library, because that was school policy. I'd have to wait until it was returned to the shelf a day later, giving someone else a chance to read it. But what other ninth grader cares about fairy tales? The book was always waiting for me, so I could check it out again and reconfirm my position as Public Loser Number One.

My mother worried. Why was a girl like me, who could easily read thousand-page adult novels, obsessed with a children's book?

I knew the answer to that, not that I was about to admit it to anyone.

Prince Oliver understood me better than anyone in the world.

True, I'd never met him. And true, he was a fictional character. But he also was what people needed him to be: a dashing hero, an articulate peacemaker, a cunning escape artist. Then again, Prince Oliver had never existed anywhere but on a page, and in some random author's brain. He didn't know what it was like to be stuffed into a locker by the cheerleading squad and left there until some janitor heard me yelling.

Today, I decide as I wake up and stare at the ceiling, is going to be different. First thing, I am going to return the book to the library. In my English journal, I'll write down that I've been reading *The Hunger Games* for my outside reading requirement (like 98 percent of the ninth grade), and I'll explain why I am Team Peeta instead of Team Gale. I'll tell Jules that we should go to the *Rocky Horror* marathon at the cheap theater this weekend. Then in Earth Science I'll finally get enough courage to go talk to Zach, my vegan lab partner who insists on feeding tofu crumbles to the class Venus flytrap, and who probably will save the whales before he turns twenty-one.

Yes, today is the day everything is going to change.

I get up and take a shower and get dressed, but the fairy tale is sitting on my nightstand where I left it before I went to bed. *This must be what an addict feels like*, I think, trying to fight the pull of one last, quick read. My fingers itch toward the binding, and finally, with a sigh of regret, I just grab the book and open it, hungrily reading the story. But this time, something feels wrong. It is like an itch between my eyebrows, a wrinkle in my mind. Frowning, I scan through the dialogue, which is all the way it should be. I glance at the illustration: the prince sitting on a throne, his dog waiting beside him.

"Delilah!" my mother yells. "I told you *twice* already . . . we're going to be late!"

I stare at the page, my eyes narrowed. What *is* it that's off? "Just let me finish—"

"You've read that book a thousand times—you know how it ends. *Now* means *now*!"

I flip through the book to the final page. When I see it, I can't believe I haven't noticed it before. Just to the left of Princess Seraphima's glittering gown, drawn into the sand, is a grid. Sort of like a bingo chart. Or a chessboard.

"How strange," I say softly. "That was never here before."

"DELILAH EVE!"

When my mother uses my middle name, it means she's *really* angry. I close the book and tuck it into my backpack, then hurry downstairs to scarf down breakfast before I am dropped off at school.

My mother is already rinsing her coffee cup as I grab a slice of toast and butter it. "Mom," I ask, "have you ever read a book and had it . . . change?"

She looks over her shoulder. "Well, sure. The first time I read *Gone with the Wind* and Rhett walked out on Scarlett, I was fifteen and thought all that unrequited love was wildly romantic. The second time I read it, last summer, I thought she was silly and he was a selfish pig."

"That's not what I mean. . . . That's *you* changing— not the book." I take a bite of the toast and wash it down with orange juice. "Imagine that you've read a story a hundred times and it always takes place on a ship. And then one day, you read it, and it's set in the Wild West instead."

"That's ridiculous," my mother replies. "Books don't change in front of your eyes."

"Mine did," I say.

She turns and looks at me, head tilted as if she is trying to figure out if I am lying or crazy or both. "You need to get more sleep, Delilah," she announces.

"Mom, I'm serious—"

"You simply saw something you overlooked before," my mother says, and she puts on her jacket. "Let's go."

But it's not something I overlooked. I know it.

The whole way to school, my backpack sits on my lap. My mother and I talk about things that don't matter— what time she is coming home from work; if I'm ready for my Algebra test; if it's going to snow—when all I can focus on is that faint little chessboard scratched into the sand of the beach on the last page of the fairy tale.

Our car pulls up in front of the building. "Have a good day," my mother says, and I kiss her goodbye. I hurry past a kid plugged into his earphones, and the popular girls, who cluster together like grapes. (Honestly, do you ever see just *one* of them?)

The school's current "it" couple, Brianna and Angelo—or BrAngelo, as they're known—are wrapped in each other's arms across my locker.

"I'm gonna miss you," Brianna says.

"I'm gonna miss you too, baby," Angelo murmurs.

For Pete's sake. It's not like she's leaving on a trip around the world. She's only headed to homeroom.

I don't realize I've said that out loud until I see them both staring at me. "Get a life," Brianna says.

Angelo laughs. "Or at least a boyfriend."

They leave with their arms around each other, hands tucked into each other's rear jeans pockets.

The worst part is, it's true. I wouldn't know what true love feels like if it hit me between the eyes. Given my mother's experience with romance, I shouldn't even care—but there's a part of me that wonders what it would be like to be the most important person to someone else, to always feel like you were missing a piece of yourself when he wasn't near you.

There is a crash on the metal of the locker beside mine, and I look up to see Jules smacking her hand against it to get my attention. "Hey," Jules says. "Earth to Delilah?" Today she is dressed in a black veil and a mini-skirt over leggings that seem like they've been hacked with a razor. She looks like a corpse bride. "Where'd you go last night?" she says. "I sent you a thousand texts."

I hesitate. I've hidden my fairy-tale obsession from Jules, but if anyone is going to believe me when I say that a book changed before my eyes, it's going to be my best friend.

"Sorry," I say. "I went to bed early."

"Well, the texts were all about Soy Boy."

I blush. At 3:00 A.M. during our last sleepover, I confessed to her that I thought Zach from my Earth Science class was possible future boyfriend material.

"I heard that he hooked up with Mallory Wegman last weekend."

Mallory Wegman had hooked up with so many guys in our class that her nickname was the Fisherman. I let this news sink in, and the fact that I had thought about Zach this morning before reading my book, which seemed a thousand years ago.

"He's telling everyone she slipped him a real burger instead of a veggie one and it overloaded his system. That he has no recollection of doing anything with her."

"Must have been some really good beef," I murmur. For a second, I try to mourn Zach, my potential crush, who now has someone real, but all I'm thinking of is Oliver.

"I have to tell you something," I confess.

Jules looks at me, suddenly serious.

"I was reading this book and it . . . it sort of changed."

"I totally understand," Jules says. "The first time I saw

Attack of the Killer Tomatoes I knew my life was never going to be the same."

"No, it's not that *I've* changed—it's the book that changed." I reach into my backpack and grab the fairy tale, flipping directly to the last page. "Look."

Prince? Yup, standing right where he usually is.

Princess? Ditto.

Frump? Wagging happily.

Chessboard?

It's missing.

It was there less than a half hour ago, and suddenly it's gone.

"Delilah?" Jules asks. "Are you okay?"

I can feel myself breaking out in a cold sweat. I close the book and then open it again; I blink fast to clear my eyes.

Nothing.

I stuff the book into my backpack again and close my locker. "I, um, have to go," I say to Jules, shoving past her as the bell rings.

Just so you know, I never lie. I never steal. I never cut class. I am, in short, the perfect student.

Which makes what I am about to do even more shocking. I turn in the opposite direction and walk toward the gymnasium, although I am supposed to be in homeroom.

Me, Delilah McPhee.

"Delilah?" I look up to see the principal standing in front of me. "Shouldn't you be in homeroom?"

He smiles at me. He doesn't expect me to be cutting class either.

"Um . . . Ms. Winx asked me to get a book from the gym teacher."

"Oh," the principal says. "Excellent!" He waves me on.

For a moment I just stare at him. Is it really this easy to become someone I'm not? Then I break into a run.

I don't stop until I have reached the locker room. I know it will be empty this early in the morning. Sitting down on a bench, I take the book from my backpack and open it again.

Real fairy tales are not for the fainthearted. In them, children get eaten by witches and chased by wolves; women fall into comas and are tortured by evil relatives. Somehow, all that pain and suffering is worthwhile, though, when it leads to the ending: happily ever after. Suddenly it no longer matters if you got a B– on your midterm in French or if you're the only girl in the school who doesn't have a date for the spring formal. Happily ever after trumps every-thing. But what if *ever after* could change?

It did for my mom. At one point, she loved my dad, or they wouldn't have gotten married—but now she doesn't even want to speak to him when he calls me on my birth-day and Christmas. Likewise, maybe the fairy tale isn't accurate. Maybe the last line should read something like *What you see isn't always what you get.*

There is still no chessboard on the sand.

I start flipping through the pages furiously. In most of them, Prince Oliver is in the company of someone or something—his dog, the villain Rapscullio, Princess Seraphima. But there is one illustration where he is all alone.

Actually, it's my favorite.

It comes toward the end of the story, after he's outsmarted the dragon Pyro and left the beast in the care of Captain Crabbe and the pirates. Afterward, as the pirates load the dragon onto the ship, Oliver is left alone on the shore looking up the cliff wall at the tower where Seraphima is being imprisoned. In the picture on page 43, he starts to climb.

I lift the book closer so that I can see Oliver more clearly. He is drawn in color, his jet-black hair ruffled by the breeze, his arms straining as he scales the sheer rock face. His bottle green velvet tunic is tattered: singed from Pyro's fiery breath and torn from his escape from shackles on the pirate ship. His dagger is clenched between his teeth so that he can grasp the next ledge. His face is turned toward the ocean, where the ship slips into the distance.

I think the reason I love this illustration so much is the expression on his face. You'd expect, at that moment, he'd be overcome by fierce determination. Or maybe shining love for his nearby princess. But instead, he looks . . . well . . . like something's missing.

Like he'd almost rather be on that pirate ship. Or any-where but where he is, on the face of the rocky cliff.

Like there's something he's hiding.

I lean forward, until my nose is nearly touching the page. The image blurs as I get close, but for a moment, I'm positive that Oliver's eyes have flickered away from the ocean, and toward me.

"I wish you were real," I whisper.

On the loudspeaker in the locker room, the bell rings. That means homeroom is over, and I have to go to Algebra. With a sigh, I set the fairy tale down on the bench, still cracked open. I unzip my backpack and then pick the book up again.

And gasp.

Oliver is still climbing the sheer rock wall. But the dag-ger clenched between his teeth is now in his right hand. Steel to stone, its sharp tip scratches the faintest of white lines into the dark granite, and then another, and a third.

H

I rub my eyes. This is not a Nook, a Kindle Fire, or an iPad, just a very ordinary old book. No animation, no bells and whistles. Drawing in my breath, I touch the paper, that very spot, and lift my finger again.

Two words slowly appear on the surface of the rock wall.

HELP ME.

n the bright side, Oliver realized, odds were in his favor that his intended bride was not in a coma, nor did she have a rope of hair for him to climb in order to rescue her. However, he was going into this endeavor blindly—knowing nothing about where this girl might be.

He had saddled his stallion, Socks, and now hesitated outside the castle walls. Glancing down at Frump, who trotted beside his master, he spoke aloud. "Which way, boy?" Oliver asked. It was extremely difficult to rescue a princess, he realized, when one had precious few clues to begin with.

Frump barked, jerking his snout in the direction of the Enchanted Forest.

Oliver cringed. Although that *was* the quickest route to the cottage of the wizard Orville—the person in the kingdom who was most likely to be able to conjure clues for Oliver's quest—it was also riddled with hazards. There were roots your stallion might trip over while galloping; there were low-hanging branches. Some bits of the forest were so thick that you could not see a foot before you. And because the woods were enchanted, the paths through them were mazes that changed constantly; the route you took the last time was never one you'd take twice.

He closed his eyes, imagining Princess Seraphima, who would be consigned to a lifetime of misery with a villain if he didn't manage to save her.

Then again, it wasn't like she was *counting* on Oliver's arrival. . . .

He reached for the compass around his neck, thinking of home, which was just a few steps behind him. Maybe his mother was right; maybe it was better to be safe than sorry. Before he could convince himself to retrace his steps into the safety of the castle walls, however, a tiny light zoomed before his face. Squinting, he could just make out the body of a fairy. Nasty little creatures, they fed on lies and gossip. They'd been known to put a grown man to sleep, and to steal all the secrets from his mind. Oliver waved his hand before his face, the way you might try to get an insect away from you, but the fairy rose, glowing, and then dove, biting Socks firmly on the hindquarter.

The stallion reared and bolted into the Enchanted Forest. It was all Oliver could do to hold on for dear life, and he hoped that Frump was able to keep up.

Sawing at the reins, Prince Oliver finally managed to stop the horse. "It's all right, boy," he soothed, looking around to get his bearings.

It was too dark to see. And then suddenly, there was a pin-prick of light. And another. A third. If he squinted, he could see the long, thin legs of the fairies illuminated against the halos of their beating wings.

One fairy hovered in front of his face, mesmerizing him. Her hair was a constantly shifting mane of sparks that crackled as she moved. Nearly translucent, her skin glowed in the dark like the face of the moon. Her teeth, when she smiled, were perfect tiny dagger points. In the blink of an eye, she darted toward his neck, and bit his skin.

"Ouch!" Oliver cried, swatting her away as she licked his blood from her lips.

"He tastes like royalty," said the fairy. "Like wine and wealth."

"I'm a prince," Oliver replied. "I'm on my way to rescue a princess."

The second fairy landed on his hand and sank her razor teeth into his thumb, making Oliver yelp. "He's lying," replied the second fairy. "I taste fear."

The third fairy landed delicately on the tip of Oliver's nose. "Fear? I know who this boy is." She looked directly into Oliver's eyes. "This is the queen's son. I'm Sparks. The one who gave you wisdom."

The first fairy came to hover beside her. "I'm Ember. I gave you loyalty."

"And I am Glint," said the second fairy. "I gave you life."

"Thank you for all of that," Oliver said politely, because a prince is nothing if not polite. "But I'd really like it if you allowed me to pass through the forest."

"You can't," said Sparks. "It's too dangerous."

Ember nodded. "A boy without bravery shouldn't take chances."

"Glint," said the first fairy, "bite the horse again so he'll gallop home."

"No!" Oliver cried out. "What if I challenged you?"

He knew very little about fairies—no one knew much about them, really. They somehow managed to learn the secrets of humans without ever letting a secret of their own slip out. But Oliver had seen the strongest of knights carried back to the castle by his peers after a hungry swarm of fairies had pulled every hidden memory from his mind. They were destructive and impulsive, and they never had any regrets.

"If I beat you at your own game," Oliver said, thinking on his feet, "wouldn't that be proof enough of my bravery?"

"A game?" said Sparks, her hair flickering with excitement.

Ember landed on his shoulder and whispered in his ear. "But we make the rules."

Glint settled on a branch in front of him, calling her sisters close. As they leaned in, their hair brightened, like combined flames. Finally Glint broke away. "You must try to cast a glow farther than any of us."

Oliver didn't miss a beat. "Done," he accepted.

The fairies looked at each other. "Stupid humans," said Ember. "They can't shine."

"What do we get if we win?" Sparks asked.

Oliver thought. "All my secrets," he said soberly. "Every last one."

The fairies clapped, creating a rain of glitter. "Me first," Glint sang, and she shimmied so that a halo of silver light rose from around her body. The forest lit, six tree trunks deep, before fading into darkness again.

"Amateur," Ember scoffed. She spun in a tight circle, holding her wings out like helicopter blades, and a warm bronze glow enveloped the area where Oliver was standing. Like that of the fairy before her, the circle of light grew and grew, this time ten trees deep, before snuffing itself out.

"Watch and learn, girls," Sparks said. She curled tightly into a ball, growing so small she was only a pinprick, and then with a sudden pop let loose a corona of golden light.

The glow was fiercer, hotter, wider—but quicker to fade to black.

"Your turn," Glint said, raising one arched silver brow.

"Wait. If I win," Oliver replied, "I want safe passage."

The fairies, blinking intermittently now, whispered to each other. "Safe passage," they agreed.

Oliver reached into Socks's saddlebags and took out the packed lunch that the royal cook had given him before he left.

Inside were two hard-boiled eggs, some cheese, and a hunk of bread. There was also a tiny drawstring bag of seasoning.

Loosening the string, Oliver gently blew across the small heap of pepper, so that it created a cloud around the fairies.

Glint, Sparks, and Ember sneezed in unison, and as they did, flashes of light burst like fireworks to illuminate the whole of the Enchanted Forest.

"Well," Oliver said, swinging himself back into the saddle. "I think it's clear that I—"

Before he could finish his sentence, Socks let out an enormous sneeze too. He reared on his hind legs, inadvertently pawing at Glint, who then nipped him in self-defense.

Once again, Oliver held on for dear life as his runaway stallion bolted into the Enchanted Forest. Finally, they broke through the thick foliage, just in time for Oliver to notice that they were approaching a cliff. At an alarming pace.

"Whoa!" he cried, yanking on the reins.

There was six feet of ground remaining before the cliff edge. Three feet. One. Miraculously, Socks halted abruptly at the edge. "Thank goodness," Oliver said.

Apparently, he spoke too soon.

Because although Socks stopped, Oliver didn't. He tumbled over the horse's head, past the edge of the cliff, and into the roiling ocean below.

OLIVER

THERE IS ONLY ONE PAGE IN THE BOOK WHERE I'M alone, where there's no other character whose dialogue I have to prompt, or whose motion I need to follow.

Because of that, I sometimes test my boundaries in the moment before a Reader starts reading.

I might sing at the top of my lungs.

Or push the limits of the story, by sitting on the ground and waiting until the book pulls me up the cliff.

Sometimes I try to get to the edge of the cliff, to the spot where the rock has a crease in it from someone who dog-eared the page years ago.

Occasionally I climb to the highest point to see past the blurry edge of the illustration.

None of it matters, because no one ever notices what I'm doing anyway, and I'm pulled back into the flow of the fairy tale.

Until today.

As soon as I realized that Delilah had noticed the chessboard in the sand—something that has nothing at all to do with the story—I started to wonder if maybe she might be the one. The one who was able to notice *other* things that aren't part of the story.

Mainly, me.

At the very least, I couldn't let the moment pass without trying. So I scratched the words "HELP ME," and she saw. I just know she saw.

I'm clinging onto the rock wall, and I'm holding my breath, because I'm so scared she is going to turn the page, just like everyone else.

Except she doesn't.

"How?" she says, and very slowly, I turn so that I am looking right at her.

I clear my throat, trying to speak out loud. It's been a long time since my voice was projected anywhere but inside a Reader's head, and speaking takes great concentration for someone who's not used to doing it. "Can you . . . can you hear me?" I ask.

She gasps. "You're British?"

"Excuse me?"

"You have an accent," she says. "When I was reading you, I never heard an accent . . ." Suddenly her eyes widen. "Oh my God, I've gone crazy. The book isn't just changing, it's talking back to me—"

"No—I'm the one talking . . ." My heart is racing, and my thoughts are coming fast and furious. This girl, this Delilah, just answered my question. She *heard* me.

She takes a deep breath. "Okay, Delilah, pull yourself together. Maybe you have a fever. This will all go away with a couple of Tylenol—" She starts to close the book, and with all of my strength I yell.

"No! Don't!"

"You don't understand," she says. Her cheeks are flushed and her eyes are wild. "Characters in books aren't real." She smacks her forehead. "Why I am even explaining this out loud?"

"Because I *am* real," I plead. "I'm just as real as *you* are." I stare at her. "And you're the only Reader who's ever noticed."

At that, Delilah's lips part. I find myself thinking about those lips, which look soft and sweet and infinitely more interesting to kiss than Seraphima's. She pulls away, so that instead of seeing just an up-close view of her face, I am able to see her dark hair, her pink shirt, her fear.

"Please," I say softly. "Just give me a chance."

I can see that she's wavering, considering whether

she should slam the book shut or actually listen. So I jump down from the cliff ledge.

"How did you do that?" she gasps. "Where are the batteries?"

"Battery? I can assure you, no one is getting a beating," I say, crawling upright again.

"You moved," she accuses, pointing a finger at me.

"So did you," I say. I decide to test things a bit, and race to the side of the page so that I can run up its edge and do a standing flip. "Did you see that?"

"Yes, but—"

"How about this?" I grab on to the cliff wall and climb it like a monkey. When I reach the top, I take a flying leap and loop my arm around the tail of a letter *g*, swinging back and forth.

"Now you're just showing off," Delilah says.

I laugh. "Do me a favor," I ask. "Turn the book sideways?"

She does, and I let go so that I drop lightly on the long edge of the page and slide down it to the illustration at the bottom.

"That's amazing," Delilah whispers, setting the book upright again. "How do you move?"

"The same way you do, I guess."

Tentatively, she holds up her hand in front of the book. "How many fingers?"

"Three."

"So you can see me too?"

"I've always been able to see you," I say. "It's a rather lovely view."

I watch her face flood with heat. "I've read hundreds of books. How come this hasn't happened before?"

"I'm not like most characters, I guess," I say slowly. "Everyone else in here seems to be happy having their lives already planned out for them, and doing what they're told to do. But I've never really fit in. I've always wondered what it would be like to be someone . . . different."

Delilah's eyes widen. "I've always wondered that too."

Brightening, I smile at her. "Look at how much we already have in common."

She smirks. "Yeah. Like, for example, I'm talking to a book, and you think you're alive. We're both insane."

"Or very, very evolved. . . ."

"Maybe it was something I ate," Delilah says, standing up and pacing in a circle. "Maybe the milk in my cereal was bad or I took an accidental overdose of vitamins and now I'm hallucinating—"

"Not this again." I sigh. "Haven't we established that I am not a figment of your imagination?"

"You can't be real," Delilah murmurs.

"Says who?" I ask. "Did you really think that a story exists only when you're reading it?"

"Um," Delilah says. "Well, yeah."

I settle my hands on my hips. "When you go to sleep at night, do you cease existing?"

"Obviously not. . . ."

"And how do you know that *you're* not part of a book? That someone's not reading *your* story right now?"

She looks at me, narrowing her eyes as the implication sets in. "But you're part of a fairy tale."

"Exactly. *Part* of a fairy tale. Which suggests that there's more to me than meets the average Reader's eye. Did you ever think that maybe what you see isn't really what's true? Take Socks, for example. Actually, please, *do* take Socks. He's not a fearless steed — he's a hopeless one. And Rapscullio — he's actually a rather nice guy! He collects butterflies and is quite the pastry chef in his time off! And Seraphima — "

Delilah sighs. "I always wanted to be Seraphima. . . ."

I snort. "You *might* want to revise your life goals, then. She has the brain capacity of a sea cucumber."

I realize that I quite like this girl. It's not just that she's so pretty the words fly out of my mind before they can leave my mouth — it's that when we're chatting, I feel like I've known her all my life. It's as easy to speak to her as it is to talk to Frump. It's been a long time, I realize, since I made a good friend.

"Can I ask you something?" I say. "Why do you keep reading this story?"

"I—I don't really know," Delilah admits. "Because of that one line, I guess. About growing up without a father." She looks away. "I liked the idea of someone else knowing what that's like."

I feel a twinge as I realize that whatever I've experienced in the story pales in comparison to what she's had to suffer through in real life. After all, I've never even met King Maurice; he is just words on a page to me.

Delilah swipes a hand across her eyes. "I mean, I have nothing to complain about. A lot of kids have no one who cares about them. And my mom, she's great. She loves me like crazy. She'd do anything for me."

I frown. "But she doesn't want you to read this book, even though it makes you happy."

Delilah looks at me, confused. "Oh, no," she says, shrugging. "She just thinks I read too much, in general. She wants me to get out more."

"May I ask you something?" I say. "Why *do* you read books, when you could be outside, living a million different adventures every day?"

"Because you can always count on a book to stay the same. Everything else changes when you least expect it," she replies, bitter. "Families split apart, and nothing's forever. In books, you always know what's coming next. There are no surprises."

"Why is that a *good* thing?"

"You of all people ought to understand why I wouldn't want to take a risk—"

I scowl. "That's just a role I have to play in the story. If I had the chance, I'd do anything to not know what tomorrow's going to bring."

"People in the real world would kill for a happily ever after, and you're willing to just throw it away?"

I look away from her. "It's hardly a happily ever after when you wind up right back at the beginning. I've never experienced 'after' at all."

Suddenly, I hear another voice in the Otherworld.

Delilah McPhee, what are you doing out of homeroom?

"What is a 'homeroom'?" I ask.

"Shut *up*!" she grits out.

Excuse me, Ms. McPhee, did I just hear you tell me to shut up?

"No, Coach Farnsworth. I would never say something like that, Coach Farnsworth. . . ."

"You just did," I point out, grinning.

Immediately, she slams the book closed.

The dark is complete. It rather catches me off guard this time. Although I hear other characters climbing down from their scenes to mingle with each other and carry on their off-time pursuits, I narrow my eyes and wait.

Sure enough, she opens the book again.

"Now see here," I command. "It's downright rude to

end a conversation without a proper goodbye. You may apologize. Now."

She snorts. "*You* can apologize first! What were you trying to do, get me detention?"

I have no idea what detention is. But I do know that never in the course of the story has anyone ever talked back to me like this. After all, I'm a prince. Which doesn't seem to matter in the least to this girl.

And instead of being angry, I'm intrigued. "What's detention?"

"It's . . . not important," she says. "Look, I can't have you speaking when other people are around."

"Believe me—they won't hear me. No one ever does."

"Well, they're going to hear *me*, and normal people don't talk out loud to books."

I grin. "In that case, I'm glad you're not normal."

"You have *no* idea. Talking out loud to fictional characters is just the tip of the iceberg."

"Fictional character?"

"Well," she says. "You may be real, but you're still stuck in a book."

"That's why I need your help."

"I don't understand. . . ."

I stare very soberly into her pale brown eyes. "I want you to get me out."

Delilah

OKAY, FIRST OF ALL, THIS IS NOT HAPPENING.

My mother is right. I need more sleep. It's bad enough that I'm talking to a book, much less entertaining the thought of how to get a character out of it.

"I don't think it works that way," I say. "It's not like springing someone out of jail—"

"I'm hardly a felon!"

"No, you're a two-dimensional, inch-high illustration," I point out. "If you were to get out, what would you do? Live in a shoe box? Be Flat Stanley?"

"Who's Flat Stanley?"

"Another fictional character," I say. I have a sudden flash of second grade, when my teacher had us take our cutouts of Flat Stanley all around the world during spring break. My mother and I took pictures of him in Boston, eating clam chowder and waving at the seals in the aquarium.

So maybe Oliver isn't the first fictional character with a hankering to travel.

"You don't know that I'd stay this size. Perhaps I'd be scaled to fit your world, if I were lucky enough to reach it."

"Why are we even discussing this?" I explode. "You can't take a character out of a book!"

"How do you know? Have you ever tried?"

"No, but it's not like Cinderella is working at Starbucks—"

"Cinderella? Starbucks?" Oliver says.

"Exactly. You wouldn't survive ten seconds in this world," I tell him. "There's so much out here you don't know."

"I know *you*," Oliver insists.

The way he looks at me, I almost forget that this is all in my imagination.

"You hardly know me. We've been talking for, like, twenty minutes."

"You're wrong," Oliver says. "I know that your bedroom is painted pink. And that you bite your lip at the part where Rapscullio and I fight. And that you say good night to your goldfish without fail. And sometimes when you get dressed in the morning you dance to the music that comes out of that odd little box—"

"You've watched me getting dressed in the morning?"

He flashes me a grin. "*You're* the one who left the book wide open."

"We don't even know if this is a one-time thing," I say. "I could close the book and you could be gone, forever."

Oliver takes a step forward. "Try it."

"Try what?"

"Closing the book."

"But what if—" I realize that I don't want him to disappear. I may not fully believe he's real; I may not understand why I can hear him speaking to me—but I sort of like it. I like knowing that of all the people in the world, I'm the only one listening to what he has to say. It makes me feel like we've been destined for each other. Which is the way things work in fairy tales, not in my ordinary, boring life. "Are you sure?" I whisper.

Oliver nods. I start to close the book, but then I hear him shout, and I yank it wide open again. "Just in case," he says, his eyes locked on mine. "Just in case it . . . doesn't work. I want you to know, Delilah. You've already been the biggest adventure of my life."

I gently touch my finger to the blank space beside Oliver. He reaches toward my hand and spreads his own, pressing it against the filmy barrier between us. I can feel the pressure of his touch, the temperature of his skin.

Before I can lose my nerve, I close the book.

[61]

I take a deep breath. Then another one. I spell M-I-S-S-I-S-S-I-P-P-I. Then I riffle through the book until I am on page 43 again.

There's the cliff, and the sea in the distance. There's the gravel that was beneath Oliver's feet. But Oliver is missing.

It feels like a punch. Tears fill my eyes, and I wonder how I could be upset over losing something I never had.

Just then, Oliver pokes his head out from behind a boulder. "It was only a jest," he says, laughing.

"*Not* funny." I start to slam the book shut.

"Wait! Wait, I'm sorry. Truly!"

I let the pages fall open again. "You owe me," I mutter.

"I promise to make it up to you," Oliver vows. "The very minute I get out of this book."

"I really do have to leave, though," I tell him. "If I don't go to Algebra, I'm going to get into trouble."

Oliver nods his head. "Of course," he says, and then hesitates. "Is Algebra quite a distance away?"

I stifle a grin. "Light-years," I say. "I'll come back later."

"And help me get out of here?"

"I don't know—"

"Promise?" Oliver asks.

I can't remember anyone else who's ever been desperate for me to return. Most of the kids in school are desperate for me to leave, and the ones who aren't are totally indifferent. There's Jules, of course, but she doesn't need me. Not the way Oliver does, anyway.

"Yes," I say. "I promise."

I suffer through Math and English and an embarrassing moment in Social Studies when Mr. Uwenga calls on me, asking for the name of the secretary of state, and I say "Oliver." Then, finally, it's my free period. Jules and I always meet at the same table in the cafeteria. It's the one where the geeks congregate. Jules could probably announce she was the love child of President Obama and a cat and they wouldn't look up from their Calculus textbooks.

She slides into a seat beside me with her hot lunch tray, sighing. "Four hours, thirty-six minutes, and twelve seconds till we're out of purgatory for the weekend."

"Maybe later," I murmur, still distracted by the day's previous events.

"So, let me show you how a conversation works. I say something, and then you say something back that actually relates to what I was talking about, as if you were even the least bit interested."

"Huh?" I say, turning to her. I shake my head. "I'm sorry. I'm kind of out of it today."

"What's up?" She pops a grape into her mouth. "Did Uwenga spring another pop quiz on you guys? And if so, can you tell me what's on it so I don't fail?"

I desperately want to tell Jules the truth about what happened. I want her to see it for herself, because if she believes it too, then I'm not crazy. After all, if anyone's going to hear me out and not judge me or call me a freak, it's my best friend. So I turn to her. "Did you ever wonder what happens when you close a book?"

Jules stops chewing. "Um. It stays closed?"

"No. I mean, what about the characters inside?"

She tilts her head. "They're just words." She peers at me. "Is this an English major kind of thing?"

"No. They're words, but they're more than words. They come to life in your head, right? So how do you know that doesn't keep going when you stop reading?"

"Like how little kids think their stuffed animals wake up and party when they fall asleep?"

"Yes—exactly!"

Jules laughs. "Once, I took my dad's video camera and let it run all night long while I was sleeping because I thought I could catch my toys in the act. I was convinced my Tickle Me Elmo was a closet ax murderer." She shrugs. "If he was, it never showed up on tape."

"I've got something better than a tape," I say. I look at the two geeks sitting across from us. They are completely enraptured by their matrices and graphing calculators; Jules and I might as well be on the moon as far as they're concerned. So I take the book from my backpack and open it up to page 43. "I need to show you something," I say. "Watch carefully."

I crack the spine a little bit, so that the book lies open. "What is this?" Jules says, laughing a little. "Did you swipe it from the last kids you babysat for?"

"Just read it," I say.

Jules raises her brows but starts to read out loud: "*Oliver grasped a root sticking out of the rock wall and hoisted himself a little farther up the cliff. With his dagger clenched between his teeth, he swung one arm up, and then the other, climbing the sheer granite, driven by the force of his determination.* Seraphima, *he thought.* I'm coming for you."

"Fat chance," I said.

"Did you say something?" Jules asks.

"Just keep watching," I tell her.

We both stare at the illustration. Then Jules nudges my shoulder. "Delilah? What exactly am I looking for?"

Although the book has been open for thirty seconds, Oliver hasn't budged, or spoken, or in any way indicated that he is more than just an illustration on the page.

"Say something," I mutter.

Jules looks at me, baffled. "Um, it's a nice paragraph?"

The fact that Oliver isn't talking to us both makes me feel sick to my stomach. For all I know, I've only been kidding myself. If I tell her now that I've been chatting with a prince in a fairy tale who wants my help getting out of his story, Jules is going to march me to the nurse or call a guidance counselor. Jules, who understands everything about me, just wouldn't understand *this* . . . and I can't risk losing the only real friend I have.

"I'm still waiting. Is he going to jump out of the page and attack me with that knife?"

If you only knew, I think. I pretend Jules has made the funniest of jokes. "Now, that would be *absolutely* ridiculous. I just wanted to show you . . . the description. This writer's something else, isn't she? It's like, when you read the words, it's actually . . . happening!"

I laugh again, a big fake laugh, for good measure. Jules looks at me like I've grown three horns out of my forehead. "Have you been sniffing Sharpies again?" she asks.

I stuff the book into my backpack. "Totally forgot—I have to go take a makeup test with Madame Borgnoigne." I silently curse Oliver for making me look like an even bigger fool than usual. "I'll call you after school," I say, and I run out of the cafeteria.

I'm not in the habit of sneaking into faculty restrooms. In fact, this is something I've never even thought of doing, but then again nothing I've done today is something I've ever thought of doing. The bottom line is I need to be alone with this book, and in a faculty restroom I can lock the door and not have to worry about any gossiping girls who might run to a teacher to snitch on the insane student who's conversing with a fairy tale.

I crack open the book once again to page 43, lean into the story, and whisper, "Hello?"

When Oliver smiles, I catch my breath. "You came back. You said you would . . . and you did."

Get a grip, Delilah, I tell myself. "What was that all about?"

"What was what all about?"

"Why didn't you talk when I asked you to?"

"I thought you didn't want me talking when strangers were around!"

"I don't!" I argue.

"I'm having a little trouble keeping up, here. . . . You're angry because I did what you asked me to do?"

"I'm angry because Jules isn't a stranger."

"She might as well be, to me," Oliver says. "She wouldn't have heard me even if I were yelling at the top of my lungs."

"How do you know that? You didn't even try."

"I've been trying for years—you're the first person who has ever noticed me."

I sigh. "But if you'd talked to Jules—if she could hear you . . ." My voice trails off.

"Then you wouldn't feel quite so crazy?" Oliver asks gently. "Can't you believe in me, if I believe in you?"

"I don't know what to believe," I say, completely honest. "Nothing like this has ever happened to me."

Oliver sits down on the ground. "And nothing *at all* has ever happened to me."

I look at him, resigning himself to an endless life trapped inside someone else's plot. I know what that feels like. If I'd written my own story, my father would never have left us, and my mother wouldn't have to work till she was so tired she fell into bed each night before dinner. If I'd written my own story, I wouldn't have broken a cheer-leader's kneecap and single-handedly turned the entire school against me. If I'd written my own story, I'd have someone like Oliver here who loved me.

Then again, maybe I *can* change my own story. Or at least try. "I think we need to do a test," I say.

"I don't understand."

"What if I cut you out of the book and you stop breathing? What if the only oxygen that works for you is in the pages?"

"*Cutting?* Who said anything about cutting—"

"And what if you *do* make it into this world but you're small enough to fit in my pocket?" My voice rises as I think of everything that could possibly go wrong.

"So by *test*," Oliver says slowly—hopefully, "you mean you're going to help me get out of here?"

"Yes. And we're going to start with a trial run. I'll meet you on page twenty-one." I hesitate. "You can see the numbers on the pages too, right?"

"If I squint," Oliver says. "They're so far up in the corners."

"It's the part where you and Frump are walking through the forest. . . . Yes! We'll try the dog first!" I say.

Oliver shakes his head. "*Frump?* You can't do that!"

"He's just a dog, Oliver. He'll probably never even know."

"Just a dog!" Oliver stands, angry. "That 'dog' speaks three languages and is brilliant at chess and happens to be my best friend. Or did you forget that he used to be a human too?"

"I guess I maybe skimmed that part," I confess, although I'd rather die than admit that I often skipped over the pages without Oliver in them. "If we can't experiment on Frump, then what do you recommend? Or does even the bacteria in your book do rocket science on the side?"

"I could give you my tunic," Oliver suggests.

"Keep your clothes on, buster. I think we'd be better off seeing what happens with something that's alive and breathing, don't you?"

"Give me a moment." He paces from one end of the page to the other, briefly disappearing into the spine for a moment before reappearing with a smile on his face. "I could get you a fish from page forty-two."

"I don't know. . . . Shouldn't you try something that

doesn't belong in the ocean? That way, if it doesn't survive intact . . . we can't blame the problem on a lack of lungs."

"You're quite right." Oliver sighs. He swats at the back of his neck, then waves his hand in front of his face. "Blasted spider."

I start to ask him where it came from, fascinated by the mechanics of what appears and disappears in his world—but then I realize there might be any number of microscopic things that readers overlook—chessboards in the sand, spiders, even princes. "Wait!" I lean closer. "Oliver, did you kill that spider?"

"It *bit* me!"

"It's the perfect sample for a trial run," I tell him.

He brightens. "Of course. And if it doesn't live, I'll actually have something to celebrate." He falls to his hands and knees and begins to search for the bug. "Got it," Oliver says, and he extends his palm. In its center is a writhing, fat spider.

"Now what?" I ask.

Oliver blinks up at me. "Well. I guess you just take it."

I gently reach down, trying to pinch the spider off the page, but nothing happens. There is a barrier between us, thinner than silk and incredibly solid. "It's not working."

"I forgot about the wall," he says. He sits down, lost in thought.

"The wall?" I ask.

"It's what keeps us safe, I suppose, if a Reader handles

the pages without much care, or folds one down right in the center of an illustration. It's like a bubble. Soft, but you can't push through it no matter how hard you try." He glances up. "Believe me, I have."

"So you need something that can poke a hole in it. . . ."

Oliver reaches for the dagger in his belt and takes a running leap directly toward me, so forceful that I find myself covering my face with my hands, as if he might burst through the pages and land right in front of me. But when I peek between my fingers, I find him flat on his back, staring up at the sky.

"Ouch," he murmurs.

"Scientific discovery number one," I say. "You can't break the barrier between us."

He sits up, rubbing his forehead. "No," he replies, "but maybe *you* can."

"You want me to poke the book with a knife?"

"No," Oliver says. "You have to rip the book."

I gasp. "No way! This is a *library* book!"

"You have *got* to be kidding me," Oliver mutters. "Come on, Delilah. Just a little tear, so that I can sneak the spider out to you."

When he offers up that smile again—the one that makes me feel like I'm the only person in his universe (although in this case that's probably true)—I am utterly lost. "Okay," I say with a sigh.

Gingerly, I take the page between my fingers and

make the tiniest, most minute, infinitesimal tear.

"Delilah," Oliver says, "I couldn't squeeze protozoa through that, much less a spider. Could you try again? A little less imaginary this time?"

"Fine." I pinch the top of the page between my fingers and give a good, solid tug. The paper tears.

"It *had* to be up at the top of the page, didn't it. . . ." Oliver rolls his eyes and wearily looks at the sheer cliff of rock before him.

"You do it for Seraphima," I point out.

"Very funny." Clenching the spider in his fist, he looks up. "How am I supposed to hold on to this thing *and* climb?" With a grimace, Oliver opens his mouth and pops the spider onto his tongue.

"That is so gross!" I cry out.

"*Mmffphm,*" Oliver says, but his eyes speak volumes. He starts to climb up the rock wall, getting quicker and quicker as he comes closer to the top. He inches to the right, to the part of the page that I've torn.

Holding his hand in front of his mouth, he spits. "That," he says, "was *revolting.*" He glances at me over his shoulder. "Are you ready?"

"Yes," I say. Feeling foolish, I hold my finger up to the rip in the paper.

Oliver extends his hand. The spider begins to crawl across his knuckles, his ring finger, his pinkie. When it reaches the edge of his skin, its legs grasp for purchase and find the seam of the paper.

And suddenly, there is the tiniest of black dots in my palm.

It's nearly invisible, and it's uncomfortably warm and wet. Before my eyes, it begins to grow, expanding into a familiar formation of eight creepy, crawly legs.

"Oliver!" I say, stunned. "I think it worked!"

"Really?" He has jumped down to the ground again and stares up at me eagerly. "You've got the spider, then?"

I glance down at the tiny arachnid. But now that I am looking more carefully, I see something's not quite right. What I thought were legs are letters, raveling and unraveling. I think I can make out a *d.* And a *p.*

It's not a spider, really. It's the *word* "spider," taking the shape of the bug and crawling across my hand.

Before I can tell Oliver, however, a knock at the bathroom door startles me. I shake the word-insect off my palm, beneath the inside cover of the book, and shut the book tightly. "I'll just be another minute," I call out.

Gingerly, I open the book again. There is no insect. Instead, written neatly on the inside cover, at a bizarre diagonal angle, I read: *spider.*

"Oliver," I murmur, although the pages are still closed, although he probably cannot hear me. "I think we need to go back to square one."

he last thing Oliver remembered was the splash. Now he was tumbling head over heels as he sank to the depths of the ocean. Two eels twined and vined, the water sizzling with electric current every time they rubbed against each other. Oliver felt his lungs burning, at the point of bursting, and he wondered if this was how he'd die—not at the hands of the villain who'd kidnapped Seraphima but simply consumed by the ocean. Suddenly, he remembered the compass hanging around his neck. *Home,* his mother had promised. It was a foolproof escape. He let the chain slip through his fingers, and with the last of his energy, he reached to grab it, but before he could, it was snatched out of his grasp.

"Noooo!" he screamed, water filling his lungs. He closed his eyes, imagining the worst.

Fingers snaked beneath his collar. A soft mouth closed over his own, and he felt a shudder run through his chest. "Seraphima," Oliver murmured, stunned to realize he could talk and breathe. He blinked to find a woman in his arms.

Her skin was blue, patterned with a web of scales. Her hair was a wild black cloud, seaweed twisted into its crown, flowing behind translucent, spiny ears. Two sets of gills undulated on her cheeks and beneath her emaciated rib cage, which tapered into a muscular, finned tail that reflected flashes of copper and gold. She had no bridge to her nose, just deep-set nostrils that flared above the cavern of her toothless smile. "Who's Seraphima?" the girl asked, her clear blue eyes flashing a deep shade of red. "I'm Marina."

Terrified, Oliver thrashed, trying to loosen himself from her embrace.

"Sister," said another female voice. "Don't keep him all to yourself." Oliver looked up to see a second mermaid, who was wearing his father's compass around her neck. And then he heard a third voice: "Oh yes, this is the one we've been waiting for."

Oliver managed to land a swift kick against Marina's tail, only to have the hair of the second mermaid twist itself into a spitting bronze eel, which wrapped its neck around his torso, immobilizing him and pulling him closer to her. "Tell my sisters that you're here for me, Ondine," she said. He tried to close his fingers around the compass that hung from her neck, but she kissed him so deeply that he started to lose consciousness again.

A webbed hand smacked Oliver across the face, scratching his cheek with long, pointed nails. He was snatched away by the third mermaid, who cradled him in her elongated arms. "Why bother with a trifle like that," she sang into his ear, "when you could have someone like me, Kyrie?"

"Ladies," Oliver said, his heart racing. "With three beautiful choices, you can hardly expect me to make a decision so quickly." If he could only get out of their clutches long enough to think clearly, he could get his compass back. And once he did that, he knew he could escape and find Frump and Socks. He backed away so that he could see his rescuers, and gave them a dazzling smile. Marina's black hair fanned through the water in slow motion as her eyes settled back to a deep, royal blue. Her slender neck was draped with beads and shells, and her shimmering tail swayed in the water behind her. Ondine and Kyrie swam behind her. When one of the mermaids reached out toward Oliver again, Marina slapped her hand away and hissed so loudly that the water pounded against Oliver's eardrums.

"You must stay for dinner then," Kyrie said.

What if I am dinner? Oliver wondered. "I can't imagine a better way to pass the evening," he said.

Ondine and Kyrie wrapped their hair around his wrists, pulling him into the current. Marina tilted his chin and kissed him once more. The kiss was foul and tasted of fish, but it filled his lungs with oxygen.

They arrived at a deep cave, with jaws of stalagmites and

stalactites that nicked at Oliver's legs when the mermaids drew him into its belly. He winced as blood welled from his calf. It curled in the water like crimson smoke, and before Oliver could even cry out from the pain, there was a sudden rush of movement as a broad silver shark sped toward him. Ondine let her hair fall away from his wrist and turned to the shark, her eyes flashing red as every scale on her body stood on edge. Gills fanned, she screamed, and every fish swimming nearby fled. As the shark dipped and swam away, Ondine's scales smoothed and her eyes dimmed, now calm and purple. "Come," she whispered, and for a moment, all Oliver could do was stare at this creature that dragged him along in her wake.

The cave's centerpiece was a giant stone table, or maybe it was an altar upon which Oliver was destined to be sacrificed. At the rear of the cave a rounded driftwood door hid another room; on the other side, a golden chest with a huge padlock sat half-buried in the sand.

Oliver looked from one to the other. It was possible that the chest held riches he could use to bribe whoever had taken Seraphima. But it was equally possible that he'd never have the chance to leave this cave alive.

"A wedding feast," Marina cried. "And I will be the bride!"

"No, Sister," Ondine screamed. "You speak too soon."

"You are both mistaken," Kyrie said. "It's my turn this time."

This time? Oliver thought. How many other men in the kingdom had fallen to a watery death at the hands of these vile creatures? He had to find a way out, and it had to be fast, because he was starting to see stars at the edges of his vision again.

Kyrie wrapped her long fingers around his shoulders and kissed breath into his lungs. "You see, my love," she whispered. "You need me just as much as I need you."

If this was what love was, maybe it wasn't worth the trouble. Oliver had grown up with a mother who'd lost half her heart and had never been able to replace it. These mermaids had been just as broken by love, albeit in a different way.

"I'm hardly dressed for a wedding," Oliver demurred.

"We have just the thing," Ondine said. She swam toward the driftwood door and slid open the latch. As the door swung on its hinges, a tumble of skeletons—hundreds stacked and thrown askew, some still rotting with flesh peeling back from the bone—drifted into the cave. Oliver screamed, backing up against Kyrie, who stroked his hair and kissed his neck. "Don't be shy," she said, pushing him forward.

The mermaids swam around one of the corpses, which was decked in the finest of white royal robes, sewn with golden thread. Oliver hardly even saw the finery, however. His gaze was glued to the face of the dead man, still frozen in horror.

"I think," Marina said, "it will be a perfect fit."

Behind him, Kyrie shrieked. "Take that off!" she cried. "It's mine." Oliver spun to find her fighting Ondine for a tattered snatch of veil. The mermaids' fingernails clawed the fine fabric to shreds as they argued.

"Ladies," Oliver said. "I don't love any of you."

The mermaids turned, eyes flashing red in unison. "How dare you?" Ondine spit.

Marina crossed her arms. "You think you're too good for us?"

"No," Oliver said simply. "I just don't think you love me either. Isn't that what true romance is supposed to be about? Finding the person who's your soul mate. Someone you dream about at night. Someone whose name is on your lips when you wake up in the morning."

Seraphima, Oliver thought.

"I'm not your destiny. I'm just someone who happened to fall into the ocean."

Marina shrugged. "Grooms are few and far between," she said. "We can't afford to be picky."

"What if I could promise you each a faithful groom? One so delighted to be in your presence that he'd never leave?"

Kyrie's eyes flashed green with curiosity. "How would you find such men?"

"Well," Oliver said. "I'd need my compass back, for starters."

The mermaids circled, creating a small whirlpool as they whispered, heads bent together. "We need to be sure you're telling the truth," Marina said.

"You have my word," Oliver vowed. He was starting to run out of oxygen. Whatever happened was going to have to happen soon.

"We need something a bit more concrete." Kyrie's hair swirled around his chest, pulling him toward a giant pink clamshell that was filled with thousands of keys. Some were rusted, some were covered with seaweed. Some were still shiny, as if they'd just dropped into the ocean this morning.

"Honesty is as rare as a man who can breathe underwater," Ondine said. "Pick a key."

Oliver reached into the half shell and waited, letting the keys sift through his fingers, hoping one might burn its silhouette onto the palm of his hand.

He fought to stay conscious. "What happens if it's the right key?" he gasped.

"Then you're truthful. You get all the riches inside, and we give you back your compass so you can find us mates."

"And if it's the wrong key?"

Kyrie shrugged. "The oxygen spell wears off. And you drown."

How on earth would he know which key to pick? One wrong choice here would be his last. Oliver blinked, struggling to swallow his panic.

"Come now," Ondine snapped, leaning over the half shell. "We don't have all day." Annoyed, she overturned the bowl of keys, scattering them into the sand at Oliver's feet.

There was the tiniest flicker in his fading vision—perhaps a ray of sun slanting through the sea, maybe the reflection of a fish's silver scale. At any rate, it drew Oliver's attention to his father's compass hanging around Ondine's neck.

Very slowly, as he watched, the needle began to jump, quivering to the right until it seemed to be an arrow directly indicating one key that had drifted and fallen a distance away from the others.

It points you home, his mother had said.

Oliver leaned down and grabbed that key. He felt his vision fading as he slid the key into the padlock. It slipped easily, effortlessly, and the hinge fell open. A black cloud of squid ink billowed from inside.

The contents were not gold, or jewels, or anything that would be considered treasure by any stretch of the imagination. The mermaids brought him, one by one, each item from inside the chest.

A fire extinguisher.

A megaphone.

A shark's tooth.

Oliver blinked, his vision blurred. "But these aren't riches," he forced out.

"What makes a treasure a treasure," Marina replied, "is how rare a find it is, when you need it the most." She reached toward Ondine and ripped the compass from her sister's neck, pressing it into Oliver's palm.

Oliver considered her words. And as he passed out, he thought that maybe this was the best advice one could ever be given about love.

OLIVER

THIS IS WHAT I KNOW ABOUT DELILAH McPHEE:

She bites her nails when she's nervous.

She sings off-key.

She mispronounces the word *schedule* in her flat, odd accent, yet insists that I'm the one who can't speak correctly.

She has the most mesmerizing eyes. It's as if she needn't speak at all, since everything she's feeling is written within them.

"You're not listening," Delilah says.

After my spending hours without her, we are finally together again. It is a little difficult to hear her, because she's blasting music from that magical box

called a radio, in the hopes that it will keep her mother from hearing her talk out loud to me. Behind Delilah's shoulders I can see the familiar bits of what I know is her bedroom—pink walls, pink lampshades, pink everything. At the edge of my vision is a fringed, furry throw pillow. And yes, it's pink.

"You keep distracting me," I tell her.

"All I'm doing is sitting here talking to you!"

"Exactly," I say, and I smile at her.

I like knowing that when I smile that way, it makes her cheeks go red. It's interesting that the same thing happens when I smile at Seraphima, but I don't find that nearly as charming.

I am looking at the way Delilah's eyelashes cast shadows on her cheeks and trying to decide if her hair is the color of milk chocolate or polished teak as she natters on and on. "I completely understand why you feel trapped," Delilah says. "But it's better to be trapped and alive—whatever that means inside a book—than free and dead."

Teakwood, definitely. Or maybe walnut.

"If something as simple as a spider didn't make it out of this book, how do you think a human being is going to fare? What if I pull you out of the book and you're only . . . a word?"

She gets up from where she is lying on her bed, talking to me, and starts pacing back and forth. From this perspective, I can see more of the room behind her: a mirror with pictures affixed around its edge, of Delilah and the girl she was speaking with earlier today; of Delilah with her arms spread wide at the top of a mountain; of Delilah and her mother making funny faces. I think that if I were to get out of this book, one of my first orders of business would be to steal one of those photos, so that I could always have her with me.

The other thing I can see from this angle is the way every inch of her figure is quite visible in the odd clothing she wears—some sort of blue hose with several rips and tears. They're so tight it's as if she's practically wearing nothing.

"Why aren't you wearing a dress?" I blurt out.

Delilah stops moving and faces me. "What? What does that have to do with anything?"

"What you're wearing is indecent!"

She snorts. "It's a whole lot more decent than what some of the girls in my school wear," she says. "Relax, Oliver. They're just jeans."

I realize that although I've seen Readers in strange garb before, they are usually so close to the page that I haven't marked the differences between their clothing and mine. On Delilah, though, I can't help but notice.

"As I was saying," she continues pointedly, "I really wish I could help you. But I've been thinking about you all day—believe me, you're *all* I've thought about—"

At this, I grin.

"—and I don't think I could ever forgive myself if I were the one who killed you."

My head snaps up. "*Killed* me? Why the devil would you do that?"

"Oliver, have you listened to *anything* I've just said? I can't risk having what happened to that spider happen to you." She sits down, looking into her lap. "I only just found you," Delilah says. "I can't lose you now."

In the fairy tale, I've never had to worry about death. I know the mermaids will not let me drown. I know I'll always beat the dragon. I know I'll always defeat Rapscullio.

But this Otherworld, it doesn't work the same way. There are no second chances. Death, here, is for real.

It hits me with the force of a blow: the understanding that I'd rather die than know I might never have a chance to truly, finally, kiss Delilah McPhee.

Maybe the reason I've never died in this story is that I've never had something worth dying for before.

"We just need to think of a different escape method," I suggest. "There has to be another way."

I hear Delilah's mother calling her name, and all of a

sudden the book is slammed shut. I wait a few moments, in the hope that Delilah might come back.

When she does, it's on page 43 once again. "Sorry," she says. She is hurrying around her room, locating a rucksack and stuffing a towel inside. "I have to go to swim practice."

"I'm sure you'll get the hang of it quickly," I reply. "I did."

"I *know* how to swim," Delilah says. "It's a sport. I'm supposed to be doing it for fun. But when you come in last place every time in the individual medley, it's hard to find the joy."

"Then why do it?"

"My mother thinks it will help me fit in."

"You should just tell her you'd prefer not to."

She pauses and looks at me. "Why don't you tell *your* mother off when she gives you a hard time?"

"That's different. I was written that way."

"Well, believe me," Delilah says. "Being a teenager isn't all that different from being part of someone else's story, then. There's always someone who thinks they know better than you do."

I offer my most charming grin. "You could stay with me instead."

"I wish." Delilah sighs. "But that's not going to happen."

"Then take me with you."

"Water and books don't mix very well."

"DELILAH!" Her mother's voice booms in the background once again.

And so she closes the book, more gently this time, and abandons me.

I sit down on the edge of page 43, already missing her, as Queen Maureen wanders into the edge of the margin. It's like that when the book is closed—any of us can wander anywhere; there's no privacy. "Oh, I'm *so* sorry!" she says, backing away. "I didn't realize anyone was on this page!"

"No, no," I say, getting to my feet. "It's quite all right. Really."

Queen Maureen isn't really my mother, of course. Technically, the author of this story is the woman who gave life to all of us. But like two actors in any long-running play, Maureen and I have become so comfortable with each other and our roles that she is the closest thing I have to a parent inside the pages of this book. I like the way she always saves me one of her fresh-baked ginger cookies from the castle kitchen when she's in a cooking mood. And from time to time, I've turned to her for advice when Frump and I have had a disagreement, or when Seraphima is so delusional that she's chasing me nonstop during our time off. I respect Maureen's opinions. In this way, I guess, my character has started to blend with the real me.

"Have you got a minute?" I ask.

"Of course." She walks closer and sits beside me on a stubby boulder. "You look like you want to kick a wall."

I exhale heavily. "I'm just so *frustrated.*"

"Who spit in your porridge?" she asks, raising a brow.

"If we're all just make-believe, are the emotions we feel still real?"

"Well," Maureen says. "Someone's philosophical today—"

"I'm serious," I interrupt. "How am I supposed to know what love really feels like?"

"Dear Lord, please tell me you haven't suddenly become smitten with that ditzy princess—"

"Seraphima?" I shudder. "No."

Maureen's eyes light up. "It's Ember, isn't it? I've seen her looking at you from the corner of her little eye."

"I'm not in love with a fairy—"

"It's not Cook, is it?"

"Cook? She's twice my age—"

Maureen frowns. "One of the mermaids? I should warn you that your dates would be impossibly soggy—"

"She's not in the book," I say.

Maureen just blinks. "Ah. Well, my boy, I don't think I can help you there."

"She's not like anyone I've ever seen before. When I'm not with her, I want to be. And when she opens the book and I see her face, I can barely remember what I'm supposed to say, much less how to speak at all." I test the words on my tongue. "I think I might be in love with her. But how can I really know, since the only love I've ever experienced was written for me?"

"Oh, darling, that's what love *is*. It's some power greater than you and me, that draws us to one special person."

Maureen sounds like she knows exactly what she's talking about. As if she's felt the same way I feel right now.

"I guess you really loved Maurice," I say.

She laughs. "Sweetheart, he's just a flashback."

I press my fingers to my temples. It's all so confusing—what's real, and what's only make-believe. In the story, I fall in love with Seraphima, but the way I feel when I'm with her is far different from what I feel for Delilah. With Seraphima, I'm going through the motions. With Delilah, everything is brand-new, brightly colored, always changing. "Then how do you know what love is?"

"Because so many stories are all about love, written by people who've felt it before. Rapscullio's lair is full of books about characters who aren't in *this* story but who are mad about each other. Romeo and Juliet, Beauty and the Beast, Heathcliff and Cathy."

"Who are *they*?"

Maureen shrugs. "I don't know, but our author wrote them onto the shelves on the illustration of page thirty-six. I've read a few, myself, during our off time. You know that anything that was in the author's mind might exist in the book, even if it doesn't show up in the proper story."

This is true. The world we live in is bigger than just the fairy tale; in fact, it's as spacious as the imagination of the woman who created us. It's why Frump and I know how to play chess, and Captain Crabbe has a passion for creating crosswords. It is as if whatever the author was thinking when she created the spaces we are in was richly imagined, three-dimensional. The castle kitchen, for example, is fully stocked with grains and flours and dishes and tableware, even though in the fairy tale, Cook is never actually seen baking. Because of this, during our off time, Maureen pores through recipe books and bakes cakes and pies and biscuits for the rest of us.

"Can I ask you something else?" I say, turning to Maureen. "I know he's just a flashback to you. But Maurice, he rode off to save you, and wound up leaving you behind forever. Is it really worth dying for the person you love?"

She thinks about this for a moment. "That's not the real question, Oliver. What you *should* be asking is, Can you live without her?"

Frump has called a meeting of all the characters, so we are gathered on the final page of the story, on Everafter Beach. He stands on his hind legs on a driftwood stump, addressing the masses. "It has come to my attention, friends," he says—he's truly the best orator of us all—"that we may be falling down on the job."

"Falling down *is* my job," says Pyro the dragon, who I must admit looks rather fetching with new fiery red rubber bands on his upper braces. "It's on page forty."

"I meant it more as a metaphor," Frump says. "None of us have gotten a lot of face time lately, because the Reader seems to be fixated on a particular page."

From my position, where I am sitting with my back against a palm tree, I freeze.

"Page forty-three," Frump adds, staring at me.

I give a flat laugh. "Well," I say. "Go figure."

"Can you think of any reason, Oliver, that the Reader's ignoring the rest of the story?"

"I'm, um, certain that it's only a coincidence," I stammer. "Perhaps she's very interested in rock climbing?"

"She?" Rapscullio says, stepping forward with a frown. "How do you know it's a *she*?"

I swallow hard. "Did I say *she*?" I shrug. "Just a guess. I mean, aren't most of our Readers little girls?"

"My point exactly," Frump says. "Which is why I think we need to amp up the action a bit. The next time this book is opened, let's leap off the page."

"Good luck with that," I mutter.

"What was that, Oliver?"

I cough. "Just a tickle in my throat."

"Right. As I was saying—mermaids, creepier! I want these kids to have nightmares! And trolls, make sure you slam Oliver to the ground when he crosses the bridge. And Rapscullio, when you've got him dangling sixty feet off the ground—"

"Hey, wait a minute!" I interrupt. "What about me?"

"Seems to me you're doing just fine." Seraphima sniffs. "Whereas *I* haven't spoken a single word in *days*. . . ."

"There's a silver lining," I murmur.

"You're absolutely right," Frump agrees, so eager to support Seraphima that he yelps. "With a voice as pure as yours, Princess, you should speak constantly. . . ."

But he might as well be talking to thin air. Seraphima completely ignores Frump, instead settling down beside me on the sand and running her fingers up my arm in a tickle. "Ollie," she purrs. "I really miss you. How about we go to page sixty and practice the kiss?"

"I promised, uh, to help Maureen in the kitchen," I say.

She sighs. "Suit yourself." Then she looks up at Frump. "Are we about done here? Because I really need a nap. Beauty sleep, you know."

"If you'll allow me to say so, milady, nothing could make you any more beautiful than you already are," Frump replies.

Kyrie, the mermaid, rolls her eyes. "For goodness' sake, Frump, you're making me seasick." One of the great ironies of this book is that the mermaids, in real life, don't have a boy-crazy bone in their bodies.

"All right, then!" Frump barks. "We all know what we've got to do to engage the Reader. I highly recommend using this off time to practice, so that we're in top-notch performance shape by the time the story is in play again."

He hops down lightly from his stump as the characters scatter. "Oh, Princess? Princess Seraphima? If you need someone to stand in for Oliver on page sixty, I'm happy to volunteer. . . ."

She turns around and points a finger at him. "Stay. Good boy."

With his tail between his legs, Frump shuffles off the beach. I am about to head after him, to try to lift his spirits—or at least to get him to abandon a ridiculous crush on a woman with the mental resources of a brick—when Captain Crabbe slaps me hard on the back. "Ahoy, Oliver. Did I hear you say that Maureen's cooking again? Dare I hope it's the pineapple upside-down cake? I'm happy to cut it into slices."

He draws his rapier from its sheath. The steel gleams, but not as brightly as his smile. Guess that's what happens when you floss daily.

Flossing daily.

Putting braces on dragons.

Moonlighting as a dentist instead of a pirate.

I take one look at Captain Crabbe and realize that this man might actually understand why I so desperately want to get out of the story. "Captain," I say, "how about you and I take a little walk?"

"Leave the story?" Captain Crabbe says, stopping dead in his tracks. The fairies, which have been accompanying us, swarm about his face like large mosquitoes. "I could never!"

"But imagine—somewhere, in another world, you might have your own orthodontics practice. You could fit retainers all day long, without ever having to stop to rig a mainsail or blow a cannon!" I offer him my widest, most hopeful smile.

He looks, for a moment, like he's considering this option. Then he says, "You know, that eyetooth on the left is just a little crooked. I can fix that. . . ."

I sigh, frustrated. "What if I told you I'd made contact with . . . the outside?"

Glint crosses her tiny arms. "Sounds like someone's been daydreaming again. . . ."

I swat at her. "Who asked you, anyway?"

"Ignore him," Sparks whispers. "He got up on the wrong side of the royal bed, obviously."

I ball my hands into fists. "WILL YOU ALL JUST LEAVE ME ALONE?"

"Well, I never," Ember mutters.

"Honestly!" Glint seconds.

Sparks lifts her chin. "Come on, ladies. We know when we're not being appreciated."

They disappear between the branches of the trees in the Enchanted Forest, and Captain Crabbe follows after them.

"Not *you*," I say. "*You* can stay."

"Oh. Aye." He faces me again. "Look, son. Even *if* what you said was possible . . . that doesn't mean I'm not happy right where I am."

"But how could you be? Doing the same thing over and over again, as if it doesn't matter whether or not you have your own mind, or your own thoughts?"

He shrugs. "I may be doing the same thing over and over again, Oliver . . . but I'm doing something I love. I get to be an actor *and* I get to do orthodontia." Captain Crabbe looks up at me. "What if instead of focusing on what you don't have, you concentrated on what you've got?"

I snort. "A supreme amount of frustration?"

"I was thinking more along the lines of a beautiful girl, in your arms, every time the story is read. A loyal sidekick who'll do anything for you." Captain Crabbe hesitates. "And fantastic gums."

"But—"

"I'm sorry, lad. But sometimes the key to happiness is just expecting a little bit less." The pirate smiles. "That way, you'll never be disappointed." With a cheery wave, he heads through the trails of the forest. "Must get back to the ship. By now, Walleye and Scuttle have probably lit the galley on fire."

As I watch him walk off, I lean against the trunk of an ancient, weathered oak. Could the captain be right? If I'd never spoken with Delilah, would I know what I was missing?

That's it. I'm going to go sit on page 43 and wait for her to come back to me, and I'll tell her she's right—that this is simply impossible. That there's no way I'm ever going to transcend the pages of this story. I'll tell her that—

"Ooomph!" I am knocked flat on my back, and for a

moment, all I can see are stars circling my face. At first I assume this is payback from the fairies, but then I hear a very clear, clipped voice behind me.

"I don't have all day. . . ."

I frown. That's the line Rapscullio says on page 45, once I've finished climbing the rock wall and have crept through the tower window where he is imprisoning Seraphima. I overhear him, and then I leap forward with my dagger drawn.

Except this isn't page 45.

Rolling onto my belly, I look up and spy Rapscullio, who is brandishing one of the pirates' fishing nets, rigged in a loop at the end. Just out of his reach is a stunningly brilliant spotted butterfly.

"Now what?" he growls.

Another line. From page 58, when he's holding his sword to my throat.

I get up, brushing dirt off my knees. "What on earth are you doing?"

Startled, he faces me—and the orange butterfly wings its way into the Enchanted Forest. "I *was* trying to kill two birds with one stone: practicing my lines like Frump suggested, whilst also catching a specimen of *Polygonia interrogationis.*"

"Gesundheit."

"You cretin. It's a species of butterfly,"

Rapscullio says. "One which has now eluded me, thanks to your interference."

I realize that Captain Crabbe and I have walked more of a distance than I intended, that we are actually not far from Rapscullio's lair: a small, dark hovel built into the wall of a cave and lit with hundreds of tallow candles. I think about what Queen Maureen told me — the rows and rows of love stories on the shelves of his library. "You know," I say slowly, "I don't believe I've ever seen your entire collection. Of butterflies, I mean."

Rapscullio's face lights up. "Oliver! Are you a closet entomologist?"

"Me?" I say. "Yes! One hundred and ten percent!" I have no idea what an entomologist is. I am hoping desperately that I haven't just admitted to Rapscullio that I like to bathe in garlic, or dress up in ladies' clothing.

"Well, come along, then! One never knows how much time one will have before the book is opened again." Rapscullio cocks his net over his shoulder and takes off through the grove at a brisk clip.

I run after him. "Do you happen to know how many species of butterflies exist?"

"But of course," he says. "There are five hundred and sixty-one. I have a book at home with illustrations of every single one."

"Huh." I pretend to mull over this information. "And how many have you managed to capture, exactly?"

Is it my imagination, or do his cheeks go pink? "Well, so far, only forty-eight. But then again, I only have sixty pages in which to collect them."

By now, we have reached the moldy wooden door of his residence. "What if I told you that you could catch the other five hundred and thirteen species?"

Rapscullio pauses, one hand on the doorknob. "You know, it's not nice to tease."

"I'm not, Rapscullio. I swear it." I follow him into his lair. I've been here a million times, of course, but it never fails to creep me out a bit. The walls are slightly damp to the touch, and mist rises from a mossy floor. In one corner is a cluttered desk that has been fashioned out of animal bones and rotted wood. The only natural light comes through a hole cut into the rock wall of the cave, and it illuminates an easel with a large canvas propped upon it: a half-finished portrait of Queen Maureen as a young girl, the crush who—in the story—led Rapscullio into a life of evil. There are a half dozen more pictures of her scattered around the small space, as well as some of dragons breathing fire.

"Here's the thing," I say, shrugging off the observation. "I think there might be a portal of sorts. A way to get out of this fairy tale into the real world. And in the real world, Rapscullio, you could spend every minute of your day hunting for butterflies you can only imagine in your wildest dreams."

"Why would I have to do that?" he says. "I can do the same thing right here."

"But you said there were only forty-eight types—"

"So *far*," Rapscullio retorts. He elbows me out of the way, his bony arm reaching behind me for a painting that I haven't noticed. Moving aside Maureen's half-finished face, he sets this new canvas on the easel.

It is a perfect, realistic replica of the exact room in which we are standing. In it is an easel. And on that easel is a canvas with an exact replica of this room as well. And so on and so on. In fact, it makes me a little dizzy to stare at the picture, as if a window has opened up directly in front of me.

"Wow," I say, impressed. "Maybe you should give up the villain thing and become an artist."

"Watch and learn, my friend," Rapscullio says. He lifts his painter's palette and dips a crusty brush into a splat of crimson. Then, with careful, fine strokes, he adds a glorious butterfly to the canvas, hovering just over the desk. He finishes with some yellow and black touches, then steps back to survey his handiwork. "Voilà," he says, and as I watch, the butterfly slowly evaporates off the painting.

And reappears four inches in front of my nose, before flitting out the window.

"Make that forty-nine species," Rapscullio says.

In one of the flashbacks of the fairy tale, we learn how Rapscullio managed to get a dragon to terrorize the kingdom and kill King Maurice. Instead of chasing one down in the Hidden Highlands, where the beasts are rumored to live, he conjures one with a magical easel. Anything painted on the canvas would peel itself free, just as three-dimensional and alive as the rest of us.

I can't believe I'd forgotten that.

"Hang on," I say, flabbergasted. "You can create anything you want just by painting it—even when the story isn't being read?"

In reply, he picks up another paintbrush and sketches a steaming mug onto the desk in the painting. It immediately appears in his hand. "Some tea?" he offers.

"Rapscullio, this is huge. This is *bigger* than huge. You can actually put anything you want into this story?"

"So it seems," he says. "I don't know why it works when the story isn't in play. Or why I can draw something other than Pyro into existence. But I must admit it's been rather handy."

"Do you ever paint anything other than butterflies?"

Rapscullio looks down, sheepish. "Last week I had the most intense craving for chocolate-covered gooseberries, and I painted a bowl of them and ate until I thought I was going to explode."

"If you can paint something *into* the story," I say slowly, thinking, "can you paint something *out* of it?"

He opens his mouth to reply, but before he does, we hear Frump's frantic voice, as if on loudspeaker:

Places, everyone! Book is opening! We have light along the seam, people! And remember, make this performance award-worthy!

And then, all of a sudden, I am falling backward and tumbling head over heels, until I land, catlike, clinging to a sheer rock wall on page 43.

Delilah

EVERY TIME I GO TO SWIM PRACTICE, I AM the last one out of the locker room. I just don't have any great eagerness to rush toward an hour of torture. I am the swimmer who comes in twenty-fifth out of twenty-five competitors, no matter what the stroke. I'm the one whose coach practically cringes each time she calls my name to get onto the blocks.

Today, though, I feel a little different. Maybe it's talking to Oliver—but I actually think that today, I might not come in last during our mock races. After all, he seems to believe in my ability to do the impossible—so why shouldn't I?

"Swimmers, take your marks," my coach says, and I

slip into the far right lane, hanging on to the edge of the pool in preparation for the backstroke. I fix my goggles and adjust my swimming cap, glancing down the row of my teammates. I'm next to Holly Bishop, who came in third in the state in the backstroke. *Awesome.* Farther down the line are some freshmen, and then in the far left lane is Allie McAndrews, the cheerleader, who (as far as I can tell) swims only because it gives her the chance to wear a bathing suit and flirt with the guys on the team.

There is an electronic beep, and I duck under the water and push off the wall, undulating in the first few meters. Already, it feels different to me, as if I am a creature of the sea—a mermaid, like the ones in Oliver's story—with a tail so powerful I could outswim a boat, much less Holly Bishop. I break the surface and stare up at the fluorescent lights of the aquatic center, streaking blindly backward. I am a machine. I am invincible.

I do my flip turn and when I surface again I can hear my fellow competitors yelling and cursing—and my coach screaming my name. *That's* how fast I'm going; nobody can believe that finally this day has come for ol' Delilah McPhee. Any moment now, I'm going to feel it— the electronic sensor board that will the stop the clock and herald my win. There is a flurry of water rushing beneath me, and my outstretched arm smacks something hard behind me—

"Owwwww!"

Sputtering, I pivot and rip off my goggles to find Allie McAndrews holding her nose, which is now streaming with blood in the deep end. "Are you *kidding*?" she screams.

I look at her, horrified, and then at some of the other girls on the swim team who are dragging her out of the pool. "Everybody out," my coach yells. "Bodily fluid in the water!"

"I . . . I'm sorry," I stammer, wondering what Allie McAndrews was doing in my lane. But then I glance around.

Somehow, I've managed to cross five pool lanes, to the far left one Allie had been swimming in. And with my killer backstroke, I've probably broken her nose.

"How was swimming?" my mother asks as soon as I slide into the passenger seat of her car.

"I'm quitting. Swim team, high school, life in general."

"What happened?"

"I don't want to talk about it." My phone beeps. There's a new text from Jules, but I don't even feel like telling *her* about my latest catastrophe. Besides, I'm sure she'll figure it out at school on Monday when I become an even bigger pariah than I already am.

My mother glances at me. "Well, whatever it was, it's nothing a double chocolate milk shake from Ridgeley's Diner can't fix. Let's stop there for dinner."

I know, for my mom, this is a big deal. We aren't the kind of people who eat out a lot. We can't afford to. "Thanks," I mutter. "But I really just want to go home."

"Delilah," my mother says, frowning at me. "Are you sure you're okay?"

"I'm fine, Mom. I just have . . . a lot of homework."

I successfully manage to avoid conversation for the rest of the ride home. When we pull into the driveway, I rush into the house and upstairs to my room. The book is lying on my bed, just where I left it.

I open to page 43 without even trying—the spine is developing a natural split there, I think—and find Oliver at the bottom of the rock cliff. He offers me a brilliant smile. "Did you enjoy swim practice?"

I've managed to hold it together through the end of practice; through the locker room, where everyone was whispering and giving me dirty glares; through the ten-minute car ride home. But now, in front of Oliver, I let go and burst into tears. As I do, droplets splash on the page. One lands on Oliver and bursts over his head like a water balloon, leaving him soaking wet.

"Sorry," I say, and sniffle. "I had a pretty lousy afternoon."

"Maybe I can cheer you up, then," he says.

Just being here cheers me up, I think, and I realize

that at swim practice, when my whole life was falling apart, the one person I really wanted to see was Oliver.

Who, technically, isn't really a person.

I wipe my eyes. "I just practically drowned the most popular girl in my school—the same one I crippled last year. Monday morning when I go to school every single student in the building is going to hate me."

"*I* won't hate you," Oliver says loyally.

I smile a little. "Thanks. But unfortunately, you don't go to my school."

"Ah, but maybe I could—sooner than you think. . . ."

My eyes widen as I realize what he's talking about. "You found another way out?" I would much rather talk about Oliver's problems than my own.

"Well, I found some kind of portal, at the very least! I met with Rapscullio, and he's a brilliant painter!"

"*Painter?* I thought he was a villain!"

"No," Oliver says. "Remember, I told you, that's just his role in the story. Anyway, he's figured out how to paint an object onto a special canvas that's an identical portrait of his lair . . . and have that object magically appear."

"That's how he creates Pyro, the dragon—"

"Exactly. But apparently the mechanism works even when the story isn't in play."

I shake my head. "How will that help? It's not like

Rapscullio lives *here*. He can't just paint you into this world."

"Yes, but I think I might be able to paint myself *out* of my own."

I ponder this for a moment. "That won't work. You'd just wind up repainted somewhere else in your story. Like a clone."

"A scone?"

"No, a cl— Never mind." I get up from the bed and start pacing in front of it. "If there was a way, though, to get a painting of *my* world into Rapscullio's lair, then maybe—"

"I thought you might need some comfort food. . . ." At the sound of a voice, I whirl around to find my mother standing in the doorway with a dinner tray. There's a grilled cheese sandwich and a glass of milk. She peers around the room. "Who on earth are you talking to, Delilah?"

"My . . . a friend."

My mother glances around again. "But there's no one here. . . ."

"Oliver's on the phone," I say quickly. "Speaker phone. Isn't that right, Oliver?" He doesn't answer, of course, and I feel myself blushing furiously. "It's a pretty bad connection."

My mother's eyebrows raise. *It's a boy?* she mouths silently.

I nod.

She gives me a thumbs-up and—leaving the tray—backs out of my room. "That was close," I tell him, and sigh.

He grins. "What's for dinner?"

"Can we be serious here?" I say. "I don't suppose you've taken any art classes?"

Oliver laughs. "Those," he replies, "are for *princesses.*"

"Oh yeah? Tell that to Michelangelo. Let's say that someone painted over that magic canvas so it *isn't* a portrait of Rapscullio's lair . . . but instead a painting of my bedroom. And then you happen to start to paint yourself onto it. Logic says that—"

"I'll wind up in your bedroom!" Oliver's eyes shine. "Delilah, you are amazing!"

When he says those words, a shiver runs the length of my spine. What if he *did* show up right now, sitting on my bed? Would he high-five me? Hug me?

Kiss me?

At the thought of that, my cheeks burn like they're on fire. I hold my palms up against them, hoping Oliver hasn't noticed.

"Ah, now I've embarrassed you," he says. "All right, then. You are not amazing. You're perfectly ordinary. Run-of-the-mill. Completely dismissible."

"Shut up," I say, but I'm smiling. "I want to try an experiment. Have you got your dagger?"

"Of course," Oliver replies. He draws it from its sheath. "Why?"

"Draw a picture of me. On the rock wall."

He blinks. "Right now?"

"No, next Thursday."

"Oh, good." Oliver starts to put the dagger away.

"I was joking! Of *course* right now!"

Is it my imagination, or does he look a little green? "Right," Oliver mutters. "A portrait." He poises the tip of the knife over the granite. "Of you." He steps forward, blocking my view as he begins to etch on the rock. Twice, he looks over his shoulder to peer at my face.

I think of all the beautiful paintings hanging in museums around the world—muses captured on canvas: the Mona Lisa, the birth of Venus, the girl with a pearl earring. "Voilà," Oliver declares, and he steps aside.

Carved onto the rock wall is a disproportionate figure with bug eyes, snake hair, and a flat line of a mouth. Apparently, to Oliver, I look like a Muppet.

"Not bad, eh?" he says. "Although, I don't think I *quite* captured your nose. . . ."

No wonder; he's drawn it as a triangle.

I hesitate. "No offense, Oliver, but you might not be the ideal choice to paint a picture of my room."

He frowns at the portrait he's drawn of me, and then smiles. "Perhaps not," Oliver says, "but I know just the fellow who is."

rince Oliver dreamed that one of the mermaids was still kissing him. He was fighting to pull away from her, struggling to breathe—and then he opened his eyes. No mermaid was kissing him, just Frump, licking his face as Socks whinnied and stamped his foot a few feet away. Oliver sat up, damp and bedraggled, on the ocean shore. He had no recollection of the mermaids bringing him to the surface, and he might have considered it all a nightmare, except for the fact that in one hand he was clutching his compass, and in the other he was holding a sack that contained the flotsam and jetsam the mermaids had claimed to be treasures.

One hour into their journey, Oliver and his faithful entourage reached the River of Regret, a mile-wide whitewater fury that had claimed the lives of many who'd tried to cross it. The only hope for passage was the Bridge of Trolls, which—it had to be said—was nearly as perilous.

It is a well-known fact that trolls either *always* tell the truth or *always* lie. And that every day they build two bridges—one safe and one designed to collapse at the first hint of weight.

Oliver dismounted, patted Frump on the head, and walked to the edge of the cliff. He could see three small, squat men shuffling about with hammers and nails on the far side. One of the bridges appeared rickety and weak; the other was strongly fashioned—but Oliver knew that looks could be deceiving.

"Helloooo?" Oliver called, but the trolls continued working, unable to hear him over the roar of the water.

Oliver turned and dug the megaphone from the mermaids' treasure collection out of his rucksack. "Helloooo!" he yelled again, and this time the trolls all looked up. "My good men," Oliver said. "Which bridge should I use to cross?"

The first troll, Biggle, glanced up. When he spoke, Oliver had no trouble hearing him; trolls were known to talk in decibel levels that could shake the Earth. "Why, what have we got here? Some fancy man with his fancy horse, and what's that? A big rat or somethin'?" Biggle stroked his long gray beard.

"Sir, I do see you're working quite hard," Oliver said with a smile. "I would greatly appreciate your advice."

Snort and Trogg, the remaining trolls, started to laugh, grunting and holding their bellies. "Ye can only ask one of us to choose for you," said Trogg, the chubby one. "Make yer pick."

Oliver thought about this. If trolls *always* lied or *always* told the truth, how to find out which troll was trustworthy? "Do you tell the truth?" he yelled through the megaphone.

Biggle replied, but at that moment, the water between them roared, so that Oliver could not make out the answer.

Snort cupped his hands near his mouth. "He said he always tells the truth!"

"No, he didn't," called Trogg. "He said he was a liar."

Oliver glanced from each hideous face to the next. Biggle, he realized, must have said he was truthful. This would have been his response if he *was* indeed truthful, because of course he'd say so; but it also would have been his response if he was a liar.

Which meant that Snort's statement *had* to be the truth.

In other words—*he* was the troll to trust.

"You!" Oliver said, pointing to the short troll in the middle. "Which bridge?"

"This one," Snort proudly answered, pointing to the rickety bridge.

Oliver mounted his stallion again and, without a moment's hesitation, crossed the bridge Snort had indicated.

"That'll be a guinea," Biggle grunted.

Oliver patted down his pockets and saddlebags, but all his spare change had fallen into the ocean when he was with the mermaids.

The mermaids.

The trolls advanced, menacing, ready to pound him into the dirt.

"Gentlemen," he said, "do you know what's more precious than gold? True love."

"We're trolls," said Trogg. "Or hadn't you noticed?"

"I happen to know three lovely ladies who could overlook that fact," Oliver said.

"Honestly?" asked Snort.

Oliver grinned. "I always tell the truth," he said.

OLIVER

"BEDSPREAD," DELILAH SAYS.

"Um . . . pink."

"Good. Number of stuffed animals on the bed?"

"Three."

"Excellent. What are they?"

I close my eyes, trying to remember. "A pig, a bear wearing a strange little shirt, and a duck with quite a sassy look on its face."

"And the book?"

"Purple leather, with gold lettering that reads *Between the Lines*."

It's odd to think of my story as a physical entity, because obviously I've never seen the outside of the tome in which we all live. But Delilah has described it in excruciating detail.

In fact, she's spent hours this Saturday evening giving me a thorough tour of her bedroom by carrying the open book from end to end. I have read fortune cookie messages tacked onto her mirror; I have met her pet fish—named Dudley; I have stared at a whiteboard she can write upon and erase, which is festooned with small favors from places she and her mother have visited: the Flume in New Hampshire, Ben & Jerry's ice cream factory, Boston, the Statue of Liberty. We realized that the only error in our plan was that Delilah could not watch the painting actually happen—since that would have to occur when the book was closed and I could meet privately with Rapscullio in his lair.

To this end, Delilah insisted that I memorize every last detail of her room, so that it could be as accurate a representation as possible on that magic canvas. Like me, she doesn't want to leave anything up to chance.

"How many lamps are in here?" she quizzes.

"Three. One on the desk, one clipped to the bed, and one on the dresser. And next to the lamp on the dresser is a music box you got from your mother for your fifth birthday; and there's a sticker on your headboard of Curious George that you put there when you were three and could never quite peel off entirely; and right now there are three pairs of earrings that you haven't put into your jewelry box yet, which are sitting next to your hairbrush." I smirk at her. "*Now* do you believe I'm ready?"

"Very," she says.

"Okay. I'm off, then."

"Wait!" I turn back to find her staring at me, biting her lower lip. "What if . . . it doesn't work?"

I reach up, as if I might be able to touch her, but of course I can't. "What if it *does?*"

She traces one finger along the edge of the page close to me. The world beside me ripples. "Goodbye," Delilah says.

Rapscullio's lair needs a thorough cleaning. There are cobwebs in the corner, and I am pretty certain a rat runs over my shoe as I enter. "Anybody home?" I ask cheerfully.

"Over here," Rapscullio calls out. I turn a corner to find him examining a butterfly that's been trapped inside a glass jar. There are holes in the lid, but the insect's wings are beating desperately as it tries to escape.

I know how that feels.

"Rapscullio," I say, "I need your help."

"Kind of busy right now, Your Highness . . ."

"It's an emergency."

He sets the captured butterfly down on a table. "Go on," Rapscullio says, folding his long, bony arms.

"I was hoping you could paint something for me. A gift."

"A gift?"

"Yes—for a friend of mine. A very special friend of mine."

Rapscullio's face lights up. "I have just the thing—I've been working on a close-up of a long-toed water beetle—"

"I was thinking of something different," I interrupt. "And maybe a little more romantic."

He scratches his chin. "Let's see . . ." he says. When he stalks into the adjacent room—the studio I've been in before—I follow him. Rapscullio pulls three canvases with Seraphima's face from the piles stacked along the walls. "Take your pick."

"The thing is . . . this isn't for Seraphima."

A slow, itchy smile twitches over Rapscullio's lips. "Well, well," he says. "Our little prince is playing the field."

"Oh, cut it out, Rapscullio. You know Seraphima and I were never really a 'thing.'"

"Then who's the lucky lady?" he asks.

"No one you know."

He laughs. "I'd say, given the size of our world, that's highly unlikely."

"Look," I say, "just do me this one favor, and I'll do anything you want."

"Anything?" He looks at me from the corner of his eye.

I hesitate. "Sure."

"Will you . . . sing something for me?"

I'll be perfectly honest, my singing ability ranks at about the same level as my drawing ability. But I nod, only to have Rapscullio turn aside, move some canvases out of the way, and pluck out a tune on an ancient piano.

I listen to the first few notes. "Do you know it?" he asks hopefully.

"Um. Yes." I clear my throat, and start to sing: *"For he's a jolly good fellow, for he's a jolly good fellow. For he's a jolly good fellow . . . that nobody can deny."*

When I finish, I look up to find Rapscullio wiping a tear from his eye. "That," he says with a sniff, "was beautiful."

"Er . . . thanks."

He clears his throat. "Sometimes it's hard being the bad guy, you know?" With one final snort, he turns his attention to me again. "Now," Rapscullio says. "Your painting?"

"Well," I begin, "I sort of need it to be painted on the magic canvas. The one you use to bring the butterflies to life."

Rapscullio scowls. "Do you have any idea how long it took me to re-create my lair perfectly in that painting? I'm sorry, Oliver, I just—"

"You *can.* Because the minute the story starts again, the canvas will be back to normal—with your original painting on it. Just like always."

I watch his face as he processes this information. "That's true," Rapscullio admits.

"It's a room. With a bed in it. A bedroom," I tell him.

"Yes, that's usually the case when there's a bed in the room. . . ."

"And it's very . . . girlie. The walls are pink."

Rapscullio picks up a brush and swirls together some pigments. "Like this?" he asks, and Delilah's walls come to life.

"Yes!" I say. I point to a corner of the canvas. "Right there's a mirror—no, the wood is more blond than brown. And it sits on a dresser. Can you redo that bit, so that there are five drawers instead of four?"

It is painstaking, asking Rapscullio to re-create a room full of things he has never seen. When he gets really stuck (a lampshade? A clock radio?) I draw a mock-up of the item in the dirt floor with a stick. "And a book on the bed," I continue. "It's purple with gold lettering on the cover, which reads *Between the Lines*."

He lifts a brow. "As in . . . the name of our story?"

"Um. Yes. I thought it was a nice touch." There's no point in explaining to him why I really need the book to be there. I continue to give instructions, making corrections when necessary: *No, the magnet is shaped like a boot, not a circle. And the sheets are more fuchsia than pastel violet.*

Finally, when Rapscullio is through, I look at the canvas and see a detailed replica of Delilah's room. "Well?" he demands.

"Perfect," I murmur. "It's absolutely perfect."

Now comes the hard part. Delilah and I have realized that if I'm to paint myself into this canvas, Rapscullio can't be watching. It's just too much to risk—what if I confide my plan to him and he tries to stop me, or tells Frump and the others that I'm attempting to leave the story? I could try to dupe him into simply painting me onto the canvas as part of the gift portrait, but what if he figures out, midway, what is happening and leaves me half in Delilah's world and half in mine? I am not an artist by any means, but it's all we've got.

Together we've devised a plan—with the help of something called Google and a search for rare species of butterflies. If I stick to the script we've written, Delilah is certain Rapscullio will leave me alone here—we hope long enough for me to pick up a paintbrush and create an image of myself on that canvas.

"Oh my goodness!" I cry, snapping my head toward the open window. "Did you see that?"

"See what?"

"I'm sure it was nothing. Just a butterfly."

"Butterfly?" Rapscullio's eyes widen. "What did it look like?"

"Tiny and electric blue . . . with a black-and-white border on its wings?"

He leaps toward the window. "An Adonis blue? You saw an Adonis blue? But they're supposed to be extinct!" Rapscullio hesitates. "You don't think it was just a Chalkhill blue, do you?"

"No, not a Chalkhill," I say. "Definitely not a Chalkhill." What the devil is a Chalkhill?

"Hmm." He glances out the window again. "Are we all set here, then? Because if you don't mind, I might take a poke outside with my net to see if I can catch the Adonis before we have to do our next book performance."

"Go right ahead," I say. "Perfectly understandable."

I wave as he sprints out of the room. Then I look at the canvas again. It is a stunning, realistic representation of Delilah's room. I only wish I had Rapscullio's artistic talent.

"Here goes nothing," I mutter, and I pick up the paintbrush that Rapscullio's left on the palette. I catch my reflection in the window glass—Delilah and I both think with the subject right in front of my eyes, I may be able to at least make an adequate copy, even if I'm no artist. I touch the canvas, leaving a faint mark the same color as my sleeve. I rinse the brush and mix a new color, one that matches my flesh.

But then I hesitate. Putting the brush down, I walk into the adjoining room, where the butterfly is still beating senselessly against the glass jar. I twist the lid, and watch it fly out the open window.

Just in case something goes wrong, at least one of us will be free.

Delilah

WHAT IS TAKING HIM SO LONG?

I've been waiting for an hour and a half, and still, zip. Nada. Nothing.

I could open the book.

I told him I wouldn't open the book.

The minute I do, of course, any headway he's made with Rapscullio will be erased, and they'll all be performing the story again.

"Oliver," I say out loud, "this is ridiculous."

"My thoughts exactly."

I nearly jump a foot when I hear my mother's voice. She is standing in the doorway, looking worried.

"Delilah, it's after midnight. And you've been talking

to yourself the whole night—don't try to argue with me, I've been listening through the door—"

"You've been *eavesdropping* on me?"

"Honey," my mother says, sitting down on the bed, "I think maybe you need someone to talk to." She hesitates. "Someone real, I mean."

"I *am* talking to someone—"

"Delilah, I know what depression looks like—and I know what it feels like. When your father walked out, I had to drag myself out of bed every day just to get you to school, and to pretend for you that everything was okay. But you don't have to pretend for my sake."

"Mom, I'm not depressed—"

"You spend all your time alone in your room. You say that you hate swimming, that you hate school. And your only friend looks like a vampire—"

"*You're* the one who told me not to judge a book by its cover," I argue, immediately thinking of Oliver. "I'm fine. Honestly. I kind of want to be alone right now."

From my mother's face, I can tell this was exactly *not* the right thing to say. "On Monday, I'm going to see whether we can get you an appointment with Dr. Ducharme—"

"But I'm not sick!"

"Dr. Ducharme's a psychiatrist," my mother says gently.

I open my mouth to argue, but before I can speak, I notice something shimmering beside my mother's left shoulder.

It's a hand.

A disembodied, floating, translucent hand.

I blink, and rub my eyes. I have got to get my mother out of this room now.

"Okay," I say. "Whatever you want."

Her jaw drops. "You mean, you're not going to fight me on this?"

"No. Dr. DuWhatever. Monday. Got it." I pull her to her feet and walk her to the threshold. "Gosh, I didn't realize I was so tired! Good night!"

I slam the door and turn around, certain that the hand will have disappeared—but there it is, and

now there's an arm attached too.

Except the arm is flat and two-dimensional. Like a cartoon arm. Which is exactly what I was afraid would happen if Oliver were to come into this world.

I'd rather have him stay the way he is than change. I just wish other people—like my mom—felt that way about me.

I grab the book and rip it open to page 43. Oliver stands at the bottom of the rock cliff. As I watch, the blue paint spattering his tunic vanishes, until he looks the same way he always does on page 43. "*What* are you doing?" he yells.

"Saving your life!"

"It was *working!*"

"Oliver, you started to show up in my room. But you started to show up flat as a pancake. Did you really want to live in my world that way?"

"Maybe I just looked like that because I wasn't finished yet," he says. "Maybe I'd puff up like a pastry at the very end."

"Even so—how would you be able to finish painting yourself out of the story? At the very least, your arm or fingers or hand would have to stay behind to put those last brushstrokes on the canvas."

He sinks down to the ground. "I hadn't thought of that."

"I know," I say sadly. "I'm really sorry."

Oliver is sitting with his knees drawn, his head bent. I wish I could tell him everything will work out in the end, but that's only true in fairy tales—the very place he's trying to escape.

"Maybe we should call it a night," I whisper. I set the book, still open to page 43, on my nightstand and crawl into bed.

"Delilah?" Oliver's voice drifts to me. "Do me a favor?"

I sit up again. "Anything."

"Can you close the book, please?" He looks away. "I kind of want to be alone right now."

These are the very words I just said to my mother. The same ones she insisted were signs of depression. I wish I knew how to help Oliver. I wonder if my mother feels this way about me.

But instead, I just nod and, as gently as I can, do what he's asked.

liver eased his way inside the tiny cottage. There were piles of books and jumbles of glass bottles in all shapes and sizes. The old wizard led him to an adjoining room whose rafters were thick with dried herbs and flowers. He stuck a bony finger between his chapped lips and wet it with the tip of his tongue, then pressed it against the dusty page of a large leather book and flipped through it, scanning the spells. Finally he smiled, and his face creased into a hundred more wrinkles. "Ah," said Orville. "Pass me that Rubicon flower, will you, my boy?"

Oliver had no idea what that was, but he pointed to a dried, crusted orange button on the stone worktable before him. When Orville nodded, Oliver handed it to the wizard, who rubbed the bud between his palms before letting the petals settle in a big wooden bowl.

"And the three bottles to your left?" Orville continued to mix and stir, to taste and test. "And the vial to your right—no, be careful with that!" Orville warned as Oliver realized how hot the glass was to the touch. He glanced down to find his fingerprint burned into a whorl pattern on its side.

Orville took an eyedropper and dipped it in the vial, then counted out three sizzling drops into the wooden bowl. They vanished with a hiss and a puff, creating a wall of orange flame. Orville squinted into the heart of the fire as the hottest bits, the blue center, began to form into silhouettes.

Oliver could see a tower, and a dragon beside it blowing fire. But where *was* the tower? There had to be a hundred like it in this kingdom alone. The flames dipped and spread, and then Oliver could see it—the cliff that rose from the edge of the ocean. The jagged rocks below, the pounding surf. Timble Tower was a former battlement, long abandoned—and the only tower Oliver had ever seen perched on a cliff. He knew exactly where it was.

"Thank you!" Oliver cried, rushing out the door.

A moment later the frantic pounding of hoofbeats sounded as Oliver galloped away. Orville turned back to the flames, which were reshaping and re-forming themselves. This time, the old wizard could see black hair falling over one evil eye, a scar that wound its way from brow to cheek, a wicked grin. He doused the fire with cornstarch and raced out the front door of the cottage, but by that time it was too late.

Prince Oliver was gone. He'd have to find out for himself that this princess of his was not alone.

OLIVER

"YOU MUST BE KIDDING," RAPSCULLIO SAYS WHEN he sees me for the third time. "What do you need now?"

I don't want to be here. I don't want to be anywhere in this stupid fairy tale. I am back to square one, actually. Although I'd believed that maybe I had found a way out of this prison, Delilah is right. I can't be the one who paints myself free, and I can't trust anyone else to do it for me, which means I'm going nowhere fast.

I'd wanted to talk to Delilah, but she was fast asleep — my own fault since I was the one who asked her to close the book. After she left, I felt so completely defeated, as if nothing I could ever do would change my circumstances. Nothing I usually did in my off time — chess, a long walk, a bracing swim in the ocean—could take me away from my thoughts. And then I remembered Delilah.

When she wanted to escape *her* life, she read books. Like this one.

Queen Maureen had mentioned an entire library at Rapscullio's cave—a room that I'd never actually reached, because I got so distracted by his magic canvas instead. But if Delilah could use stories for distraction, maybe they would work on me too.

"I'm looking for a good read," I tell Rapscullio. "I hear you've got quite a large selection?"

Rapscullio brightens. "Oh, yes, indeed I do. I'm particularly fond of troubadour ballads and folktales, but my shelves seem to have a bit of everything: romances, horror, comedy. Even some plays by a fellow called Shakespeare. He's not half bad."

"Maybe I could browse?" I ask. "I don't really know what I'm looking for."

"Be my guest," Rapscullio says, extending one emaciated arm toward a tunnel in the rear of the lair. "You go have a look around, and I'll make us some tea. Chamomile. You seem a little . . . high-strung these days."

"I don't want you to go to any trouble—"

"No trouble at all." He elbows me and grins with half his mouth; the scar immobilizes the other half of his face. "Maybe you'll even tell me more about that girl of yours."

"Girl?" I can't tell him about Delilah. I feel like she's my own personal secret. Like if I tried to explain her to anyone inside here, it would be giving a piece of her away.

"The one you had me paint the picture for—"

"Right." The girl I made up, as an excuse. I wait for Rapscullio to unearth his teapot from under a moldering flutter of old maps on a broad table, and I turn and duck through the narrow passageway into another part of the lair.

The small room is musty and slightly damp, with floor-to-ceiling shelves carved out of gnarled walnut. Books are stacked and tucked and jumbled in piles. There are astronomy tomes and volumes about insect species and a whole shelf about Renaissance painters. I read some of the spines. *An Herbologist's History of the World. War and Peace. A Tale of Two Cities.*

Rapscullio's teakettle begins to whistle. Any minute now he's going to come back here and expect me to rhapsodize about a make-believe maiden who lives somewhere in this kingdom. I pluck a book off the shelf. Maybe one of these stories will inspire me to come up with a good lie that he'll believe.

When I pull the book free, though, another one tumbles to the dirt floor, having been jammed behind the first on the shelf. I pick it up and dust it off, about to replace it more carefully, when I realize I've seen this one before.

It's purple leather, with gold lettering.

BETWEEN THE LINES, I read on the cover. I flip it open and see a picture of myself on the very first page, as if I am staring into a mirror. "Once upon a time," I murmur aloud.

Maybe one of these stories will inspire me.

"Milk or sugar?" I hear Rapscullio's footsteps in the narrow corridor, so I slip the book beneath my tunic and hastily reach for another one, which I pretend to be thumbing through when my host arrives with the tea.

My whole connection to Delilah started with words — a message etched onto the cliff wall. Why couldn't it end the same way?

I may not be able to paint myself into another world, but perhaps I can edit myself out of this one.

Delilah

MY MOTHER IS THE REASON I'M HOOKED ON fairy tales.

After my father left, my mom and I got hooked on Disney movies, the ones adapted from darker, creepier fairy tales. In the Disney version, the Little Mermaid doesn't commit suicide and become foam—she winds up having a gorgeous wedding on a boat and sails away forever with her prince. The original Cinderella had stepsisters slicing off parts of their feet to try to fit into the glass slipper. My mother and I needed the whitewash that Disney provided. We'd sit with a big bowl of popcorn, wrapped together in a queen-size blanket, and would escape to a place where magic was ours for the taking, where men rescued the people they loved, instead of abandoning them. A place where, no matter how bad things looked at that moment, there would always be a happy ending.

It's silly, I know, but I sort of imagined my mother as the Disney Cinderella. She cleaned houses all day long and then came home and helped me with my school-work or cooked dinner or did our laundry. When I was younger, every time the doorbell rang and a UPS truck driver or the mailman or the pizza delivery guy was standing on the other side, I'd wonder if this was the prince who'd sweep her off her feet and give her a completely different life.

It never happened.

I don't think often about my father. He lives in Australia now with his new wife and two twin girls, who look like little princesses, with yellow curls and baby-blue eyes. It's as if he started his own fairy tale, half a world away, without me in it. Although my mother swears I had nothing to do with my father leaving, I have my doubts. I wonder if I wasn't smart enough, pretty enough, just . . . *enough* to be the daughter he wanted.

Once or twice a year, though, I dream about him. It's always the same dream, where he's teaching me to ice-skate. He's holding on to my outstretched hands, skating backward in front of me so I can balance. *You've got it, Lila,* he says, because that's what he always called me. He lets go of my hands, and to my surprise, I don't fall. I just glide forward, one foot in front of the other, as if I'm flying. *Look,* I cry out, *I'm doing it!* But when I look up, he's gone; I'm all by myself in the freezing cold.

When I have this dream, I always wake up shivering, and lonely.

This time, when it happens, I stare at the ceiling for a moment, and then I roll onto my side and pick up the book where I left it last night. I open it to page 43.

"Thank goodness!" Oliver shouts. "Where have you been?"

"Sleeping," I say.

He looks up, doing a double take when he sees my face. "What's wrong?"

"Nothing." I seem to be saying that a lot lately.

"Then how come you're crying?"

Surprised, I touch my cheeks and realize they're wet. I must have been crying while I was asleep. "I was dreaming about my dad."

Oliver tilts his head. "What's he like?"

"I haven't seen him in five years. He's someone else now, with a whole new family. A whole new story." I shake my head. "It's sort of stupid. The reason your book even appealed to me was that one line in the beginning, about you growing up without a father. But Maurice wasn't really ever your father, I guess. He's just another actor."

"I still know what it feels like," Oliver says quietly. "To be overlooked. You have no idea how many times I shouted, in my mind, trying to get a Reader to see me for more than just what she needed me to be: some stupid character in a book."

"Until me," I say.

He nods. "Yes, Delilah. Until you." Even my name on his lips sounds softer than it does on anyone else's. "I *do* understand you," Oliver says. "If I didn't, you never would have heard me."

"Well, nobody else does. My father ditched me, and now my mother thinks I'm crazy."

"Why?"

"I don't know. Because instead of joining the debate club or going out on Friday nights with guys who watch Lord of the Rings marathons and speak Elvish, I spend all my time lost in a book that isn't age-appropriate for me."

"Well, I'm not crazy, and I spend all *my* time lost in a book that isn't age-appropriate for me. . . ."

I smile at that. "Maybe we can be crazy together."

"Maybe we can," Oliver says, grinning widely. "I found another way out."

My eyes widen. "What are you talking about?" I whisper. "Why didn't you tell me right away?"

"Because you were crying," he says, truly surprised. "That mattered more."

Zach, the vegan lab partner I was recently crushing on, couldn't even remember to hold the door open for me when we were heading into class. This chivalry thing Oliver's got going on—I could get used to it.

Oliver reaches beneath his tunic and pulls out a leather-bound book with gold lettering—an exact replica of the one I'm reading. "I found this on Rapscullio's shelves. The author painted it into the illustration of his lair, along with hundreds of other book titles. You don't even notice them when you're paying attention to the story—but they're there. And they *stay* there when the book is closed. And look"—he leafs through it so I can see—"it's exactly the same, isn't it?"

It seems that way. As Oliver flips the pages, I see Pyro breathing fireballs and Frump trotting through the Enchanted Forest as fairies dance in circles around him. I see a tiny illustration of Oliver too, standing at the helm of Captain Crabbe's ship as the wind ruffles his hair.

I wonder if that very small fictional prince is, at that moment, wishing for someone to notice him and get him out of his own story.

"It makes perfect sense that I couldn't paint myself

out of this story—because a book isn't a painting. But you've already noticed things that I've drawn or written before on the pages—like that chessboard, and the message on the cliff. Perhaps rewriting the story in *my* copy will rewrite the story in *yours* as well."

"I guess it's worth a try," I say.

"What's worth a try?"

My mother's voice sinks through the blanket I'm hiding beneath. I emerge from under the covers. "Nothing!" I say.

"What's under there?"

I blush. "Nothing, Mom. Seriously!"

"Delilah," my mother says, her face settling grimly. "Are you doing drugs?"

"What?" I yelp. "No!"

She rips aside the covers and sees the fairy tale. "Why are you hiding this?"

"I'm not hiding it."

"You were reading under the covers . . . even though there's nobody in your room."

I shrug. "I guess I just like my privacy."

"Delilah." My mother's hands settle on her hips. "You're fifteen. You're way too old to be addicted to a fairy tale."

I give her a weak smile. "Well . . . isn't that better than drugs?"

She shakes her head sadly. "Come down for breakfast when you're ready," she murmurs.

"Delilah—" Oliver begins as soon as the door closes behind my mother.

"We'll figure it all out later," I promise. I shut the book and bury it inside my backpack, get dressed, and yank my hair into a ponytail. Downstairs, in the kitchen, my mother is cooking eggs. "I'm not really hungry," I mutter.

"Then maybe you'd like this instead," she says, and she passes me a plate that has no food on it—just a single young adult novel. "I haven't read it, but the librarian says it's all the rage with girls in your grade. Apparently, there's a werewolf who falls in love with a mermaid. It's supposed to be the new *Twilight*."

I push it away. "Thanks, but I'm not interested."

My mother sits down across from me. "Delilah, if I suddenly started eating baby food or watching *Sesame Street*, wouldn't you think there was something wrong with me?"

"This isn't *Goodnight Moon*," I argue. "It's . . . it's . . ." But there's nothing I can say without making things worse.

Her mouth flattens, and the light goes out of her eyes. "I know why you're obsessed with a fairy tale, honey, even if you don't want to admit it to yourself. But here's the truth: no matter how much you might wish for it, princes don't come around every day, and happy endings don't grow on trees. Take it from me: the sooner you grow up, the less you'll be disappointed."

Her words might as well be a slap in the face. She slides the eggs onto a plate and sets them in front of me before leaving the kitchen.

Sunny side up? Yeah, right.

No one ever asks a kid for her opinion, but it seems to me that growing up means you stop hoping for the best, and start expecting the worst. So how do you tell an adult that maybe everything wrong in the world stems from the fact that she's stopped believing the impossible can happen?

I usually say I hate Biology, but it's possible we just got off on the wrong foot. My teacher, Mrs. Brown, completely lives up to her name: she is addicted to self-tanner and Crest Whitestrips, and spends a lot of time talking about her favorite spots in the Caribbean instead of helping us prepare for the next day's lab. I think it's fair to say I'll be teaching myself about cell division, but I'm totally set if I need to plan a vacation to the Bahamas.

I spent Sunday in my room, plotting Oliver's escape with him. Sometimes we forgot the task at hand because we went off on a tangent. I told Oliver things I've never been brave enough to tell anyone else: how I worry about my mom; how I panic when someone asks me what I want to be when I grow up; how I secretly wonder what it would be like, for an hour, to be popular. In return, Oliver confided his biggest fear: that he will pass through his lifetime—whatever that may be—without making a difference in the world. That he will be ordinary, instead of extraordinary.

I told him that—as far as I was concerned—he's already been successful at that.

I told him I'd rather die than go to school on Monday and face Allie McAndrews. But here it is, third period, and she's absent.

Maybe Oliver's right; wishes *can* come true.

"Does everyone have a frog?" Mrs. Brown says. I glance down at the poor, dead amphibian in front of me. Usually my lab partner is Zach, but he's taken a conscientious objector position on this lab, due to his veganism, and instead of doing a dissection he is writing an independent paper on growth hormones in dairy cows.

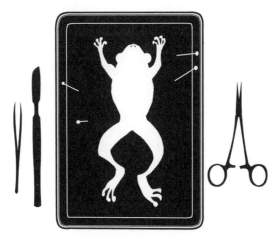

The door opens, and in walks Allie McAndrews, with two black eyes. She looks like a raccoon, and has a criss-crossed strip of tape over the bridge of her nose too. She hands Mrs. Brown a hall pass. "Sorry I'm late," she says.

"Better late than never," the teacher says. "Allie, why don't you pair up with Delilah?"

Allie shoots me the look of death as she takes the stool beside me. "Touch me," she whispers, "and I will make your life miserable."

"Now, class, pick up your frog. I want you to measure the posterior appendages . . ."

I turn to Allie. "Do you . . . want to go first?"

She glares at me. "I'd rather join Chess Club."

I joined Chess Club last year. "Okay, then," I say. *Sorry, buddy,* I think as I lift the frog into my palm and pick up a ruler.

Allie's boyfriend, Ryan, drags his stool toward our lab table, even though he is supposed to be working with someone else. "Hey, gorgeous," he says, grinning at her. "So what do you say you and I get some takeout and download a movie and *not* watch it tonight?"

"I'm not in the mood," she says, glancing at me. "I have to go home and *ice.*"

"It was an accident," I tell her. "I didn't purposely cross five lanes of the pool just to smack you in the face." Although, I admit, I might have daydreamed about doing just that.

"You're the only girl in the school who could make two black eyes look hot," Ryan says.

Allie twines her fingers with his. "You're just saying that."

"Cross my heart," Ryan answers.

"I love you, babe," Allie says.

Ryan grins. "Love you more."

I thought there was a good chance I would feel like throwing up during a dissection lab, but I figured it would be because of the frog, not the conversation.

Mrs. Brown winds past our lab table. If she notices that Ryan is now our third partner, she doesn't comment. "Now, class, I want you to examine the chest area. . . . What skeletal feature is missing?"

I wait for Allie to pick up the frog to examine it. "You, um, want a turn?" I ask her.

"To smack *you* in the face? Break *your* knee?"

"Right, then," I say, poking at the frog again.

"What kind of takeout should I get?" Ryan asks. "Chinese? Indian? Italian?"

"Ribs," I announce.

They both look at me with disgust. "Who asked you?" Allie says.

"No . . . the frog. The skeletal part it's missing . . . is ribs."

She tosses her hair. "Who cares?"

"Gently," Mrs. Brown warns a boy to my right, who is

squeezing his amphibian so tightly that its head is swelling. "Dissection is both an art *and* a science. Show your frog a little love."

Suddenly, Ryan grabs the frog off our lab table in one hammy fist. "Yeah . . . show your frog a little love." He shoves it so close to my face that I can breathe in the scent of chemicals and death. With all my might I push away from him, knocking over the lab stool and causing enough of a commotion that the entire class stops to watch.

"My bad," Ryan says. "I thought it said it was a prince. . . ."

The class bursts into laughter. I turn seven shades of red.

"That's enough!" Mrs. Brown says. "Ryan, go to the principal's office; you and I will be seeing each other at detention this afternoon. Delilah, take the bathroom pass and go clean yourself up."

As I grab my backpack and stumble out of the classroom, the students are silent. And then, just before I cross the threshold, I hear it: "*Ribbit. Ribbit.*" It's one of the kids in the back, and suddenly everyone is snickering and Mrs. Brown is trying (and failing) to get them to quiet down.

The girls' bathroom is empty. I scrub my hands and face and blot them dry with paper towels. Jules used to be my go-to girl whenever something horrendous happened—the person I could count on to make me feel better. But now I find myself searching through my back-pack. Just like after my dream, the only person I really want to talk to right now is Oliver.

I rummage in my backpack, past my Biology textbook and my English binder and my lunch, but the book is missing.

"No," I mutter, and I pull the textbooks out of the bag. All that's left now is crumpled paper, nubby pencils, bits of crushed granola bars, and forty-two cents.

The fairy tale—which I had put in my backpack that morning with my own two hands—is gone.

It doesn't take me long to decide that I'm not going back to Biology class. I'll just tell Mrs. Brown I was so trau-matized I was in desperate need of a guidance coun-selor. Instead, I hurry to the library, where I find Ms. Winx pasting bar codes into new books. "Ms. Winx," I ask, "has anyone returned *Between the Lines*?"

"Aren't you the one who has it checked out?"

"I'm pretty sure I left it by accident in the cafeteria before homeroom. . . ."

"Well, if anyone turns it in, I'll let you know."

As I leave the library, in the pit of my stomach is a stone. What if I can't find the book? What if it's gone forever?

What will I do without him?

I've never been in love, but I've always imagined it—weirdly—like some sort of OxiClean commercial. The TV host shows a scene from an ordinary day, and then takes a big old sponge soaked in love and swipes away the stains. Suddenly that same scene is missing all the mistakes, all the loneliness. The colors are like jewels, ten times richer than they were before. The music is louder and clearer. *Love*, the host will say, *makes life a little brighter*.

When I'm talking to Oliver, I feel like there's nobody in the world but the two of us.

When I'm talking to Oliver, I want to keep talking forever. I want to know how old he was when he learned to ride a horse, and what his favorite color is, and what pops into his mind just before he falls asleep.

When I'm talking to Oliver, I wonder what it would be like if he held my hand.

In spite of what Ryan and my mother think about me and fairy tales—it's not that I've been looking for a prince.

It's that, without even trying, Oliver makes me feel like a princess.

Seventh period Jules and I have Driver's Ed, the only class we share this semester. The third kid in our car, Louis Lamotte, who always smells like soup, is at the wheel. Which means that Jules and I are stuck in the back while Mr. Barnaby tries to keep Louis on the right side of the road.

"So are you going to tell me why you're pissed off at me, or do I have to play Twenty Questions?" Jules says.

"I'm not mad at you!"

"Yeah, right. You don't answer my texts all weekend, you don't wait for me after school, and today at lunch when you were totally ignoring me and I told you I had an asteroid growing out of my butt, you said, *That's nice.*"

"I'm just a little distracted," I tell her. "Really, I'm not angry."

"Girls," Mr. Barnaby says, "you're supposed to be *observing.*"

Jules totally ignores him. "When you accidentally tripped Allie McAndrews last year during the hundred-meter dash at Field Day and she broke her knee, I was the first one to know. You called me up hysterical and told me I had to run off to Mexico with you because you weren't coming back to school. Today, I found out that you broke Allie's nose from that kid who chews gum too loud in the library." She looks at me. "I don't even know that kid's *name* and he knew something about my best friend that I didn't."

"Look," I tell Jules. "I'm not hiding anything from you. And you're still my best friend. Things at home are just . . . crazy right now. My mother wants to take me to a shrink."

Jules shrugs. "Big deal. My parents take me two or three times a year. Just tell them you have deep-seated issues with your father and they'll say you're cured."

"Girls!" Mr. Barnaby says, over his shoulder. "Louis needs to focus."

"Louis needs a lot of things," Jules says under her breath. "Starting with a shower."

I can't help it; I stifle a laugh. Jules glances at me sideways and bumps shoulders with me. "Don't shut me out, okay?" And just like that, I'm forgiven.

I felt like I was in a sort of frantic fog, mentally retracing my morning steps to figure out where I could have misplaced the book. By the end of school, it still hasn't turned up. I shuffle to the curb where cars are lined up to retrieve kids, and find my mother's van.

"So," she says as I open the door, "how was your day?"

I shrug. "The same as usual."

"Oh, really? I thought you might have missed this." She reaches beside her and pulls out *Between the Lines.*

"Where did you *find* that?" I shout, grabbing it out of her hands. I know it will send Oliver and Company into a tizzy, but I open the book quickly and flutter through the pages without reading it. Then I hug it to my chest. "Thank God! I thought I lost it!"

My mother shakes her head. "That's exactly why we're going to Dr. Ducharme, Delilah."

"*Now?*" I thought at least it would take my mother a few months to get an appointment. And by then, she might have totally forgotten about the psychiatrist, and we could just not show up.

"It's nothing to be ashamed of. He's only going to chat with you for a little while. Help you get in touch with what's making you sad."

Angry tears spring to my eyes. I'm *not* sad; I'm tired of being told by someone else what I'm allegedly feeling. "You're one to talk," I say. "You're taking me to a psychiatrist when *you* haven't opened up for five years! I guess it's perfectly normal to just work yourself to the bone, because then you don't have time to realize how depressing your life is!"

My mother reels back as if I've slapped her. "You have no idea what my life has been like, Delilah. I had a daughter to raise on my own, with no income. I can barely cover the payments on my mortgage. Somehow, I have to find the money to send you to college. Someone has to be the grown-up here, and that means knowing the difference between what's real and what's make-believe."

"I know the difference between reality and make-believe!" I cry out. But even as I'm saying it, I wonder if that's a lie. If it makes a difference, when you keep wishing they were one and the same.

liver had lost count of how long it had been since Scuttle and Walleye locked him in the brig. The ship pitched and dove in the storm; every now and then, Oliver felt the timbers shake with the force of the lightning and thunder.

Whatever rescuing a princess entailed, he was pretty sure that becoming a pirate captain's sacrificial slave was not part of the deal.

He tugged at his chains, but they held fast. On the floor was the dinner tray he'd refused—the one with crackers that were moving. Or rather, the crackers weren't moving. Just the worms baked into them.

He wondered why they would bother to feed a prisoner who was ultimately being transported as a gourmet peace offering for a very cranky, very hungry dragon. The same one that Rapscullio had conjured sixteen years earlier—the one that had killed Oliver's father—now nested on the Cape of Passing Tides, preventing the ship from continuing its journey. Maybe Oliver had to put on some weight in order to qualify as a tasty morsel.

He wondered what had become of Socks and Frump, whom he'd last seen on the shoreline as the shipmates dragged him into the brig. He wondered how long it would be before Captain Crabbe himself showed up to bring his prisoner abovedecks, to make Oliver walk the plank onto the waiting fiery tongue of the dragon.

There was a strafing of metal against metal as the door to his cell slid open. The pirate captain stepped inside and narrowed his eyes. "My boys tell me ye aren't cooperatin'," Captain Crabbe said. "Ye know what we do to slaves who don't cooperate?"

He crossed to the table that was bolted to the floor so that it wouldn't overturn as the boat pitched and tossed. From his spot chained to the wall, Oliver watched the captain take out a velvet roll. He untied it, spreading the fabric open to reveal pockets full of gleaming instruments of torture.

Except they weren't daggers and thumbscrews and knives.

Last year, Queen Maureen's tiara had fallen off while she was horseback riding through the unicorn meadow. Although it was retrieved, it was badly dented and in need of fixing. She put out a call for crown repair, and the man who came to the castle, to everyone's surprise, asked her to take a seat in her throne and open her mouth wide.

Apparently, there were the sorts of crowns one wore on one's royal head . . . and then there were the sorts of crowns that sat on one's teeth when one had severe dental problems.

In Captain Crabbe's velvet pouches were explorers, extractors, probes, and mirrors.

"You're . . . you're a dentist?" Oliver asked.

At first Captain Crabbe's eyes bugged out, surprised. Then just as quickly he recovered. "Nay. I'm a fearsome pirate, and you, my lad, are an appetizer."

"Maybe," Oliver said, "but you're also a dentist."

Captain Crabbe gasped and rushed over to Oliver, clapping a hand across his mouth. "You won't tell anyone, will you? I have a reputation on the high seas to uphold!"

"That depends on whether you let me go," Oliver said.

"I can't," the captain said, shaking his head. "If I don't feed *you* to Pyro, I'm likely to wind up as a meal myself."

Oliver considered this. "What if," he suggested, "I told you there was a way to get you around the Cape of Passing Tides . . . *and* at the same time, to find you the best dental patient you'll ever have in your life?"

OLIVER

I'VE BEEN WAITING PATIENTLY ALL DAY FOR Delilah to get out of school and come back to me. I want to talk to her more about the fairy tale I found at Rapscullio's. I want to know if she thinks this new plan will work better so that I won't wind up as a flat blue stick figure in her world. I want to ask her opinion on what I should write in the book and where, since she seems to have great experience as a reader. I want to form a plan about what we'll do if—*when*—I get out of here.

Who am I kidding? What I want is simply to spend time, more time, with Delilah.

I think that when you live in a world with limits, as I have—when you've met everyone and seen everything you're ever going to see—you lose the hope that something extraordinary will happen in your life. Your actions and interactions will always be shades of the same old routine. But with Delilah, everything is new and fascinating. Who knew, for example, that there is a huffing sort of air gun to make wet hair dry, so that the ends don't freeze when you're riding on a cold morning? Who knew that there are devices that have just a single page, but with the click of a button fill that screen with new text over and over? For every question I ask Delilah, she has one for me: Are other books like this one, and do all characters exist when we're not reading? (I have to beg off answering that, because all I know is my own experience.) When did I first become aware that I was trapped inside a story, instead of just assuming that I was living my life? (Again, hard to answer, as I have always been and always will be sixteen in here.) And then there are the questions she asks me in a whisper, when night falls and it is just the two of us in the dark: *Who would you be, if you could be anyone? Where would you go?*

I don't always have a ready reply. But the mere fact that Delilah is asking is magical to me. Never before has anyone ever thought I might be anything other than what I appear to be on the page. No Reader has assumed that there are thoughts in my head other than the ones put there by an author.

Last night, Delilah asked me if I believe in Fate.

"I don't think so," I said. "Since I just can't accept that my destiny is to play a role in someone else's story."

"But what if that isn't the case?" Delilah whispered. It was late, after midnight, and the moon had silvered half of her face. It made her look otherworldly, magical. Like someone who'd belong in a fairy tale.

"I'm not following you. . . ."

"What if you and I were meant to be together?" she said. "What if the reason Jessamyn Jacobs wrote this story in the first place was because some higher power— Fate, Destiny, whatever—compelled her to do it, since it was the only way for us to meet?"

I liked that idea. I liked thinking that whatever Delilah and I had between us was so strong that there was no boundary between the true and the imagined, the book and the Reader. I liked the idea that although I started my life as a figment of someone's imagination, that didn't make me any less real.

Today, while Delilah is in classes, I'm sitting on a crooked, twisting branch in the Enchanted Forest. The fairies flutter around me, chattering. Although they *do* like gossip, unlike the characters they play they're actually not nasty little creatures at all. They're always happy to be pawns when Frump and I play chess, and they are good sports about shimmying down cracks and crevices too tight for the rest of us to pick up a dropped penny or a lost button. They're also the strongest creatures in the story, with more strength than even the thuggish trolls, and they don't mind helping Queen Maureen redecorate by hauling furniture up and down the castle steps. I've seen a single fairy roll aside a boulder that had blocked the road to the castle without even breaking a sweat.

"Glint, can I borrow your poisonberry lip gloss?" asks Sparks.

"Get your own," Glint says. "I'm tired of you using all my stuff." But she tosses an acorn to Sparks, who twists off the cap and dips her finger into the cosmetic. She leans toward a dewdrop to see her reflection and then swipes her tiny finger across her lips. I try to read the book in front of me, but branches block out the light. Suddenly, a hovering glow illuminates the page. I squint at it and see Ember shining.

"Thanks for that," I say.

She flashes a brilliant smile. "No problem."

I flip through the pages, absently wondering if in some other world, there is a cast of royalty and mermaids and pirates all racing into position so that I can enjoy my story.

I wonder if in some other world a prince is pining away for a girl he loves.

"Love?" I say out loud.

"*Love?*" Glint repeats.

"Did someone say *love?*" Ember asks.

"Love?" I hear again, followed by an echo, and another, and another, as every fairy in the forest repeats the word.

"Oh yes," Sparks says, "I totally called this."

"Remember yesterday, when you walked into a tree?" Ember asks.

"That," Glint says, "is when we started taking bets."

The fairies perch on my shoulders and arms. "Who's the lucky princess?" Ember asks.

I have no intention of telling them; I couldn't betray Delilah that way. "You wouldn't know her. She's not from around here."

"Uh . . . who *isn't?*" Sparks says.

All of a sudden I hear a bark from across the woods. "Frump," I say with relief.

"I'm pretty sure Frump is from around here," Sparks replies.

Waving them away, I hop off the tree branch and land on the ground just as Frump skids to a stop at my feet.

"Hey, buddy . . . you got a minute?" he asks. The look on his face is one I've seen before—mostly when he's under the table begging for scraps.

With reluctance I tuck the book beneath my tunic. He leads me out of the forest, away from the keen ears of the fairies. As soon as we clear the woods, Frump breaks into a run. I have to sprint to catch up to him.

We race past the cliff walk and the turnoff for the trail to where Orville the wizard lives. "Is there a reason we're in a hurry?" I pant.

"We have to get to the unicorn meadow in time," Frump shouts back to me.

"What's in the unicorn meadow?" I ask as we break into its center. The field is full of snowy, horned crea-tures grazing on lush silver grass.

"You are," Frump admits, coming to a stop. "I told Seraphima you'd be here."

"*Why?*"

He looks down at the ground. "So she'd come. If it had just been me, she'd never bother."

Frump was, according to the backstory we all know by heart, once human. My best friend, as a matter of fact, until Rapscullio stole some herbs from Orville, intend-ing to kill the young prince (namely, me) he saw as an obstacle to his love for Maureen. The draught into which he mixed the herbs, however, was mistakenly drunk by

Frump. He would have died without Orville's interven-
tion. The wizard couldn't reverse the curse, yet he managed a transfiguration: Frump would live, but in the
body of a different creature. In this way, he'd be safe
from Rapscullio's wrath.

This, anyway, is what the text says during the course
of our story. But I have known Frump only as a dog,
because that's what he is when the fairy tale begins. He's
a boy only in flashbacks, and flashback characters don't
exist the way the rest of us do, flesh and blood even when
we're offstage. It's why I've never met King Maurice; it's
why Frump is a hound . . . with the heart and mind of a
young man.

One who is utterly, incomprehensibly, madly in love
with Seraphima. Who wouldn't give him the time of day,
even if he *didn't* have fleas.

"Aw, Frump." I scratch behind his ears. "You don't
need me to get a girl interested in you."

"Oh yeah? Then how come she lit up like a firecracker as soon as I mentioned your name?"

I wince, thinking of Seraphima. "Doesn't it bother
you to know she can't tell the difference between when
the book is closed and when it's open?"

"Not really. I keep telling myself that's why she isn't
interested in me. To her, I'm just a dog."

I suppose it could be argued that Delilah doesn't

have the best track record either, when it comes to telling reality from fiction. "Can I ask you a question?"

"Sure."

"How do you know she's the one for you?"

Frump wags his tail. "Well, she's got that beautiful, shiny blond coat . . . er . . . I mean, *hair* . . . and there's that little space between her front teeth . . . and did you ever notice how, when she's nervous, she sings? Off-key?"

"You *like* that?"

"Well, that's the thing," Frump says. "I think her flaws make me love her even more. She's not perfect, but she's perfect to me."

I think about Delilah—how she snorts when she laughs, how she bites her nails when she's thinking hard about something. How she doesn't seem to know the simplest things—like that if one has an ache of the head, a leech—not some small round white candy—will do the trick. How she makes wishes on eyelashes and stars or when her clock reads 11:11. "Yes," I say softly. "I understand."

Frump lets out a painful yowl. "You love her too?"

"Seraphima? No. A million times no."

He gives me a look that betrays just the slightest doubt.

Even if I didn't want to kiss Seraphima, the book would pull me into the embrace. And she's pretty enough. So kissing her isn't really a hardship, and if I *have* to do it, I might as well pretend I am having fun.

Still, my intimate moments with Seraphima always leave me feeling guilty. Not just because of Frump, but because I know she is putting all her passion into that kiss since she thinks it's real, when for me, it's a day's work . . . with some pleasant benefits.

"Then you've got to help me, Oliver," Frump begs. "How do I get her to notice me?"

For a moment, I let myself consider this. Delilah saw me all on her own, and I doubt that even if Frump mowed the word HELP into this field, it would do anything but annoy the unicorns. "What about a gift?" I suggest.

"I gave her a bone—the best one I've ever buried. She threw it away!"

"What did you do?" I ask.

Frump shrugs. "I fetched."

I start pacing. "The problem is that Seraphima always sees me as the conquering hero, when she needs to look at *you* that way. Which means, my friend, that you need a damsel in distress." Several unicorns whinny as I pass by too closely. "That's it." I snap my fingers. "I'm going to die."

"What?"

"Not for real. Just pretend. Then you can rescue me in front of Seraphima."

"Ollie, no offense, but you make

a really ugly princess. And I'm not going to kiss you to wake you up from your fake sleep, no matter what."

"You don't have to, Frump. We're going to pretend I've been gored by a unicorn. All you have to do is stop the fake bleeding." I bend down in front of a sugarberry bush and grab a handful of the fruit.

Frump looks anxiously off in the distance. "Could you maybe pick berries *afterward*? She's going to be here any minute."

"I'm not going to eat them," I mutter, mashing the berries between my hands. They are a red, runny mess. Opening my tunic so that my white shirt shows through, I smear the berry juice into the fabric. A red stain bleeds from the center of my chest.

"There's just one problem," Frump says. "No one's ever been gored by a unicorn. They're the sweetest creatures in the book."

"Well . . . maybe I made one really angry," I suggest. I lie down with my head against a boulder and cover my fake wound with my hand.

Frump is turning in nervous circles. "It's not going to work, Oliver. She's going to figure it out. I can't act. . . ."

"Are you kidding me? You act like a dog every day. Surely this has to be easier."

Suddenly we hear a high, off-key tune floating over the meadow. The unicorns bleat and scatter. "Oh, Oliver . . ."

Seraphima trills. "Are we playing hide-and-seek, my darling?"

"Oh, that's good, that's really good," Frump whispers, glancing at my face. "You look really sick."

"Focus," I hiss. "Fr . . . ump . . ." I gasp. "Help me . . ."

Seraphima races across the field, but when she sees me fallen and bloody, she shrieks. "Oliver!"

Frump leaps onto my chest. "Hang in there, my friend," he says. He turns to Seraphima. "One of the unicorns went berserk. Oliver's lost a great deal of blood." Frump presses his paw down in the center of the wound. "Take off my collar," he orders.

"I beg your pardon!"

"For a tourniquet," Frump says.

Out of the corner of my eye, I watch Seraphima stare at Frump in a way I've never seen her look at him. But it's not adoration I'm seeing.

It's competition.

She lifts him up with two hands and hurls him off my body. "Out of my way, puppy," she grunts, and she kneels in front of me. "Don't go with the angels, Oliver!" she cries. "Stay with me!"

With that, she leans down and seals her lips over mine in a massive huff that is supposed to be artificial respiration but feels more like a sloppy, wet kiss. Sputtering, I sit up and push her off me.

"I did it! I saved you!" Seraphima cries, pulling me into her arms. "Oh, Oliver. I don't know if this is life imitating art or art imitating life. . . . I'm just so glad to know that you and I will have our chance to live happily ever after!"

I groan. "Where's the unicorn. . . ."

"Far, far away, my love. Why?"

"I was hoping it could run me through again."

Frump shuffles closer, his tail between his legs. *Sorry,* I silently mouth.

Seraphima plops herself down on the ground beside me and starts tearing the bottom of her skirt to make bandages. "We need to get you to Orville for a poultice. . . ."

The last thing I want is for Seraphima to stay here playing nursemaid—or worse, to treat me for an injury I've never had. Thinking quickly, I frown and whip my head to the left. "Did you hear that?"

Frump barks.

"Right, old buddy. It *did* sound a lot like Rapscullio. . . ." I know that will put Seraphima into a panic. For someone who can't tell the difference between real life and the story, Rapscullio is a constant threat.

"Rapscullio!" Seraphima gasps. "What if he finds me?"

"Quick—run away." Steeling myself, I give her a fast, firm peck on the lips. "Your life is more important than mine. I'll come as quickly as I can. Frump, can I trust you to keep Seraphima safe?"

Frump smiles slowly. "It would be my honor and my privilege, Your Highness," he says. "My lady?" He holds out a paw, and after a reluctant moment, Seraphima takes it.

I watch them hurry across the meadow, a delusional princess who can't distinguish reality from fiction, and a lovesick basset hound. Well, there have been stranger couples, I suppose. "Good luck," I whisper to Frump, although I know he cannot hear me. "I'll miss you, if I ever get out of here."

Not if, I tell myself. *When.*

As I'm changing into clean clothes, I wonder about the seeming discrepancies of my life in this book. Why is it that I have a closet full of tunics and doublets I am never  seen wearing during the course of the story, but Frump, who by text used to be a boy, is never seen in that form? Why is the barn where Socks lives stocked with geese and chickens and cows who play no other discernible role in the fairy tale but Seraphima doesn't recognize that the part she plays isn't necessarily who she is? These are contradictions I don't understand and, to be honest, haven't considered before. Before meeting Delilah, that is.

I am still mulling over this when I hear Frump call a full-book alarm. "All fairy-tale personnel, report immediately to the stables," he commands. "I repeat, this is an emergency—not a drill!"

On the way down the castle staircase, I nearly bump into the queen. "Oliver, dear," she says. "Do you have any idea what's happening?"

I don't. But my heart is pounding and my hands are shaking . . . and I am hoping like mad this has nothing to do with me and Delilah. Has Rapscullio discovered the book is missing? Have the fairies figured out more from our earlier conversation? "I don't know," I tell the queen, "but I don't like the sound of it."

The sound actually gets worse as we approach the stables. There is a frantic snort and a series of low grunts. Overhead is the telltale sliver of light that indicates the book is about to be opened. But if that's the case, why are we all just milling around?

Because I am a main character, I am able to push my way through the crowd to the open stable door. There, Frump paces back and forth on a clot of hay as chickens scurry and flap to get out of his way. "Frump, what's this about?" I ask.

He turns. "Thank goodness you're here." He glances up at the slice of sky that is growing wider. "It's Socks. He's talking about a strike."

"Strike? What did he strike?"

"No, he's *on* strike. He refuses to come out of his stall for the next telling of the story."

I hesitate. No one in this story has ever resisted the telling of it. That is, every time the book opens, characters scramble into position. I'm the only one I know of who's ever defied it in any way—and I know from experience that the book will correct itself and yank Socks into position whether he likes it or not. But if I admit that out loud, I'll create an even bigger stir, because everyone will realize that I have been actively resisting the book too.

"What's the worst that could happen?" I say lightly. "So I'm missing a trusty steed. No one will ever notice." *No one will ever notice,* I think, *because the minute we're all back on page one, Socks will have been dragged against his will to meet us where he belongs.*

"We can't take that chance. We're trying to buy some time." Frump jerks his chin up to the corner of the barn, where Orville teeters on a ladder, pointing his wand at the crack of light. *"Obscurius manturius . . ."* he intones, and a shower of sparks creates a gummy seal across the line of light, falling to the hayloft and igniting several small fires that Rapscullio, standing below, stomps out.

"Someone's opening the book even now, Oliver," Frump says. "I don't know how long we can hold it shut."

I am knocked sideways as the trolls lumber past me

into Socks's stall. "From the back, boys," Frump orders. "Give him your best shove."

I approach the open stall door. Socks is standing with his face in the corner, head ducked. "Socks?" I murmur. "What's going on, buddy?"

"Just go away," the pony sobs.

"Whatever it is, I'm sure we can work it out. I'm here for you. We're all here for you."

He tosses his mane. "I am a hideous, monstrous beast. Please let me wallow in my own misery."

"I'm afraid I can't do that, Socks. I mean, a lot of people are counting on you. We've got a story to tell. And you—you're one of the stars of the show."

He hesitates. "I . . . I am?"

"How else would I get anywhere?" I say. But there is a part of me wondering if I'm right about what will happen if Socks just stays in his stall. Will he be ripped into position on the page, like I was? Or will he do what I so badly crave: change the way this story goes?

"*Ein . . . zwei . . . drei . . . stoß!*" the trolls shout, and Socks whinnies as they shove at him, trying to make him budge.

"Frump," Orville shrieks, "I'm afraid I can't make this hold any longer!"

I glance up. By now, long streaks of light are falling on the floor of the barn. "We're on it!" Glint calls. A battalion of fairies flutters up to the corner of the scene. Like an acrobatic circus troupe, they arch their bodies over the growing gap, their small faces twisted with determination as they struggle to keep the pages shut.

Stepping into the stall, I sink down to the ground so that I can shimmy underneath Socks. He immediately averts his nose. "I can't. I can't."

"Socks," I beg. "Please. At least tell me what the problem is so that I can fix it."

"It's too horrendously embarrassing."

"As embarrassing as the time I fell overboard on the pirate ship?"

"Worse," Socks groans. "I have . . . I have . . . Oh, I can't say it out loud."

"Chicken pox?" I guess. "Poison ivy? Heartburn?"

"A zit," Socks bursts out. "A huge, red, swollen zit on my nose."

"Horses don't get zits, Socks," I say gently.

"Oh, great. So now I'm a zoological abnormality with acne."

"Let me look." Gently, I pull his velvety muzzle down to my face. I scrutinize from nostril to nostril, finding no blemish of any kind. "Socks," I say, "there's nothing there."

"You're just saying that to make me feel better!" he wails. "I cannot go out in public with a big red clown nose, Oliver!"

There is a commotion as Captain Crabbe comes through the crowd. He is wearing his dentist's coat and carrying a blue-paper-wrapped pack of sterilized instruments. "Did someone call for a surgical consult?" he asks.

Socks's eyes widen. "Surgery! Who said anything about surgery?"

"Don't worry, my little horseshoed friend. You'll only feel a pinch," Captain Crabbe promises.

He motions the trolls out of the way and stands directly behind Socks. As he unwraps the sterilized tools, several points of light shimmer from the corner of the scene onto Socks's back, dappling his hide. "Frump," Sparks grits out from the top edge of the page, "it's T minus ten . . ."

Is Delilah wondering why the book is stuck? Is she attributing the trouble to humidity, faulty binding, a smear of jam?

Captain Crabbe brandishes the dental scraper, a blinding silver hook.

"Nine," Ember says.

He holds it up to a shaft of light, examining the point. "Eight . . ."

Socks twists his neck, looking at the tool with dread. "Seven . . ."

I swing my leg over the pony and lean down against his mane. "It's your call, Socks. You can do this your way, or his way."

"Six . . ."

"I love a good lancing at twilight," Captain Crabbe says with a sigh.

"Five . . ."

"Well?" I say. "What's it going to be?"

"Four . . . three . . ."

Socks shifts nervously. "Um . . . um . . ."

"Two . . ."

Captain Crabbe raises his arm high as several fairies fall, exhausted, to the barn floor in small puffs of golden glitter.

"One!"

"Wait!" Socks cries, but Captain Crabbe has already jammed the tool into his hindquarters, sending the pony crashing through the wall of the barn. The wooden wall splinters and shatters just as the sky above us becomes blindingly white and the rest of the fairies lose their hold on the seam of the scene. "Places, everyone!" Frump screams. Even though I dig in my heels, Socks runs blisteringly fast, and I can barely hang on. I look back to see utter chaos—characters trampling each other to get to their correct spots, words jamming and tangling as they rearrange themselves on the page, the barn shattered by Socks in his escape.

Except, it's not.

As Socks continues his gallop, I stare over my shoulder and watch the wooden boards that have been torn from the barn frame slowly knitting themselves back together, until the wall that was broken a moment before is just as good as new.

Rapscullio.

Why didn't I think of Rapscullio?

Every time we tell the story, it ends with a fight between us. There I am, unarmed, as Rapscullio swings his sword back and forth. Eventually, he backs me up against the tower window. Sixty feet below me, the angry ocean crashes against a stony cliff. The sea mist sprays upward in a plume. "Goodbye, Prince Oliver," Rapscullio says with a sneer, every time. But as he lunges toward me with his sword pointed, I duck to the side. Without the resistance he's expecting, Rapscullio falls forward through the open window and shrieks to his death below.

Here's the thing:

After the next few pages are finished and Seraphima and I have our wedding on the beach, the book closes, and there's Rapscullio walking around from page to page — chasing another butterfly, or doing needlepoint, or trying out a new lemon square recipe with the trolls as his willing taste testers. In other words, he's no worse for wear.

He falls sixty feet onto jagged rocks and pounding surf, and winds up as good as new.

Now that I'm thinking about it, there are plenty of

instances I've witnessed where something happens on the page, only to undo itself moments later. Pyro's braces vanish the moment the story's over. The bridges that the trolls have built collapse again.

So even if I write myself out of the fairy tale . . . I might wake up the next morning to find myself right back where I started.

What this calls for, I realize, is a test. A personal test. As scary as it is, I have to be the one to get hurt—because that's the only way to know whether my story has any hope of changing for good.

"I'll show you," Delilah says, her voice filling every corner of my mind. "I'm not making this up." Suddenly, I am clinging to the rock wall for dear life, looking up at the tower that houses Seraphima.

In other words, the book is open again, and I'm on page 43.

Who is she talking to?

I glance over my shoulder and see Delilah—with another face peering down at me.

Some fellow I've never seen before, with a sweep of brown hair and kind blue eyes.

He seems a bit old for her, but that doesn't stop me from feeling a burning jealousy in my belly. If I took my dagger out from between my teeth, could I throw it at him? Would it just bounce back against the barrier between us?

"Oliver," Delilah says.

That's more like it, sweetheart.

"Say something."

I freeze. I'm completely confused. Am I supposed to speak out loud or not? Delilah seems to change her mind about this as frequently as Socks changes horseshoes. She wants me to be quiet when her mother is nearby; but then she's angry when I don't speak for her friend Jules. I honestly don't know what she wants of me this time.

"Oliver!" Delilah groans. She turns to the man. "I don't know why he's not talking to me."

"And how does that make you feel?" the man asks.

She leans closer to me. "Oliver," Delilah whispers. *"Speak!"*

I can feel her breath ruffling my hair. She seems to want me to speak, but then again, maybe this is a trick. And besides, even if I yell at the top of my lungs, Delilah is the only person who's ever heard me loud and clear. Better to be safe than sorry, to stay the course so that Delilah doesn't come off as completely mad.

I carefully remain frozen on the page.

"Fine, then. Let's try *this* scene," Delilah says, and she flips through the book. I find myself tumbling sideways, smacking into several trees, the letter *y,* and Socks's considerable rear end before landing in Seraphima's embrace on the final page. Her lips are locked against mine, and her

body is pressed along the length of me. The other characters stand in a semicircle around us. I roll my eyes upward,
only to see those famous last words: THE END.

"Hmm. Let's look at that again," Delilah says, her voice
sugary sweet, as she flips backward a few pages. This time I
tumble across the slick deck of the pirate ship, splash into
the frigid ocean, and get my tunic caught on the *c* of the
word *captain* before finding myself facing an angry dragon.

Pre-orthodontia.

Pyro barely has time to blow a stream of fire at me
before Delilah flips back to the last page, slamming me
once again into Seraphima's sloppy kiss.

She is totally doing this on purpose. Well, two can
play this game. I tighten my arms around Seraphima and
kiss her like . . . like . . . well, like she's Delilah.

Seraphima melts against me, her eyes widening.

Twice more Delilah jumps between the scene with
Pyro and the last page of the book. By the time Seraphima
leans in for a fourth kiss, I can't even pretend it's fun anymore. She's mauling me, and from behind, I can hear the
slightest whimper escape from Frump.

That's it. I am ready to say anything Delilah wants
me to.

"I give up," I cry out, and immediately, Delilah turns
to the strange man.

"Did you hear that?" she says, and she lets the book

fall open, mercifully to the page with Pyro instead of the one with Seraphima.

"You heard something?" the man asks.

"Didn't you?" Delilah says.

Pyro is snorting small puffs of smoke.

It is the strangest feeling, to have words drawn out of your throat like water from a well, as if you have no control over stopping it from happening. I know these same words will float across the minds of Delilah and this man as they read the story. "Wait!" I cry, my mouth twisting into a conversation I've had a hundred times. "I didn't come here to fight you. I'm here to help!"

The dragon's scales shimmer in the strong sunlight. He pulls himself upright, to a full muscular height of twelve feet, and his teeth gnash as he takes a step forward. He belches, and sparks shoot from his nostrils.

I cannot take my eyes off Pyro's mouth, the smoke seeping through his lips. One more line and he is going to shoot a fireball that sets a tree beside me into flames.

Suddenly I realize: this is my chance.

Pyro's huge jaws open, and a blazing streak curls off the run of his tongue. I grab the fairy-tale book I've stolen from Rapscullio, hold it up to cover my face, and leap forward, setting myself on fire.

The last thing I remember is hearing Delilah scream.

Delilah

ACROSS FROM THE COUCH IN DR. DUCHARME'S
office is a huge aquarium full of tropical fish. I know it's
supposed to be pretty, or relaxing, but it just makes me
depressed. I'm quite sure they'd all much rather be
doing the backstroke somewhere in the Caribbean.

"So," the psychiatrist says, "tell me, off the top of your head, five places you'd rather be than here."

I look up at him. "In England during the Black Plague, at the dentist getting a root canal, at a taping of *Teletubbies,* locked inside a Porta Potti, and . . . taking the SATs."

He steeples his fingers together, considering these. *"Teletubbies?"* he says after a moment, wincing. "That bad?"

"That bad," I say, but my lips twitch.

He has a nice smile, and all his hair, and he's about my mom's age. "Your mother says that you are somewhat less than thrilled to meet with me," Dr. Ducharme says.

"Don't take it personally. There's nothing wrong with me."

"I'm glad to hear that. But that's not why your mom is concerned." He leans forward. "What worries her is that you seem to be isolating yourself lately. You've become dependent on—maybe even obsessed with—this book."

When I don't reply, he clasps his hands. "When I was your age, I used to watch *A Christmas Story* every Christmas at least ten times. '*You'll shoot your eye out!*'" he quotes.

I stare at him blankly.

"Guess you've never seen it," the doctor says. "My point is, I used to watch that movie over and over because it was easier than admitting to myself that Christmas is a really crappy day for a kid whose parents are divorced. Sometimes the things we treasure for comfort are just masking a deeper symptom." He looks at me directly. "Maybe you can tell me why this story means so much to you?"

I don't know how to respond. If I say Oliver speaks to me, I look insane.

"I don't read it because I miss my dad or I hate my mother or any of the other juicy things psychiatrists always think. It's really not a big deal."

"Your mom seems to think it *is* a pretty big deal to you," Dr. Ducharme replies. "I don't know many fifteen-year-olds who spend their time reading fairy tales."

"It's not just a fairy tale," I blurt out.

"What do you mean?"

"It's a one-of-a-kind story. The only copy in existence."

"I see," the psychiatrist says. "You're intrigued by rare books?"

"No," I admit, blushing. "The main character. I can relate to him."

"How, exactly?"

I think for a second, watching the fish in Dr. Ducharme's tank swim in trapped circles. "He wishes his life could be different."

"Do you wish *your* life could be different?"

"No!" I say, frustrated. "It's not about me. It's what he's *told* me." Immediately, I panic—I've just admitted exactly what I promised myself I wouldn't.

"So . . . you hear him talking?"

The psychiatrist thinks I'm nuts. Then again, why would I be here if I wasn't? "I'm not hearing voices. I'm just hearing Oliver. Look," I say, "I'll show you."

I skim through the book until I land on page 43. There's Oliver frozen, clinging to the rock wall, dagger in his mouth. "Oliver," I demand, "say something."

Nothing.

"Oliver!" I groan. "I don't know why he's not talking to me."

"And how does that make you feel?" Dr. Ducharme asks.

Oliver knows I'm here. I can see it, in the way his eyes slide toward mine when he thinks the psychiatrist isn't looking. Can't he understand that I need him more than ever? That this isn't the time to fool around? That our entire future together might be dependent on him actually emitting a sound right now? I lean in and press my nose to the book. "Oliver," I grit out. "*Speak!*"

There's no response.

Well, if he wants to play games, I'm perfectly happy to do just that.

"Fine, then. Let's try *this* scene." I turn to the last page in the book, where Oliver and Seraphima are locked together in a perfect kiss.

I think I see him squirm.

It serves him right.

"Do you ever have trouble telling the difference between . . . for example . . . a dream you've had the night before and reality?" the doctor asks.

"I'm not making this up," I insist. "Hmm. Let's look at that again." Angry, I flip back and forth between a scene where Oliver is fighting the dragon and the final page. Is it my imagination, or is he actually kissing Seraphima as if he's *enjoying* it?

Angrily, I open and close the book a few more times. Then, faintly:

"I give up."

"Did you hear that?" I cry.

"You heard something?"

Oliver. I heard Oliver, loud and clear. "Didn't you?" I ask, but I already know the answer. Oliver told me that in all the years he's been in this fairy tale, I'm the first reader who ever listened.

The psychiatrist gently pries the book out of my hands and places it on the coffee table between us, still open to the page where Oliver stands toe to toe with Pyro.

"Delilah," he says quietly, "I know sometimes it's easier to make believe than to have to deal with the truth."

"This isn't make-believe!" I glance down at the book, and my eyes widen. Something's wrong, terribly wrong.

My eyes fall on the text across from the illustration:

"Wait!" Oliver cried. "I didn't come here to fight you. I'm here to help!"

The dragon took a menacing step forward and roared.

Because I have read this book a hundred times, I know what comes next. Pyro snorts and lights a tree on fire. Except now it reads differently:

As Pyro snorted, Prince Oliver rushed headlong into the ball of fire.

"Oliver!" I scream. "No!"

The illustration quivers and re-forms, like a pond after a stone's thrown into it. Before my eyes I see Oliver being burned alive as the dragon rears its head behind him.

I reach for the book, hoping to slam it closed, but it singes my fingers. "Ouch! You have to help him," I sob, grabbing at the psychiatrist's sleeve. "Please. Before it's too late . . ."

Dr. Ducharme puts his hands on my shoulders. "It's all right, Delilah. Take a few deep breaths."

I do what he says, but my eyes are on the book that's on the table behind him. It's glowing red, like coals, at the edges of the page.

"I'm going to get your mother to join us for these last few minutes," Dr. Ducharme suggests. "Are you all right now?"

I nod. The minute he steps out of his office, the book bursts into flames.

BETWEEN THE LINES

Oh my gosh. I grab my coat, and using it as a giant pot holder, snatch the book from the table and thrust it into the enormous fish tank. Two angelfish scuttle out of the way as the book bubbles and fizzes down to the plastic-pebbled bottom.

With a small smile, I realize I've rescued the prince, instead of the other way around.

The book is dripping wet, so I hold it over the tank as I turn to page 43. Oliver is healthy and intact—if a little bit damp. I remember my tears splashing on him as well; whatever seal is between us must be porous to liquid. "What were you trying do? Kill yourself?" I yell.

"Exactly," Oliver says, taking the dagger from between his teeth so that he can talk to me. "I was proving a hypothesis."

"Like whether you could burn this office down?"

"What office? Where are you, anyway?" Oliver asks. "And why am I sopping wet, down to my undergarments?"

"Long story . . ." I suddenly realize what he's said to me. "You . . . you want to die?"

"No—I want to get out of here. But everything that changes in this story winds up fixing itself in the end. I've seen it with my own eyes. Dead men walk again; broken barns fix themselves. What good would it be for me to write myself out of this book if I'm going to wind up right back inside it sooner or later?"

I remember the words on the page shimmering and changing before my eyes. "Hang on," I say, and I flip to the page that has Pyro and Oliver fighting on it.

The text has gone back to the way it used to be.

I hurriedly turn again to page 43, where Oliver and I can speak freely. "You're right," I tell him.

"Obviously. I didn't burn to death." He sniffs at his sleeves. "Not even smoky. Delilah, I'm afraid I'm stuck here, destined to be part of this story forever. Nothing from this book will ever break through to the outside world."

I think about how water has permeated that barrier— but in both cases, it was water from *my* world entering his, a one-way valve. The only time we tried to extract something from the book—that spider—it didn't work.

Except, this time, something *did* escape.

"Oliver," I say, "you're wrong."

He lifts his face toward mine. "How so?"

"When you ran into Pyro's flames, were you holding the book you found at Rapscullio's?"

"Yes."

"Well, that must be the difference. When it caught fire," I say, "so did the book I was reading. And it wasn't just words like *inferno* and *blaze* writing themselves all over the place—it was actually *flaming*."

Oliver's eyes widen. "You mean—"

"Yes." I laugh. "You did it!"

"*What* did you do?" My mother has come into Dr. Ducharme's office. They are both staring at me as I stand in front of the fish tank talking to an open book.

"I, um, was just . . . proving a hypothesis," I say, borrowing Oliver's phrase. "In Biology we're studying the ability of, uh, sea creatures to recognize the written word." Closing the book, I wrap it in my coat and hug it to my chest. It leaves a damp spot on the front of my shirt.

If the psychiatrist didn't think I was crazy already, seeing me reading to his angelfish will have sealed the deal. Knowing there's no way to get out of this one, I smile at Dr. Ducharme. "So," I say brightly. "Same time next week?"

In a way, Oliver could argue that his whole life had led up to this moment: when he stood toe to toe with the beast that had killed his father.

The dragon's red scales shimmered in the heat of the day. His eyes were as black as the heart of the man who'd conjured him. His clawed feet scrabbled for purchase on the bald rock of the Cape of Passing Tides. As Oliver watched, Pyro tilted back his long throat, drew in a deep breath, and bellowed a plume of fire into the sky.

Oliver's pulse was racing. He was so close to the dragon that he could smell charred flesh and ash. This was danger, up close and personal, in a way he'd never experienced and had carefully avoided his whole life. He wondered, as he had many times during his childhood, what his father had been thinking at this moment.

Had King Maurice stood, steadfast, with no fear as he brandished his sword and ran toward his death? Had his last thoughts been of his beloved wife? The son he would never meet?

I cannot get out of this alive, Oliver thought.

He reached around his neck for the compass his mother had given him. If there was ever a time to turn tail and run back home, this was it. But as his fingers closed around the small disk, he imagined his father clutching it even as he battled this same dragon. Oliver wanted to be the sort of son that his father would have been proud of. The one who faced his fears, instead of falling prey to them.

He let the compass drop back beneath his shirt.

Maybe he did not have his father's skill with a sword, or the kind of courage that inspired epic poems and legends. But that was not the only way to win a battle.

"Wait!" Oliver cried. "I didn't come here to fight you. I'm here to help!"

The dragon took a menacing step forward and roared. Flames singed the hair around Oliver's brow.

He remembered a childhood story that his mother used to read to him at night. "My," Oliver said softly, "what big teeth you have."

The dragon proudly flashed his massive overbite, gnashing his teeth inches away from Oliver's face.

Instead of flinching, however, in the cloud of smoky breath, Oliver just frowned. "Well," he said, "no wonder you're in so much pain."

The dragon, about to swipe his tail at him, hesitated.

"Look, dental issues are nothing to be embarrassed about."

Pyro snorted, the fiery ball igniting a tree just to Oliver's left. "Denying it will not make it any better," Oliver insisted. "Do you or do you not have a smoky aftertaste in your mouth?"

The dragon blinked.

"Classic symptomology. You, my friend, suffer from an impacted firecuspid. If left unattended, it can lead to scaly skin, flaring of the nostrils, charred tongue . . ."

With each recognizable symptom, the dragon backed away, eyes wide.

". . . and untimely death."

The dragon sat back on his haunches and clamped his mouth firmly shut.

"Lucky for you, I have some experience with orthodontia." Oliver took a step forward. "Just close your eyes, and open your mouth wide."

The dragon slowly, warily, opened his massive jaws.

This was the place his father had died. Holding his breath, Oliver cautiously climbed onto the dragon's spongy tongue. He stared at the teeth, large as boulders, with bits of flesh and blood caught between them. His boot slipped, and as he fell to his knees, something winked at him. It looked like a silver filling.

Oliver narrowed his eyes and realized that it wasn't a filling at all. It was a knight's helmet, a piece of the armor he'd created with Orville—made of the strongest, most fireproof material in the kingdom—reduced to a shredded ball of foil.

This knight had died. Oliver's father had died. This dragon could swallow Oliver whole. No amount of skill with words and lies and ruses could protect him from bodily harm.

As if to underscore this fact, the dragon belched, and a gust of flame rushed toward Oliver like a wave. He reached into his rucksack and closed his fingers around the fire extinguisher that the mermaids had given him.

He pulled out the metal key to activate it and carefully positioned the canister between two enormous molars. "Now," he said, gingerly backing out of the dragon's mouth and wiping his tunic clean of saliva, "I need you to bite down very gently."

Pyro clamped his mouth shut. Oliver counted to three under his breath, and suddenly white foam began oozing out from between the dragon's gums. "Ah," he said. "I can see it's working. . . ."

The dragon began wheezing. His mouth opened, but instead of a burst of flames came a sad, weak cough. Like any cornered animal, Pyro began to lash out with his claws and his tail, slicing the air. Oliver leaped out of the way, hiding behind a rock as the dragon retreated down the hill to the ocean.

When he heard the dragon's cry growing fainter, Oliver edged forward. Pyro's head was beneath the surface of the water, and he was drinking greedily to flush out the taste of the chemicals. While he was submerged, Scuttle and Walleye crept from their hiding places and threw their nets over Pyro, trapping the dragon, who let out a feeble snarl. Then Captain Crabbe emerged with a huge tank. "Now, now, my friend, you won't feel a thing." He placed a tube into the dragon's mouth and released laughing gas into the beast's lungs. Pyro's overbite softened into a drunken smile. His huge eyelids drooped, and his roar dissolved into loud, smoky hiccups. Then he collapsed, creating a small earthquake around him.

Oliver started walking away from the dragon's lair, a victory route his father had never taken.

OLIVER

THE NEXT TIME DELILAH OPENS THE BOOK, I FIND myself in a place I've never been. Missing are the bureau and mirror and the pink bedspread I am used to seeing in Delilah's bedroom. I climb to the edge of the page, trying to see more of this new location. "Where are we?"

"Somewhere I used to come to a lot when I was little. My fort." Delilah steps away so that I can see better. The walls are made of wooden slats, and there is a poorly sawed window. Shelves are filled with tin cans containing colored pencils, pennies, and stones. A stack of newspapers crowds a corner, their edges curled with age and humidity.

I must say, I am not impressed. I have never seen a fortress in such disrepair. "It's a wonder the enemy didn't sack you ages ago," I murmur.

"No, but the neighbor's dog came pretty close one time," Delilah says. "It's not a real fortress. It's a pretend one."

"Why would you pretend to be at war?"

"Because that's what kids do," Delilah explains. "You'll see, when you're here."

At those words, we both grow silent. It's time to try to write me out of this fairy tale.

"I brought you here on purpose," Delilah says. "I thought it would be safer."

"How so?"

"Well . . . for one thing, we don't know how loud this is going to be. . . . Second, if my mother hears me talking to a book one more time, I'll definitely be locked up." She hesitates. "And third, if it does work, I don't think she'll be too thrilled to find a strange guy in my bedroom."

"Good thinking," I say. I look down at the copy of the fairy tale I took from Rapscullio's bookshelf. In spite of its brush with fire, it is in perfect condition, healed of whatever scars and burns it once bore.

"So now what?" Delilah asks nervously.

"I guess I need to rewrite the ending." But now that the moment has arrived, my heart is pounding. What if this doesn't work, and instead of appearing in Delilah's world, I resurface in another book—one whose story I don't even know? Or stuck within the barrier that exists between my world and Delilah's? What if rewriting the story just creates a new book, and I find myself in the same situation, but one layer deeper and that much harder to escape?

And even worse, what if it *does* work, and Delilah decides she doesn't want to be saddled with a clueless former fairy-tale prince who doesn't know the first thing about real life? What if the reality of me pales in comparison to the guy she's been imagining?

"What are you waiting for?" Delilah asks.

And perhaps, most frightening of all, what if I start this and it ends *me*? What if the place I go to is not her world or my former world, but nowhere at all?

I look at Delilah's face, at the way she bites her bottom lip. I want to taste that bottom lip. I want *her*. None of these risks compares to the horror of staying here and knowing I never took the chance to be with Delilah.

"Right." I reach into my tunic and pull out a piece of charcoal, which I tucked into a pocket after my last scene with Pyro—it's simply not practical to carry around a quill and ink in one's clothing—and I sharpen the edge against the cliff where I'm standing. "Here goes," I say, and I flip to the last page of the book.

Studiously avoiding the illustration on the facing page, I slide the charcoal across the words THE END.

Suddenly I am flying head over heels through the pages, struggling to hold on to the charcoal and the copy of the fairy tale. Branches from the Enchanted Forest strike my face, stinging; a rogue comma hooks the edge of my hose and rips a hole; I am plunged into darkness and back into light; I am dragged through water and wind and fire, and finally land facefirst on the sand of Everafter Beach.

I push myself up onto my elbows, spitting out a mouthful of dirt and wincing at the ache of every muscle in my body. Surrounding me are all the characters awaiting my wedding to Seraphima. I sneak a glance at the book I'm still holding—and see that I have not fully crossed out the words. Grabbing hold of the charcoal, I strike the last letter in THE END.

"Oliver!" Frump barks. "What are you *doing*?" But even while he is speaking, I can see the edges of his shaggy ears and the point of his tail becoming transparent as he disappears. I swing my head to the right, just in time to see Seraphima reaching her hand out desperately toward me as she too fades away. Each of my friends in this story vanishes, leaving behind a white silhouette and utter silence, until there is just me, sprawled on the beach, and blank holes in the shapes the characters used to be.

"Good Lord," I whisper, and just then, the entire beach drains of pigment, until I am completely surrounded by nothing at all.

I am still holding the book and the sliver of charcoal. With shaking hands I spread the page flat and write:

And he lived happily ever after with Delilah Eve McPhee.

As soon as the last letter of Delilah's name is complete, the white space before my eyes begins to burn, opening in the center the way a flame eats its way through paper. The white curls back, revealing every color and inch and stitch and knot of the ratty old fortress into which Delilah had brought me.

That growing flame of color burns away a bit more of the white, and I begin to see Delilah's shocked face. "Oliver?" she says.

But then her voice fades, like Frump's did before, until it sounds like she is speaking to me from the opposite end of a long tunnel. The holes in the white space begin to narrow, closing themselves so that I can no longer see the tin cans with their colored pencils or the stack of newspapers in the corner. Frantically I look down at the open book in my lap and watch with horror as the last letter I've written, the *e* in *McPhee*, unravels itself from the tail to the loop, and then quivers and disappears. The same happens with the previous *e*, and the *h* and the *P* and so on, until my revised ending has been completely erased.

Then there is a slam of force against my chest, knocking my breath out of my lungs and causing me to see stars. When I get my bearings again, I'm in Seraphima's arms, and all around me the characters from this story are cheering and clapping and celebrating my new marriage.

Or in other words, I'm right back where I never wanted to be.

Before Delilah and I can talk about what went wrong, her mother calls her. I hear Delilah say she'll be back as soon as she can, but I don't acknowledge her. Instead I accept the congratulations of the pirates and offer pecks of consolation to the mermaids, who are in tears, and all the while I am praying that Delilah will close the book and free me from this recurring nightmare.

The minute she does, Frump yells, *"Cut!"*

I grab him by the collar. "Where'd you go? And why did you come back?"

"Go?" Frump shakes his head. "Buddy, I think you've got sunstroke. No one's gone anywhere. We've been watching the wedding like always," he says with a grimace.

"But I saw you vanish . . . and . . . and . . . everything went white . . ."

This must be how Delilah feels, when nobody believes a word she's saying. How could no one remember the beach evaporating? And where did they all disappear to?

Their memories have been wiped clean, I realize. Just like always, the book's reset itself. It is as if that last scene I was trying to rewrite never happened.

And that's probably for the best, because otherwise, they'd want to lynch me.

Frump looks at me strangely. "You might want to go to Orville and get that checked out."

Before I can respond, a tree smacks into me from behind. Or so I think, until I turn around to find Snort—the shortest troll—clapping me on the shoulder. He pushes me aside so he can talk to Frump. "Boss," the troll says, "I'm having a little trouble giving my character credibility in the last scene. Am I still holding a grudge against the prince, or do I just plain want to kill him?"

"It's a happy ending, Snort."

The troll furrows his brow. "So, then I want to kill him?"

Frump sighs. "I don't care what you're thinking. Just look happy while you're thinking it!"

To my right, Socks and Pyro are locked in deep discussion. "You know the illustration puts on ten pounds," Socks says.

"So true, so true," Pyro replies.

"That's why I'm on a no-carb hay diet," Socks admits. "It's doing wonders for my waistline."

Ducking my head so that I won't have to field any invitations for a game of chess or a swim with the mermaids, I slip away from Everafter Beach.

What happened back there?

Everything seemed to be working. Why did it stop?

I have walked halfway to the wizard's cottage before I even realize where I'm headed. Perhaps Frump is right—maybe all I need is one of Orville's potions to set my head straight again.

He lives in a rickety old cottage that looks, now that I think about it, something like Delilah's fortress. Outside, hanging from the beams of the porch, are bundles of drying herbs and wind chimes made of rusty spoons. I knock on the door and hear an explosion and a crash inside.

"Orville?" I yell.

"Everything's fine!" the wizard responds. "Just a slight backfire!"

A moment later he opens the door. His skin is blackened with ash, in stark contrast to his snowy beard and wild cloud of white hair. "Ah, my dear boy. Don't tell me the queen sent you. I *promise* I'll get around to the Fountain of Youth potion by the end of the month. . . ."

"The queen didn't send me," I say. "I need your help, Orville."

"What can I do for you?" the wizard asks, stepping aside to invite me in.

It's hard to believe that he can see well enough in the dim light to concoct his potions. There are books upon books, old tomes so dusty that I find myself coughing uncontrollably. A table sits in the center of the room, missing one of its legs — which has been replaced by a stack of grimoires. On its surface are several large cast-iron cauldrons, each with a spoon that is stirring itself. "Orville," I say, "I think that one's boiling over."

The wizard turns to see a thick, glowing green ooze bubbling over the edge of one pot. He gasps, sticks his hand in a jar of eyeballs, and tosses three into the mix. Immediately, the liquid hisses at him.

"What the devil *is* that?" I ask.

"Jealousy," Orville says, gesturing at the contents of the cauldron. "Nasty, foul stuff." He wipes his hands on his apron, leaving behind two glowing palm prints. "Now, Prince Oliver, what's your fancy?" He grins, gesturing to the floor-to-ceiling shelves full of glass canisters, all labeled carefully in Orville's spidery writing: STRENGTH. PATIENCE. BEAUTY. GIGGLES.

I rub the back of my head, making my hair stand on end. "I blacked out a little while ago. Frump thought maybe you'd have something that could make me . . . I don't know . . . a little more focused."

"Ah, certainly," Orville says. He starts moving jars, handing me a container of serpent's teeth and another of dragon claws as he rummages. "I know it's around here somewhere," he mutters, and he climbs a dodgy ladder to the top shelf, knocking down a long, gauzy spool of memory and a cobalt blue shaker full of fairy dust, which overturns in a fit of glitter and sends us both into paroxysms of uncontrollable sneezing.

"If you can't find it," I yell out, "I'm happy to make do with a couple of leeches. . . ."

"Aha!" Orville cries. He clatters down the ladder, holding a muslin sack. He unties the drawstring and shakes a handful of iridescent clamshells into his palm. Choosing one, he pries it open with a knife to reveal a pair of perfect white pearls inside. "Take two of these and call me in the morning," he says cheerfully.

I put the pearls into my pocket just as there is a fiery explosion across the room. The heat blasts me flat onto my back on the floor and sends Orville flying. He ends up tangled in the wrought-iron candelabrum that hangs from the ceiling. "Excellent! It's ready!" Orville says.

"What's ready?" I ask, sitting up.

"Just a little something-something I'm trying out." Orville walks toward a black pedestal that looks a bit like a birdbath but is filled with purple, hazy smoke. He rubs his hands together with glee, then extracts a chicken egg from his apron pocket. "Cross your fingers," he says to me as I come to stand beside him.

He drops the egg into the purple smoke, but I never hear it hit bottom. Instead, the smoke rises into a tall column and forms a lavender screen. After a moment, a chicken materializes upon the smoky display.

"I . . . I don't get it," I say.

"What you're looking at," Orville explains, "is the future."

Or the past, I think. After all, what came first—the chicken or the egg—

Orville interrupts my thoughts. "Pretty ingenious, don't you think?"

"But that . . . you can't . . ."

"Let's try something else." The wizard glances around the shack and then plucks a caterpillar off the lopsided window frame. He drops it into the mist, and a moment later, a butterfly made of violet smoke rises in a spiral from the pit of the pedestal.

"Orville!" I cry. "That's incredible!"

"Not bad for an old guy, huh?" He elbows me, then reaches up to pluck a hair from his head. "Here goes nothing. . . ."

He drops his own hair into the mist, and a moment later, there he is, clear as can be—if a little more wizened and lined in the face. This future Orville is bent over a cauldron that suddenly explodes in a purple blast.

"Yessir," Orville says. "Looks entirely accurate."

"I want to try. I want to see *my* future."

The wizard frowns. "But why, Oliver? You

already know what happens to you. You live happily ever—"

"Yeah, yeah, right. But still. You never know. I mean, will I live in the kingdom or move away? Have kids? Start a war? I just want some details. . . ."

"I don't think it's a good idea. . . ."

Before Orville can stop me, I yank a hair out of my head and toss it onto the pedestal.

For a long moment, there is nothing but a swirling lavender whirlpool. Then a geyser of mist sprays toward the ceiling, raining down in a dome. Inside this snow globe made of smoke, I can see myself.

The first thing I notice is that I'm not wearing a tunic.

I'm not carrying a sword or a dagger.

And I'm not standing in a scene from this fairy tale.

Instead, I am dressed just like the people in the photographs I've seen in Delilah's house. I'm sitting in a room that reminds me of Delilah's bedroom . . . except different. There is a fireplace, for example, that Delilah's room doesn't have. And there's a bookcase behind me, with every shelf filled. I can't understand some of the writing on the volumes; it is in tongues I do not recognize.

Still, this looks awfully promising for a future outside this story.

Or so I think, until I see a girl walk in and wrap her arms around me. I can't see her face from where I'm standing.

Orville suddenly rushes forward and waves his hands through the purple smoke so that the image dissolves. "Your Highness, this is obviously still in the testing stages," he says nervously. "Still working out several glitches . . ."

I grab the wizard by the throat. "Bring it back!"

"I can't, sire. . . ."

"Do it now!"

Orville is trembling. "You won't want to see it," he whispers. "The person you're with . . . is not Princess Seraphima."

I pluck another hair from my head and throw it into the fountain. Again, the dome of smoke rises and the scene appears, exactly as it was a moment before. "If you touch it," I mutter to Orville, "those frog eyes go straight down your throat."

The girl in the purple mist wraps her arms around me. Slowly, she turns so that I can see her features.

Orville was right.

I didn't want to see this at all.

Not because it's not Seraphima, but because it's not Delilah either.

I used to think that all I ever wanted was to get out of this stupid book. Now I realize that one must be careful what one wishes for. Getting out might not be my wildest dream — but my biggest nightmare.

I tried to write myself out of the book, and it didn't work. I saw my future, and Delilah wasn't a part of it. I can live without leaving this fairy tale, but I can't live without her.

I need help. And I need it fast. And so, even with the uncomfortable knowledge that what I am about to do could hurt someone else, I begin to run toward Rapscullio's lair.

By the time I arrive, I am sweating and out of breath. The lair is open, and there is a heavenly vanilla scent wafting out the door. I poke my way inside to find him baking sugar cookies in his kitchen. As he's dusting the tops with pink sprinkles, I clear my throat to get his attention.

"Ah, Your Highness! You're just in time to taste the first batch. They're still warm!"

"Rapscullio," I say, "this is no time for cookies. I need your assistance."

Sensing my urgency, he puts down his spatula. "I have twelve to fourteen minutes before the next batch comes out of the oven," he says solemnly.

I grab his hand and drag him into the library—the one where, not long ago, I tried to paint myself out of this book and failed miserably. "I need you to draw something for me."

"Again?" Rapscullio says. "This is your emergency? You're having an artistic epiphany?"

"Just do it," I argue, frustrated. "I need a picture of

a young woman. I'll tell you what she looks like, and you create it on that special canvas of yours."

His eyes brighten. "You mean a *wanted* poster!"

Well. Truer words were never spoken. "Exactly," I say.

"I've done several, you know. My masterpiece is the one I painted of the Knave of Hearts after he stole the queen's tarts. It's still hanging in the castle jail."

"Great." I sit down on a stack of books, and a cloud of dust rises around me. "Now—she has dark hair that comes down to her shoulders. It's straight, with a bit of a curl on the ends."

"I'll have to start with a sketch first." Rapscullio takes a pad and begins to scribble. "How tall is she?"

I realize I have no idea. I have no reference point for that.

"Medium height," I say, guessing.

"And her eyes?"

"They're brown."

"Limpid chocolate brown, or dark-corners-of-the-soul brown?"

I shrug. "Warm brown, like honey. And her mouth . . ."

"Like this?"

Rapscullio shows me a tiny bow, lips pursed together, but that's not Delilah at all. Her mouth is always on the verge of a smile. It makes her look like there's something amazing she needs to tell me, even when it's just *hello*.

We continue in this fashion long after the next batch of cookies has burned to a crisp, as I suggest and tweak and correct Rapscullio's portrait. "Hurry," I say, wondering how much time I have before Delilah opens the book again and all this hard work is lost.

"Genius takes time," Rapscullio says. But he finally turns the pad around so that I can see it. And sure enough, there is Delilah, staring straight back at me.

"Yes," I say, nodding.

Rapscullio is pleased with himself. "So what's the rush?" he asks. "What did she do?"

"Do?" I say.

"What crime did she commit?"

Then I remember the ruse I've used to get him to draw Delilah. "She's a thief," I say.

It's not really a lie, after all. Because she's totally, unequivocally stolen my heart.

Delilah

WE ARE SO CLOSE—THERE IN FRONT OF ME
in the quiet corner of my old tree fort, I can see Oliver's
face appearing. But before he is more than just a misty
hallucination, he's gone.

While I'm still trying to figure out what happened—
and what *didn't*—I hear my mother call my name.

"Now?" I mutter. *"Really?"*

"Delilah?" Her voice is getting closer. She's standing at
the base of the tree fort. "What are you doing up there?"

I quickly close the book and shove it between the old
newspapers. My mother's head bobs at the top of the ladder. "I'm cleaning it out," I announce. "Turning over a new
leaf. No more fairy tales, no more tree forts." She looks at me

dubiously. "Dr. Ducharme thought it would be a good idea for me to have some more age-appropriate things to do."

The words have the intended effect. "Well, then," my mom says, surprised. "Good!" She shakes her head, as if she cannot quite believe me, and why should she? "Jules is here. She's upstairs in your bedroom."

"Jules?"

The last thing I want to do is hang out with Jules when what I really need is to speak to Oliver. I've realized something: he's not the one who can rewrite the ending. I have a new plan, and I am desperate to share it with him.

I take the fairy tale and tuck it under my arm, heading back to the house. When I get to my room, Jules is lying on my bed, listening to my iPod. I slip the book quickly between others on a shelf so that Jules doesn't start asking questions about why I'm still reading a kids' fairy tale. Then I sit down and pull the headphones out of her ears. "I wasn't expecting you," I tell her.

"Since when do I have to make an appointment to be with my own best friend?" Jules asks. "And since when do you listen to Justin Bieber?" She shakes her head. "Maybe you *do* need psychiatric counseling. I don't have any problem with you breaking Allie's nose, but if you keep downloading songs like this, I may have to kill you." She flops over onto her belly and looks up at me. "So how did it go?"

"How did what go?"

"Your shrink appointment?"

It seems like that happened a thousand years ago, not three hours. "It was a nonevent," I say.

"Good, because I need you to have all your brains in place to help me get out of the worst situation ever." She sits up, crossing her legs. "Remember my aunt Agnes?"

"The one who smells like beets?"

Jules winces. "Oh, God, why did you remind me of *that*? My parents said they're sending me to her place for the summer to get a taste of the country. Can you imagine me in East Nowhere, Iowa, milking cows?"

"They have cows?"

"No, but they might as *well*. That's not the point. The point is that I'm being shipped off like a FedEx box to the loneliest town on Earth." She hesitates. "They still have *dial-up*, for God's sake."

I want to feel bad for Jules, seriously. But my head is filled with thoughts of Oliver and what we are going to do next.

"Maybe it won't be that bad," I say. "Summer's over before you know it."

She stares at me. "Wow. Zero sympathy whatsoever."

"I don't mean it like that—of course I feel bad for you—but I mean, it's not the end of the world, Jules."

"Can you tell me something? Where's Delilah? Because the friend I used to know would actually care."

"That's a little dramatic," I say, forcing a laugh.

"Is it? I came over here because I wanted someone to commiserate with me. To tell me that my summer's going to suck and that you're sorry. To take my side. I'll probably still have to go to Iowa and it's going to be hell, but it sure would be nice to go knowing that there's someone here who doesn't want me to leave."

I can feel my cheeks heating up. I've been so obsessed with Oliver, I haven't had time to spend with Jules. And the fact that she can't hear him only makes her seem even more distant from me right now.

It will be different, I tell myself, when we get Oliver here. Then Jules can meet him, and get to know him, and be happy for me because I've finally got a boyfriend. These arguments we keep having are little roadblocks; eventually we'll find a way around them. "I've just got a lot on my plate right now."

Jules stands up. "I used to be on that plate," she says. "I used to matter."

"Jules, don't say that. You're still my best friend—"

"You know what? You don't get to decide that. It takes two people to make a friendship work, and these days, I've been doing more than my fair share."

"Jules," I say. "Come on." I reach toward her, but she steps away.

She looks at me. "Just remember—I had your back

when the whole world hated you. I thought that counted for something."

She walks out of my bedroom and slams the door behind her. I let out a defeated sigh. I'll make this right again, I swear I will, but first I have to finish what Oliver and I have started.

My mother sticks her head inside the door. "Is every-thing all right with Jules?"

"Fine . . ."

"Funny, she didn't look fine when she ran out the front door."

My eyes fill with tears. "I don't want to talk about it," I tell her. I've lost two friends in one day.

My mother sits down beside me on the bed. "Well, if it's not fine, it *will* be," she says. "And when you're ready to talk about it, I'm here."

It feels good to have her arms around me, to pre-tend, for a little while, that what she's saying is true. To believe that in the end, everything works out. She drops a kiss on the crown of my head. "I have an idea," she says. "Why don't we watch a movie?"

I look up at her. "Like old times?"

"I'll make the popcorn," my mother says. "You get *The Little Mermaid.*"

If I have any thoughts about why my mother would have a philosophical problem with me reading a fairy tale but be perfectly fine with me watching a Disney cartoon, they vanish in the anticipation of an evening spent believing that dreams can come true. "Okay," I whisper, and she hugs me a little tighter.

When she leaves, I go to the bookshelf to retrieve the story. I plan to just quickly pop to page 43 so that I can tell Oliver my brilliant idea. But then I think of my mother, downstairs, of how hard she's trying to make me happy. For right now, anyway, Oliver can wait.

I keep the Disney movies in a cardboard box in my closet, on the upper shelf. I can't quite reach it, so I drag my laundry basket closer, overturn it, and use it as a footstool. Reaching up, I grab the edge of the box. But suddenly everything around me grows brighter and silvery, the way the world looks when it snows overnight. I find myself squinting against all this light, and then suddenly I am falling, tumbling head over heels through a big, wide wasteland of nothing.

I start to scream. I'm falling so fast that I can hear the wind in my ears, and my eyes are watering. It's as if I've been pushed out of a speeding plane. I can dimly make out black shapes as I streak by them. Then I am abruptly yanked to a halt. My T-shirt has caught on a hook, and I find myself bobbing, the wool bunched up around my shoulders.

Except it's not a hook. When I look around, I realize that I am hanging from a gigantic letter *J*.

Until the curl of the *J* snaps beneath my weight and sends me free-falling once again.

As I tumble, color begins to bleed into the space around me—faint at first, and then growing darker and more full of pigment, until I am sure I'm going to smack against the ground at any moment. I cover my face with my arms and try to curl into the smallest ball possible, so that I won't get hurt when it happens.

"Oomph!" With a blow that knocks the breath out of me, I land on a hard stack of something. A pile of books scatters, and a cloud of dust puffs up around me. I gingerly get to my feet, taking inventory of my bones to make sure nothing's broken. From the corner of my eye, I see movement, and I whip around with my arms in a karate pose, as if I might be able to intimidate whoever else is here.

The intruder makes the same exact movement.

I take a step forward, and realize that I am looking into a mirror. At least, I think it's a mirror—even if the reflection I'm seeing isn't quite me.

Once, my mother took me to Montreal. We went to a town square, which had come alive at dusk with street performers and vendors. Artists sat beneath umbrellas, drawing sketches of fidgeting children. My mother had a portrait drawn of me just for fun. You could certainly see that there was a resemblance, but to be honest, the picture kind of freaked me out. It made me look flat and two-dimensional, not really me at all.

The image I'm staring at in the mirror looks exactly the same way.

Slowly, I reach out a finger to touch this odd girl who might or might not be me— When there is a high-pitched shriek to my left. I am knocked off my feet and pinned down by a scarred, goateed man I'd recognize anywhere.

"You thief!" Rapscullio cries. "If you're as awful as the prince says, you'll be a dragon's meal before nightfall."

I am making this all up. That's the only explanation I have for the fact that I am being dragged along by a fictional character through the Enchanted Forest. But if I am making this all up, then how come the rope Rapscullio has wrapped around my wrists is rubbing them raw? How come I can smell woodsmoke coming from Orville's cabin and feel the fairies—the size of mosquitoes on steroids— tugging at my hair and pulling at my clothes?

I know I should be freaking out, but I'm too busy looking around at this world I've dreamed of for so long. Above me, where there should be sky, are distant, dan- gling bits of letters. Beyond them, I can barely make out colors and shapes, as if I'm looking at the sun from the bottom of a pool.

"Oh my gosh." I gasp. "Is that the royal castle?"

"No, it's a loaf of bread," Rapscullio mutters. "Oliver told me you were a felon, but he didn't mention that you're feebleminded . . ."

If this is the castle, then I'm about to see Oliver.

Really see him, for the first time.

I dig in my heels, stopping Rapscullio. With my bound hands, I try to smooth my hair and adjust my shirt in a way that doesn't show the rip from the letter *J*. "Do I look all right?" I ask my captor.

"I suppose, if you're into that starving-androgynous-plebeian look." He tugs me forward, and as if by magic, the metal portcullis rises and four heralds trumpet my arrival. Rapscullio unties my wrists and shoves me forward, so that I land on my hands and knees in the middle of a circle of nobles and ladies-in-waiting.

"What do we have here, Rapscullio?"

I look up to find Queen Maureen staring at me. Her crown glistens with diamonds and sapphires and rubies, blinding me. There are braided gold threads in the fabric of her gown. Soft ermine fur lines the inside of her majestic purple cape. The details I can see here, up close, are nothing like the illustrations in a book. This looks so real . . . because it *is*.

It's like a dream. Haven't you ever had one of those, where you are utterly and thoroughly convinced that you are awake and alive? That everything surrounding you is so detailed you could draw it from memory? That what's happening is real?

Queen Maureen gasps. "Get the poor girl a blanket. She's practically in her undergarments!"

A nobleman throws a horse blanket at me, and I wrap it around myself, although I'm fully dressed in a T-shirt and shorts. Thinking fast, I wonder what explanation I can possibly make for myself. The book is clearly closed, as nothing like this happens in the story. Which means everything that Oliver told me was true: there is a completely different world that happens between the lines.

"Your Majesty, I bring to you a despicable, detestable, reprehensible thief!" Rapscullio says, smiling sheepishly at the queen. "I've been using that thesaurus you bought me for Christmas."

I stand up, hands on my hips. "For your information, I'm not a thief. And I'm not despicable, detestable, or reprehensible. In fact, some people would call me astute, intuitive, and perspicacious." I lift my chin a notch. "English. Straight As."

"Astute-Intuitive-and-Perspicacious," Queen Maureen repeats. "That's quite a mouthful, dear. Have you got a nickname?"

"No—my name is Delilah—"

"Then why didn't you say so?" the queen asks.

"Because"—I jab a finger in Rapscullio's direction—

"*he* was too busy accusing me of being a thief."

"I have it on direct authority from His Royal Highness Prince Oliver that this girl is a criminal." Rapscullio sniffs.

Queen Maureen stares down at me. "She hardly looks like a felon. More like a vagrant."

"I'm neither," I say. "Go ask Oliver. He'll explain everything."

"You know the prince?" Queen Maureen asks. She looks me over from head to toe, in utter disbelief.

"Your Majesty?" a familiar voice says. "Did I hear you calling for me?"

And then, suddenly, I am only three feet away from Oliver. My heart starts hammering beneath my ribs. He is taller than I thought he'd be, and his eyes—well, they're not the color of the ocean at all. They're more like the sky at twilight. But his voice, it's exactly how I've heard it. And the way his smile tips up on one side, that's how I know it's really him.

"Oliver!" I cry, and I lunge forward with my arms outstretched—

Smack.

I find myself flat on the ground, with three guards sitting on me.

"That's quite enough," Oliver says, pushing the guards out of the way and rolling me over. "Are you all right?" he asks, reaching to pull me up.

But I can't say anything. And not because those guards knocked the wind out of me either.

Because for the first time, we are touching. Holding hands.

I think Oliver realizes this at the same moment, because we wind up staring at each other, transfixed.

A line from the fairy tale pops into my head:

This was why there was music, he realized. There were some feelings that just didn't have words big enough to describe them.

"I'm afraid there's been a misunderstanding," Oliver manages, getting to his feet. "Delilah here is an old friend."

"Then why did you need me to sketch a Wanted poster for—"

"I thought she was lost!" Oliver says, and then he grins widely. "And look at how well it worked, Rapscullio, since here she is! You deserve a reward. Queen Maureen, didn't we get a rare Japanese water caterpillar as a state gift last month?"

"Oh, yes." She claps her hands, and one of her footmen runs off to fetch it. "Funny," she says, scrutinizing me. "I make it my business to know all the characters in the book, and yet I don't think we've ever met. How could that be?"

"This is Delilah," Oliver says, quickly glossing over her question. "Delilah, Queen Maureen."

I stick out a hand, only to have Oliver elbow me in the side. "Curtsy," he coughs.

Right. I sink into my best curtsy, which isn't very good, given that I'm wearing a horse blanket.

"Where do you hail from, Delilah?"

"Oh, I live in New Hampsh—"

"Page twenty-two," Oliver interrupts. "Delilah works in the butchery."

"Butchery?" I whisper under my breath. "Really? That's the best you could do?"

"How . . . intriguing," Queen Maureen says. "You must come see our cattle sometime."

"That would be . . . great," I reply.

"Well, we'd better get going," Oliver interjects. "Delilah was planning to show me how to trim out a roast."

Queen Maureen shudders delicately. "I didn't know you were interested in the trades, dear," she says. "Have a lovely afternoon."

Oliver grabs my hand (again!) and pulls me through the courtyard. We pass gardens filled with lady slippers and bluebonnets, a small sitting area with stone benches, and the royal croquet court. Finally, we come to the entrance of a maze. Oliver leads me into the center, where the boughs of trees form a tangled roof over our heads.

"It's you," he says. "It's really you!" He pulls me into his arms and hugs me tight.

I thought I knew Oliver from reading this book over and over, but here are the things I didn't know: that there is a spot near the hollow of his collarbone where I seem to fit perfectly. That he smells of freshly cut hay. That when we are touching, I can't seem to hold a single thought in my head.

"I don't know what happened," I tell him. "I was reaching up in my closet one minute, and the next, I was falling through the pages." I pinch my own arm. "Am I dreaming this?"

"No," Oliver says. "You're really here. Isn't it remarkable? I can't believe it worked." He smiles at me. "Your freckles seem a lot smaller when your face isn't the size of the whole sky."

Embarrassed, I cover the bridge of my nose, and then I replay his words. "You can't believe it worked," I repeat slowly. "What do you mean by that?"

Oliver leans his forehead against mine. His breath smells like maple syrup. "When I tried to write myself out of the book, it failed. Since it didn't seem like I was going to be able to leave any time soon, I had Rapscullio draw you *into* the book instead."

I push away from him. "You did *what?*"

"I thought this way, we could be together. I knew

you wouldn't get hurt. I've seen him paint butterflies that come to life right off the page."

"Wasn't the whole point to get you *out* of the book? Now we're *both* stuck here. Not to mention the fact that you didn't even *ask* me before ripping me out of my life!"

Oliver shakes his head, confused. "But you told me you wanted to be with me."

"Not like this," I say, as the enormity of this situation washes over me. "What if I never get to leave?"

"As soon as the book's opened up, it will correct itself," he says, thinking out loud, but I can tell he hasn't considered this beforehand.

"And who's going to open that book, since I'm inside here?" I point out. "It's jammed in a bookshelf at home with dozens of others. Plus, even if someone *did* find it and open it, how do you know I'll wind up back in my world, and not disappear completely?"

"Then stay with me." Oliver grips my arms. "Forever. Would that be so bad?"

"I'd never see my mom again," I say, tears springing to my eyes. "She'd wonder what happened to me, and she'd never know the truth. And I'd never be able to tell Jules I'm sorry—" I break off, thinking of the fight we had. "It takes two people to make a friendship work, Oliver," I say, repeating Jules's words to me. Now I get it. Now I understand how devastating it is when one of the parties is thinking only about himself or herself. "Did you ever consider how I'd feel, being dragged here, to a place you're dying to escape? Did you ever consider asking me for permission? Did you even think about me once before you went to Rapscullio?"

Oliver's eyes are fierce, locked on mine. A muscle works in his throat. "You were *all* I was thinking about."

I have never felt so alone, even with Oliver standing in front of me. "*You* wanted to leave *your* life," I say. "I never wanted to leave *mine.*"

Tears stream down my face as I blindly run through the maze. I don't know where I'm going, but it doesn't really matter. Nothing does, if I can't get back home.

I don't let myself turn around to see if Oliver's following me. I'm afraid he will be.

But I'm even more afraid he won't.

My exit from the castle is much less eventful than my entrance. Several ladies-in-waiting nod at me as I pass through the courtyard, and the same guard who was sitting on my butt to restrain me wishes me a nice day as I leave. I find myself in a kingdom that's not mine, in a world that's not meant for me.

As soon as I am outside the castle walls, I start to run. I pass scenery that I recognize, but I don't stop to take a second look. All I can think about is my mother, who is waiting for me downstairs with a bowl of popcorn. I wonder how long it will take her to figure out that I've gone missing. If she'll call the police, what sort of explanation they will make for my disappearance. I wonder who'll be there for her when she is devastated. Without me, my mom has nobody. It's always been just the two of us.

The one ally I have in this place is someone who betrayed me. And if I can't trust Oliver, then there's no reason to be here. I suppose it's stupid to think that anyone could be as incredible as I've made Oliver out to be in my mind. Clearly, that's just been a figment of my imagination.

Here's what no one ever tells you about love: it hurts, having your heart broken.

I find myself sitting on a rock at the edge of the water, where other jagged rocks stick up like sharks' teeth. In the distance, Captain Crabbe's boat bobs along the horizon. Timble Tower looms on the cliff overhead.

I hug my knees to my chest. What seemed exciting—trying to get Oliver out of the book—is absolutely terrifying now that I'm stuck inside it myself.

I reach beside me and pluck a dandelion, then close my eyes to make the wish: *I just want to get out of here.*

A little voice inside me says, *That's all Oliver ever wanted too.*

This makes me cry harder.

The only person who understands how I'm feeling right now is the very same person I yelled at and ran away from.

"I've got to go back and talk to him," I say out loud. But just as I am about to stand up, something grasps my arm at the wrist and yanks me headfirst into the ocean.

Panicked, I start splashing and striking out, trying to get to the surface, but I am wearing clothes and sneakers and sinking fast. I cry out and swallow water. What if I drown? What if I die here? I thrash even harder, desperate to get free.

A shark is swimming toward me. I go very still as I see its silver body cut through the water like a knife through butter. Its black eyes fix on me as I try to remember everything I learned from watching the Discovery Channel. Am I supposed to punch it in the nose or poke it in the eye?

The shark snaps its jaws so close to me that the water is sucked in like a vacuum, stirring the hairs on my arm. Before it can swim past me again, something wraps around my wrists and waist, restraining me. I struggle, only to hear a voice in my ear. "Don't fight it," a woman hisses. I realize that my bonds are tendrils of her hair, long and silver. Her face, close to mine, is sunken and terrifying, pocked with scales. Gills ripple on her neck and her ribs. Her entire lower half is a thick, muscular tail.

Right now I should be watching Ariel and Flounder

dance happily across a television screen. I open my mouth to scream, but the mermaid grabs my face and plants a kiss square on my lips.

"What was *that* for?" I sputter, pushing away from her. I realize two things at that moment: The shark has drifted away. And I can breathe.

It is as if I have an astronaut's helmet surrounding me. I take a few tentative breaths and then a bigger gulp. "How did you . . . I mean . . ."

As my vision clears beneath the water, I realize that all three mermaids are swimming nearby. Among the most unsettling parts of the fairy tale, when I first read it, were these women, with their tangled seaweed hair and emaciated bodies, the spiny fins on their forearms, the bloodred ridges of their gills flaring with each breath. Little girls dream of being mermaids, but not ones like these. They are, I realize, even more terrifying up close and personal than in an illustration. I have to keep reminding myself of what Oliver has told me: the characters in the story are nothing like the people they are when the book is closed. Maybe this means that the mermaids *don't* intend to kill me.

"Where did you come from?" asks Kyrie, the mermaid who saved me from the shark.

"That's a very long story," I say.

"Oh, tell it," cries Ondine, clapping her hands. "We haven't had a new story in the longest time."

"Sisters," Marina murmurs, swimming closer to me. "Don't pressure the boy. Can't you see he's scared?"

A boy? They think I'm a boy? That is enough to panic me into speaking out loud, because I know too well what these mermaids do to boys who fall into the waters near their home. "I'm not a boy," I say.

Ondine twirls around me in a circle. "You're dressed like one."

"This is how all the kids dress, where I live."

"Which is where, exactly?" Marina asks.

"In New Hampshire." I hesitate. "It's a kingdom pretty far away."

"What brings you here?" Kyrie asks.

There is no way to explain to three characters inside a book that a world might exist beyond their imaginations. It's why people don't believe in aliens, and why no one else believes in Oliver. "It wasn't exactly my idea to come," I mutter. "This guy sort of *summoned* me."

The mermaids look at each other. "Of course he did," Ondine says.

"Leave it to a man to mess things up," Marina agrees.

Kyrie shakes her head. "Men. You can't live with them . . . you can't legally drown them."

Marina slips her arm through mine. "Honey, you've come to the right place. Whoever this guy is, you don't need him."

My jaw drops open. These mermaids, who are man-crazy in the fairy tale, are . . . hard-core feminists?

"What did he do to you?" Kyrie asks. "Flirt with another girl?"

"Call you fat?" Marina suggests.

"Talk about his ex?" Ondine says, and the others groan.

"We've been there, sister," Marina says.

"No, none of those things," I tell them. "He dragged me here against my will. He didn't even *ask* me first."

"That's positively barbaric," Ondine agrees.

Marina nods. "Good thing you managed to get away from him."

Hearing those words, I feel an ache in my chest. After all this time I've spent trying to be near Oliver, it hurts to have swung to the other extreme. "The thing is," I say very quietly, "I sort of wish I hadn't."

Marina sighs. "Love's a tidal wave," she says.

"Because it sweeps you off your feet?" I ask.

"No. Because it sucks you under and you drown."

"But sometimes," I point out, "it's the only thing that keeps you afloat." I realize that as angry as I am at Oliver for doing this to me—ripping me out of my home and my life and away from my mother—I've hurt him just as much by saying to his face that I don't want to be here. After all, on the outside, I have Jules and my mother. Oliver has nobody but me.

"I think this one's a lost cause," Kyrie says to her sisters.

Marina sniffs. "If you're not going to turn your back on that jerk, as least don't be a doormat."

"I don't understand. . . ."

"Make him sweat a little," Ondine says. "Make him realize what he's got to lose."

This reminds me of the end of my first conversation with Oliver, when he bossed me around because he's a prince and simply expected me to be his subject and didn't realize I could close the book on him at any time. But now I don't have that upper hand . . . not that I've needed it. These days, we're equals.

"Oh, Lord," Marina says. "She's gone all moony-eyed."

I thought I understood Oliver, but I really didn't—not until I found myself here against my will. Stuck in this world that he so badly wants to escape, I completely, viscerally see what's at stake for him.

Maybe in his shoes, I would have been as desperate. Maybe I would have drawn *him* into the book too.

"I've got to find him," I announce.

"Are you sure?" Kyrie asks. "There's plenty of other fish in the sea."

"But not like him," I say. I look at the mermaids. "Thank you. For the hospitality, and the oxygen. But I have to get to the surface."

Marina smirks. "Not like that," she says. "You're practically wearing undergarments."

Why does *everyone* here keep saying that?

Before I can protest, Kyrie and Ondine link their arms through mine and swim me deeper into the sea, toward the mouth of an underwater cave. I recognize the small rounded driftwood door in the rear, behind which is a collection of skeletons.

They pull me through a crevice I remember seeing in an illustration—except there's no picture of what waits on the other side. The small cubby is filled with golden doubloons, jeweled goblets, and heaps of shining gems. "This . . . this is worth a fortune!" I gasp.

Marina nods. "When ships don't make it around the Cape of Passing Tides, we collect what's left behind." She picks up a diamond tiara. "You just never know when the stuff is going to come in handy."

Kyrie dives into a pile of gleaming coins, sending them spinning in slow motion in the water. She emerges a moment later, holding a swath of indigo velvet. "I think this one will bring out her eyes," she says, shaking out a gown with lace at the neckline and sleeves. Golden embroidery crisscrosses the bodice. It's prettier than anything I've ever seen.

Ondine unlaces the back of the gown as Kyrie helps me out of my clothes. I step into the puddle of billowing fabric. The mermaids pull it up around me and tie me in tight. They swim back, examining me.

"What?" I say. "Is it awful?"

"There's something missing . . ." Marina muses. She reaches into a wooden chest beside her and pulls out a rope of pearls, fastening it around my neck. "There. *Perfect.*"

"You think?" I ask shyly, and in response, they reach for my arms again and swim me out of the watery cave, up to the surface. I find myself balanced on the same rock where I'd been sitting earlier, crying.

I look at my reflection in the water. I'm stunning. If a little damp.

The mermaids bob in the waves, the sleek caps of their hair glistening in the sunlight. "This time," Marina says, "that guy will never let you out of his sight."

That's what I'm hoping. I want to go home, but I want Oliver to come with me. Which means we both owe each other an apology.

I look at each of the mermaids in turn. "I can't thank you enough," I say.

They all sigh, or maybe that's just the sound of the ocean crashing against the rocks, because when I look back they've disappeared, and if not for the fact that I'm wearing a very pretty, very soggy gown, I would think I've imagined the whole thing.

* * *

I am halfway back to the castle when the ground beneath my feet starts rumbling. I look overhead, expecting a thunderstorm, but all I can see are the dangling bits and pieces of words. Suddenly, there is a cloud of rising dust and a distant whinny, and I can make out the figure of Oliver riding his horse at a breakneck pace in my direction.

When he sees me, he pulls back on the reins, and Socks rears, his front legs pawing at the air in front of him. Oliver dismounts and rushes toward me. Before I can even apologize, he grabs me and hugs me tight. "I'm so sorry," he says. "I wasn't thinking of how much you had to lose. Only of how much I had to gain."

I hug him back. "I know. We'll find a way to get me home. But you're coming with me."

Behind me, I hear sniffles.

"That"—Socks gulps—"is just *so* romantic!"

Oliver clears his throat. "Socks? I think you know the way home?"

"That I do," Socks says proudly.

"Good. Then why don't you go there. Now."

"Oh! You mean . . . Yup, right, third wheel. Got it." Sheepishly, he bows his head and trots back along the path he rode in upon.

"I don't think I really understood how you felt until now," I admit. "To want so badly to be somewhere else."

"I should never have assumed you belonged only to me," Oliver says. "I wish there was a way to tell your mother you're all right."

At the mention of my mother, a cloud passes over my features.

Oliver touches my cheek gently. "Is there anything I can do to make you happy?"

"You can hold me," I say, and in that instant, I am pulled into his arms again. I can feel his heart beating against mine, and the heat of skin. I can feel his fingers spread across the small of my back. He is every bit as real as I am. "Oliver," I repeat slowly, the magic of this miracle truly sinking in. "You can *hold* me."

"That's not all I can do," Oliver says. He frames my face with his hands and gently, tenderly, presses his lips to mine.

This is *so* not like Leonard Uberhardt, the first boy who kissed me, or rather swallowed half my face. This is sweet and soft. It's like there is a whole story Oliver is telling me without words, as if what he's feeling can't be described, and has to be experienced instead.

When we break apart, I am breathing hard, and I cannot take my eyes off his.

"You have no idea how long I've been waiting to do that," Oliver says.

I wind my arms around his neck. "Let's do it again," I suggest.

He puts his hands on my wrists and pulls me away. "I should think you, of all people, would realize we've got other things we need to do first."

He's right, of course. I want to go home. But that doesn't mean I'm not disappointed, just a little.

Oliver seems to notice, for the first time, what I'm wearing. "What happened to you?"

"Mermaids," I explain.

"I'm surprised they didn't try to convince you to stay away from me," he says. "They're generally not too fond of men."

"So what's your plan? How do we get back home?" I ask.

"Well," Oliver says, his face flushing. "I'm still trying to figure it out."

"But you *always* know what to do. No matter what situation you're thrown into, or whatever scrape you wind up in, you figure a way out."

"That's just the way I'm written," Oliver confesses. "If I were truly clever, I'd be out of this book by now."

"But in the book you always—"

"In the book I also fall in love with Seraphima every

time," Oliver interrupts. "And believe me, that's an act."

I feel chilled all of a sudden. The enormity of my situation is becoming more clear. I'm stuck in a fairy tale that may never be opened again. After reading the story so many times, I've confused bits of the true Oliver and the fictional Oliver. I'm just not sure anymore what's real.

I don't realize I've said it aloud until Oliver reaches for my hand. "*We* are," he says. "*This* is."

By now the sun has slipped lower in the sky and has painted the horizon a vivid orange. "We'd best be getting home," Oliver says, and I sit up a little straighter. "And by *home*," he says, wincing, "I meant the palace."

He tugs me to my feet and leads me down a beaten path through the field. I can feel the warmth of his shoulder against mine, and I can smell the scent of pine, which clings to his tunic. In front of us, fairies dance like fireflies, writing our initials in the dusky violet sky. I find myself smiling at their acrobatics, amazed to see the tiny creatures right before my eyes. As much as I want to leave this world, it's breathtaking.

I am so wrapped up in the moment, in fact, that I don't even see Seraphima until she is three feet in front of us. She stands with her eyes wide, her pale blond hair cascading down her back, her perfect features frowning in confusion. "Oliver?" she asks.

"Oh, um, hi, Seraphima," he says. "Have you met . . . my cousin Delilah?" Oliver turns to me, whispering. "It's not her fault she's clueless. I don't want to hurt her. Just go along with me."

Seraphima bestows the sweetest smile upon me. "Delilah!" she says, grasping my hands in her own. "I just *know* you and I are going to be the best of friends!"

I muster a smile in response. "I bet," I manage.

"It's getting late, and my mother's expecting us," Oliver says.

"Of course!" Seraphima replies. She gives me an impromptu hug. "Maybe we can go shopping tomorrow in the village square?"

"Um . . ."

"Delilah's got a full schedule tomorrow," Oliver interjects. "But maybe the day after." He tugs me away and starts walking down the path.

"Oliver!" she calls out. "Aren't you forgetting something?"

He stops, turns toward her again. "I don't think so . . ." he says, grinning through clenched teeth.

Seraphima runs the short distance between them and throws her arms around his neck, kissing him full on the mouth. Pulling away, she bats her eyelashes. "Dream about me," she says shyly.

The minute we turn a hairpin bend in the road I elbow Oliver in the ribs. "Your *cousin*?" I say.

"It was the first thing I could come up with," he says. "I feel bad for her, okay?"

"Still, you didn't have to kiss her!"

"She kissed *me*!" Oliver argues.

"You didn't exactly fight her off," I point out.

Oliver beams. "Someone's a bit jealous."

I toss my hair. "You wish."

He twines his fingers with mine. "I did," he says. "It came true."

By the time we reach the castle, night has fallen. There are torches lining the drawbridge that leads to the doors, and the knights that stand at attention on either side like statues bow as Oliver walks by. "I can see how you might wind up with an inflated ego," I murmur.

"I prefer to call it confidence," Oliver says.

When we walk inside, we are in a huge stone hall. Tapestries line the walls, woven with pictures of princesses and knights from the past. A crystal candelabrum ringed with burning candles hangs overhead, casting long shadows on the floor. A footman approaches, dressed in dark blue velvet, with the royal crest embroidered over his chest. "Your Highness," he says. "Queen Maureen has retired with an ache of the head, but she wishes your guest to know she's welcome to stay in the north turret. The chamber's been prepared."

"Thank you," Oliver says. "I'll see Lady Delilah there myself."

"As you wish," the footman says, and he offers the candle he's holding to Oliver.

My stomach rumbles. "Is there any chance I could just make a quick peanut butter and jelly sandwich before we go upstairs?" I whisper.

"What's a sandwich?" Oliver asks.

"A snack," I correct. "I'm sort of hungry."

He grins. "If I know Queen Maureen, you won't have to worry about that." The footman has vanished, leaving us alone in the Great Hall. I follow Oliver, holding on to his hand so that he can guide me through the dark. As we start up a spiral stone staircase, the candlelight jumps on the walls, revealing our silhouettes.

We climb seven stories. Finally, Oliver pulls me onto the landing and stops in front of a heavy wooden door. "I know it's not home, but I hope this will do," he says, and he pushes it open.

The chamber has high, vaulted ceilings and an ornately carved four-poster bed draped with gauze netting. A fire blazes in the hearth. Two red velvet chairs are arranged in front of the fireplace, and on a low wooden table nearby is a feast: a roast chicken, a bowl of fresh fruit, a platter of tiered cakes, two loaves of bread, and dishes piled high with vegetables. "Oliver," I say, "how much does she think I eat?"

He smiles. "Cook tends to go a bit overboard."

"Well, I'm not going to let it go to waste. Come on in and grab a fork."

He looks horrified. "I can't come into your chamber."

"Why not? You've been in my room dozens of times."

His face reddens. "It's different in here, somehow."

"No, it's not. Besides, we're seven stories up in a tower. Who's going to know?"

For the next few hours, Oliver and I sit in front of the fire making a small dent in the sumptuous meal. He regales me with stories of practical jokes he's played on Frump, and gives me brief verbal sketches of each of the characters I am likely to meet. I tell him about my fight with Jules and how my mother tried to cheer me up. Then our conversation turns to a brainstorming session as we try to figure out what we can do to force an exit from the story.

"As soon as the book is opened," Oliver says, "you'll disappear, because you aren't part of the story."

"Even if that's true—which you don't know for sure—you wouldn't go with me. We'd be right back where we started."

"But isn't it better to have at least one of us on the outside, instead of neither?"

I can't answer that, not honestly. Before, I wanted Oliver by my side, but I didn't really know what I was missing. Now that I understand what it feels like to be near him, it's going to be that much harder to have it taken away.

"The book is stuck on a shelf in my bedroom. No one's ever going to notice it, much less open it."

"Then we have to force its hand," Oliver says. "There must be a way to get a book to open itself."

"Magic," I suggest, joking.

Oliver looks up at me. "Of course," he says, raising his brows. "We need to start with Orville."

I stifle a yawn with my hand, but Oliver sees me do it. "You," he says, getting to his feet, "have had a very long day. It's time for you to go to sleep."

He takes the candleholder he used to lead us upstairs and walks to the door. "You can't just leave me here alone," I say, panicking. What if I go to sleep, and when I wake up, this is all gone? I don't know the rules of this world. I don't know what's likely to happen.

"I'm right downstairs," Oliver says. "One flight. Stomp on the floor and I'll come running."

We are standing at the threshold to my chamber. "Aren't you forgetting something?" I say, repeating Seraphima's words.

He grins, then leans down and kisses me good night. We are both still smiling when we break apart. Oliver starts down the stone steps. "Dream about me, Cousin," I call out.

I can hear him laughing all the way down the stairs.

PAGE 44

liver could feel the mortar of the stone tower beneath his fingernails. He didn't know how much longer he was going to be able to hold on. But then again, below him there were only crashing surf and jagged rocks. One false move, and he would surely be dead.

With a mighty heave, he hoisted himself onto the wide stone ledge of the tower window.

But instead of seeing a beautiful princess, the girl of his dreams, the one he'd traveled far and wide to find—he saw a tall, caped man pacing back and forth. "Well?" the man demanded.

His voice was like fog crawling over the horizon. His hair fell like a raven's wing over one brow, and a scar that ran the length of his face curved his mouth downward. His fingers were long and bony, tapping impatiently on his arms.

"I don't have all day," he said.

No one had told him to expect anyone other than his true love in this tower, but in retrospect, Oliver knew that he should have anticipated this. If it had been easy, someone else would have rescued Seraphima by now.

Before he could begin to wonder how he—a boy who didn't even carry a sword and who had promised his mother he wouldn't fight— could defeat a villain who was at least six inches taller and forty pounds heavier, Seraphima emerged from behind a folding screen.

She was wearing a dress so white it was dazzling, beaded and jeweled at the bodice, and with sleeves that tapered down to her fingers. On her head was a gossamer wedding veil.

Immediately, over Rapscullio's shoulder, she saw Oliver.

Oliver's eyes lit upon her silver hair, her violet eyes, her heart-shaped face. And just like that, something inside shifted very subtly, so that all the empty spaces in him suddenly disappeared, so that his breath was timed to hers, so that his blood sang.

This was why there was music, he realized. There were some feelings that just didn't have words big enough to describe them.

Seraphima's lips parted. "Finally," she whispered, as if she had known he was coming all along.

But that one word was enough to make Rapscullio turn around, his cape billowing like a cloud of smoke. "Well, well," he said, every word a whipping, "look who's crashed the party."

OLIVER

THE NEXT MORNING, I ARRANGE FOR A PICNIC breakfast with Delilah in the tower where I rescue Seraphima. I figure that before we start out to Orville's cottage, we should be fortified.

And I kind of want to spend a few more minutes alone with her, instead of letting Queen Maureen grill her over the banquet table.

I thought I'd memorized everything there was to know about Delilah—from her freckles to her favorite blouse to the way she always gives her goldfish an extra helping of food—but as it turned out, there was so much left to learn. Like the fact that her skin is as soft as a feather, and that her hair smells of apples.

Her hand fits mine like the last piece of a jigsaw puzzle.

Delilah scrambles up the tower steps ahead of me, kicking her skirts out of the way. "Stupid dress," she mutters.

"It may be stupid," I reply, "but it looks quite nice on you."

She looks over her shoulder at me. "I bet you'd feel different if *you* were the one wearing it. Have you ever traipsed through a meadow in heels? I think *not.* . . . ."

"I don't traipse. Men don't traipse. We . . . swagger."

Delilah bursts out laughing. "Swagger? You?"

Affronted, I pause on the steps. "What? What's the matter with the way I walk?"

But before Delilah can answer, she reaches the top of the tower and gasps. "Oliver," she says, "when did you do all this?"

"Every now and then, having a castle full of servants is a real perk," I say. I peek over her shoulder and see that they have exceeded my expectations. A sheepskin blanket has been draped over the middle of the floor, and a feast is spread across it. There's an entire roast turkey, and apricot chutney, and stuffed figs. There are olives and grapes and plums piled high in the queen's best china bowls. A carafe of blackberry cider sits beside two golden chalices.

"I'm going to gain ten pounds before I leave this place," Delilah mutters. "A piece of toast would have been fine."

Doves coo in the rafters above us as she sits down on the blanket, her loathed dress whispering around her. She pops a grape into her mouth and sighs. "This is so unreal. I feel like a princess."

She couldn't have given me a better opening for the conversation I've been hoping to have.

"Funny," I say. "I was thinking the same thing."

Delilah frowns. "You feel like a princess too?"

"No!" I shake my head. "I just . . . well, I think *you'd* make a wonderful one." I force myself to meet her gaze. "I've never done this before. I mean, not for real, any-way." Swallowing hard, I get down on one knee and take her hand in mine. "Delilah, will you marry me?"

"What? What! *What* are you doing?" She shoves me backward, so that I topple over. "Oliver, I'm fifteen! I'm not getting married before I even go to prom!"

"Maybe we could travel there on our honeymoon?" I suggest.

She stands up, frustrated. "You don't understand."

"I thought you wanted us to be together," I say.

She moves to the open window, a flashback to the cli-max of this fairy tale. "In my world, you don't get married when you're fifteen," she says. "Unless you're pregnant and have been on an MTV show. I want a boyfriend. I want to go to movies and hold hands and have inside jokes. I want to take silly pictures with the camera on my phone. I want to get a Valentine's Day card that's not from my mother." Delilah looks up at me. "I want a date with you."

"A date. You mean like . . . the first Thursday in July?"

She smiles. "Not quite. It's when you go somewhere and get to know the other person a little better."

The picnic suddenly seems garish, over the top, a lousy idea. "We don't have to get married," I say. "All I really ever wanted was to be with you."

"I thought that was all I wanted too—but it turns out, I was wrong," Delilah admits. "I also want to wake up in my own bed. And wear pants. And—oh my gosh, I can't believe I'm saying this—go to school." She puts her hands on either side of my face. "I want you in my life. But I want it to be *my* life."

Guilty, I break away from her. "I know it's all my fault. But when I realized that I was never going to be able to leave the book, I couldn't stand the thought of—"

"Back up," Delilah says. "What do you mean, you were never going to be able to leave the book?"

My face turns red. "I saw my future, when I was with Orville," I whisper. "And you weren't part of it." I hesitate. "There was another girl in the vision he showed me."

"What?" Delilah says. "Who? Seraphima?"

"Please. Ugh."

"Then who?"

"I don't know. I've never seen her before."

Delilah considers this. "The future's always chang-ing," she points out. "A week ago, you wouldn't have pic-tured me in this book, for example. For all we know, if Orville manages to cast a spell that sends me home, your future might be completely different." She reaches for my hand and pulls me across the stone floor. "There's only one way to find out."

If I didn't know any better, I'd say Orville was flirting.

I've never seen the old coot move so quickly before. He's been blushing like a schoolgirl since I introduced him to Delilah, and he's showered her with all sorts of magic tricks: the disappear-ing newt, the violin that plays itself in midair, and his latest project—a duck that speaks fluent Hungarian.

In return, Delilah is apparently telling him everything she ever learned in science class. "You mix the zinc into the sodium hydroxide, and then heat it till it's practically boiling. Then you add the pennies, and they'll turn silver. If you heat up those same pennies, they'll turn to gold."

"Alchemy!" Orville gasps.

"Well, not really. It's the zinc and copper fusing together to make brass. But it looks like gold, anyway," she says.

Scowling, I fold my arms. "If you two are finished exchanging notes, I'd very much like to see my future again . . . ?"

"Oh, yes, of course," Orville says. He leads Delilah into his workroom and lugs the stone birdbath onto the wooden table, along with several colored glass bottles. He begins to pour a mixture into the bowl, stirring rhythmically.

Delilah and I have come up with a plan, of sorts. We know from my experiment with Pyro that the small book I carry, which is a replica of the story I'm living, has the capacity to effect change in Delilah's world. After all, somehow, it made the book in which we exist catch fire. Likewise, if we can find a way to explode the replica of *Between the Lines,* maybe the one we are living in will fall from Delilah's bookshelf and land open. Presumably, at that moment, all of us characters will be pulled into our usual positions. When the book realizes Delilah doesn't belong, she'll be sent back home.

Or at least, that's what I'm hoping.

Orville keeps his potions and ingredients under a spell unless he's in his workroom using them. Which means that we can't very well break into his cottage and find some concoction to cause an explosion. Instead, we have to distract him when he's present, and when the spell has been dismantled by Orville himself. It was Delilah's idea to ask him to replicate the magic that showed me my future. That way, we'd be killing two birds with one stone.

The liquid in the birdbath bubbles and evaporates almost immediately into a purple mist. "Let's give it a test," Orville says, and he looks around for something he can toss into the smoke. Delilah arches her brows at me and mouths a single word: *Now?*

I shake my head. "Not yet," I whisper.

Orville scans the bottles and jars on the shelves behind him. Then he brightens, reaching into his pocket and pulling out a small cloth bag. "Afternoon snack," he explains, and he extracts a seed and drops it into the mist.

The purple smoke plumes and peaks, taking the shape of a sunflower.

"Now," I tell Delilah. She falls back, ostensibly to let me get a better look at my own future, but in reality she starts grabbing every small bottle she can off the shelf behind Orville's head. She tucks them into her pockets and up her sleeves.

"It's all yours," the wizard says. He plucks a hair from

my head and lets it waft down into the haze. Just as it did last time, the mist forms a tall column that spreads wide as a movie screen, playing my future. I can see myself on a couch in a small room with bookshelves.

Delilah pauses, her fists still full of bottles and herbs, but she is drawn by the image too. "What's the matter with this future?" she asks.

"Give it a second," I say.

Sure enough, a girl walks in and embraces me. I can feel Delilah stiffen behind me.

"It gets worse," I tell her.

The girl turns, so that we can see her face. Now, upon second sight, I realize this isn't a girl as much as a woman. A woman I still have never seen before in my life.

Delilah gasps. "I know her!"

"You *do?*"

"Yes! That's—"

Before she can finish her sentence, though, the door to Orville's cottage slams open, smacking against the wall. Frump races inside, hurtling toward me with his teeth bared. I am so startled that I freeze. "Frump?" I cry. "What in the name of—"

He cuts me off, snarling, jumping at my throat. We fall to the ground in a blur of limbs and fur. I barely have time to notice Seraphima standing in the doorway too, her face ravaged by tears.

"You bloody liar," Frump barks. "You broke her heart."

"You don't have a cousin," Seraphima wails. "You don't even have an aunt or an uncle."

Before I can explain myself, I feel the weight of a vicious dog being lifted off me. I look up to find Delilah yanking Frump by the collar, pulling with all her might to get him to release his clenched teeth from the neckline of my tunic. Finally, the fabric tears, and Delilah and Frump roll backward in a somersault, crashing against Orville's shelves so that a hail of bottles rains down over them.

"Delilah," I cry, scrambling toward her. "Are you all right?"

"I'm fine," she mutters, standing up. There are wet splotches on her dress. "But I smell like feet."

Orville peers down at the mess. "Looks like troll snot. Nasty stuff."

"For God's sake, Frump, have you contracted rabies? What's gotten into you?" I yell.

Suddenly, Orville's eyes dart upward. "Move!" he bellows. "Take cover!" He dives beneath his workbench, and I shield Delilah with my body as a box teeters on the uppermost shelf. It's made of cast iron and is wrapped in chains and padlocked. "Don't let it—"

The box shudders and tumbles to the floor, landing directly between Delilah and Frump and breaking open.

"—fall . . ." Orville finishes weakly.

Rays of light begin to squeeze through the cracks in the iron box. They form an iridescent hovering ball. Slowly, the sphere begins to shake, and then it violently vibrates, before shooting like a firecracker into the ceiling. Plaster falls on our heads, but the ball of light bounces, ricocheting off the walls and the floor. The more it moves, the more energy it seems to gain.

"What is that thing?" Delilah cries.

"Pandemonium," Orville says. "You have to stop it before it destroys this place."

The light whizzes past Seraphima's cheek, and she shrieks, swatting at it. But she misses, hitting Orville across the face. He falls backward, knocking me to the ground as the light zooms in a spiral over the shelves, shattering every last standing bottle and slicing the hanging herbs off at their stems. It dips into the birdbath, sending up a spray of purple sparks before corkscrewing into the dirt floor, creating a deep black burrow.

For a moment, we all gather our senses, wondering if it's finished. Orville and I creep closer to the tunnel, peering down.

It explodes like a volcano, zipping past Frump—

Frump?

My trusty, loyal hound is gone. Lying on the floor, quite naked, is a human.

"Frump?" I say, stunned. "Is that you?"

"I didn't mean to go after you like that, Ollie," he says, sheepish. "I just got so angry when Seraphima came to me all upset. . . ."

Frump's voice is the same. His mannerisms are even a bit hangdog. But he's clearly not who he used to be. "Buddy," I murmur. "Erm . . ." I point to his bare bottom.

He looks down, yelps, and grabs the nearest covering he can—a tablecloth sewn with silver stars—which he wraps around his midsection. He's about my age, wiry and muscular, with shaggy hair the same color his fur had been. "What's happened?" he whispers, grinning widely as he feels his arms, his hands, his nose.

"Frump?" Seraphima repeats. I see her eyes lock on his the way they've always locked on mine, like she cannot bear to turn away.

Behind me I am dimly aware of the Pandemonium still wreaking havoc everywhere it touches down—creating a giant fissure in the center of Orville's worktable and singeing the tip of his hat.

The curse. The one that turned Frump into a dog must have been reversed, but how?

I turn to Delilah, but it's too late to warn her as the Pandemonium skitters beneath her feet. As she falls to the ground, I notice the splotches on her dress.

Some combination of the potions and herbs Delilah had squirreled away must have seeped onto Frump when they went tumbling backward. I dare-say she couldn't replicate that accidental spell if she tried. But the end result is that Frump is once again the boy he used to be.

"Oliver!" I turn my attention away from my friend in time to see the Pandemonium rocketing directly toward Delilah.

"Shield yourself!" Orville cries.

It is moving too fast for her to roll out of the way. Delilah looks frantically around for something to block the impact. At the last moment, she grabs an object that is lying within arm's reach away on the floor. It isn't until she holds it splayed wide open in front of her face that I realize what it is.

The copy of *Between the Lines* that I stole from Rapscullio, which must have fallen from my tunic during the scuffle with Frump.

The Pandemonium drives itself full force into the pages of the book, with the spine absorbing its impact. Delilah slams the book shut, trapping the light inside. "Gotcha, sucker," she says triumphantly, holding the tome against her chest.

The book begins to shudder so hard that Delilah is having trouble keeping it closed. I take a step toward her, hoping to wrest it from her grasp, but before I can, the fairy tale leaps out of her arms and bursts wide. The Pandemonium whooshes upward, rupturing a hole in the roof of Orville's cottage, so that mud and branches and rock shower down. I shield my eyes and reach for Delilah, to pull her to safety. I can't quite grasp her, though. Once the book leaves Delilah's hands, they freeze in position as a thick crack runs the length of her arm. The crack spreads and branches at the shoulders, creeping up her neck, splintering her features—her wide eyes, her open mouth. I see it as if in slow motion—that book tumbling toward the ground until the moment it strikes, and Delilah shatters into a million pieces, vanishing into nothing but dust.

Delilah

THE FIRST THING I SEE WHEN I OPEN MY EYES

is the book, peeking out from beneath my bed, wide open.

I roll from my stomach onto my back and blink at a purple ceiling, with little glow-in-the-dark stars. "My room," I breathe.

It worked. Our plan worked.

"Well, of course it's your room," my mother's voice floats to me.

I try to sit up, but a hand eases me down. "Take it slow, Delilah," says a voice that I cannot quite place but that seems familiar.

I look to my left to find Dr. Ducharme standing beside my mother.

My mother sits down on the edge of the bed. "You've got a nasty bump on your head," she says. "You must have fallen when you were trying to reach the box of videos in your closet."

Wincing, I touch my forehead; it's tender. "How long have I been gone?"

"Gone?" Dr. Ducharme grins. "Well, you've been asleep—but you haven't gone anywhere. Your mom even got a doctor to make a house call last night to make sure you were all right. And she called *me* when you started talking in your sleep."

I struggle to a sitting position. "What was I talking about?"

They exchange a look. "That's not important," my mother says. "You need to rest. And you're going to have a nasty headache."

I glance over her shoulder and catch a glimpse of myself in the mirror. On my forehead is a giant goose egg and an impressive bruise.

But I couldn't have just hit my head. I was in that book with Oliver. I *know* I was.

I think back to what might have happened. The last I remember, we were at Orville's cottage, and I'd managed to recapture the Pandemonium. Almost as quickly, my arms had begun to fracture, sprouting fine cracks, like a disintegrating marble statue. Gasping, I grab for my right arm with my left hand.

It's perfectly intact.

What is going on?

"What day is it?" I ask.

"Tuesday," my mother replies. "It's nearly three o'clock."

"I'm, um, starving. . . ."

"Then we'll get you something to eat." She gives me a quick embrace first. "I was so worried you weren't coming back," she whispers.

My arms close around her. "Me too," I murmur.

She stands up, and as she leaves the room, Dr. Ducharme puts his hand on her shoulder.

There's something about that casual gesture that makes me relieved. While I was in the book, I worried about my mother being left alone. But maybe, one day, she won't be.

As soon as I hear the door click shut, I scramble under the bed and grab the book. Sitting up, I see my reflection in the mirror. There is something sticking out of the collar of my T-shirt that looks remarkably—and terrifyingly—like a tattoo.

I pull down the collar, afraid to peek.

Strung around my neck is a line of backward cursive. I slip a fingernail under one edge and peel it off my skin like a Band-Aid. Then I drape the letters over the edge of my bedsheet.

pearlspearlspearlspearlspearls

Just like the spider I pulled from the book days ago, the mermaid's necklace—on the outside—has transformed into words. But I saw a vision of Oliver in Orville's cottage—a vision where he was in the future, in *this* outside world, and he wasn't just letters on a page.

Focus, Delilah, I tell myself. I grab the book and open it to page 43, where Oliver looks up at me with obvious relief.

"You're alive!" he cries.

"What happened?" I say. "It was real, wasn't it?"

Oliver's face falls. "Don't you remember?"

"Yes," I whisper. "But I want to make sure I didn't make it all up."

"Just because it's fiction doesn't mean it's any less true," Oliver replies. He squints at me. "You're hurt?"

"Just a bruise," I tell him. But that reminds me of the Pandemonium, and the devastation it caused. "What about you? Are you all right? And Orville? His poor home!"

"It's all intact again," Oliver says. "The minute you opened the book, everything went back to the way it used to be." He looks away from me.

"Frump?" I ask.

Oliver nods. "Just a dog."

"But it worked, Oliver. Exploding your copy of the fairy tale set me free."

"And I'm still here," he says sadly. "So we're back to square one."

"No, we're not. Remember the vision? Your future? I know who that woman is. It's Jessamyn Jacobs."

"Who?"

"She's the author," I tell him. "The woman who created you."

Oliver's eyes light up. "So that vision," he says. "I'm in her house?"

I hear footsteps on the stairs. "Soup!" my mother sings out.

I slam the book hard, stuffing it under a pillow and yanking the covers over me. The door creaks open. "Thanks," I say. I take a sip of the soup to satisfy my mom.

She sits down on the edge of the bed and watches me take one spoonful, then another. I blot my mouth with a paper napkin. "You're not going to watch me eat the whole thing, are you?"

My mother looks flustered. "Yes. I mean, of course not." She hesitates. "I just don't want you to fall asleep. Steve says that's the worst thing possible after a concussion."

Steve? "Mom," I say, "when's the last time *you* slept?"

"You don't have to worry about me," she says, squeezing my hand.

"I may not *have* to," I tell her. "But I *do.*"

She smiles, but she doesn't move.

"Mom?" I say. "If I promise you I'm not going to conk out, can I eat in privacy?"

She's reluctant, but she stands up. "Call me when you're done," she says.

The headache she promised is emerging. I know that Oliver expects me to open the book and finish our conversation, but there's something I have to do first. I get out of bed and gingerly walk to my desk, where my laptop sits. Opening a search engine, I type in *Jessamyn Jacobs*. All the websites connected to her are listed. I click the first one, and a photo of the woman in Oliver's vision fills the screen. I start to read the text below it:

> Jessamyn Jacobs was born in New York in 1965. After graduating from NYU, she got a job as an editor at *HorrorFest* magazine. But she realized quickly that she didn't want to correct other people's words—she wanted to write her own. Her first thriller was published when she was only twenty-six years old, and she wrote ten consecutive best-sellers. However, after writing one children's book, the author retreated into anonymity. She has not published since 2002, choosing to live quietly in Wellfleet, Massachusetts.

After writing one children's book, the author retreated into anonymity.

My whole life, and its current obsession, has been reduced to a throwaway sentence in the biography of a famous thriller writer, who hasn't been writing for years.

But at least I know where to find her.

I unplug my cell phone from its charger and text Jules.

I'm a jerk, I write.

I count all the way to sixty-two before there is an answering beep.

I know, Jules has replied.

My thumbs work furiously over the tiny keyboard. Ur Aunt Agnes is Voldemort in drag. If I could I would hide u in my closet 4 the summer. In fact, why don't we try? Might work.

Another beep: I'm closetrophobic.

I grin. Jules, I text. I know I have no right 2 ask, and you can tell me 2 go jump in a lake if u want, but I need ur help. Have 2 get to MA ASAP. I hesitate. Will explain when I see u.

This time it takes Jules even longer to respond. I can be at ur house in 5 mins. Dad's car is in the garage.

You don't have a license, I text back.

There is another beep. That doesn't mean I can't drive, Jules writes.

The hardest part is leaving my mother again—just moments after I've returned. I consider reasoning with her, but what excuse can I make that would convince her to take an impromptu trip to Cape Cod, particularly when

I am still fresh from a concussion? If I insist, she'll probably take me for a neurological exam. No, the only way to do this is to leave her out of it.

The one immediate challenge to that strategy is that in order to leave the house, I have to walk downstairs, right past her.

I'm not the most graceful person—okay, I'm a bona fide klutz—but again, desperate times call for desperate measures. If I think it's unlikely that my mother will agree to a four-hour car ride, it's even more unlikely that she'd let me go with the unlicensed Jules as my chauffeur. So I throw open the sash of my bedroom window, eyeing a tree with branches close enough for me to reach.

I used to have romantic fantasies about a guy throwing pebbles at the window, climbing up to my room, kissing me in the moonlight, stealing me away.

Wrong fairy tale, I think wryly. *I'm* the one who's going to save the prince.

I grab the notepad on my desk and rip off a sheet of paper. I write:

Be back soon. Don't worry.
I'm fine.
Really.
Love,
Delilah. xoxo

My mother is going to worry anyway—but at least when she finds me missing, Dr. Ducharme will be there. And maybe he can keep her calm long enough for me to explain why I had to do this. After all, if it works, Oliver will be here—alive and three-dimensional and very, very real—and he'll confirm this whole crazy story.

I dig around in my underwear drawer for the small jewelry box I use to store my allowance and the money I have from babysitting: three hundred and twenty-two dollars. It's not a fortune, but I tuck it into my backpack, then grab the book and stuff it inside too. I look around my room to make sure I haven't forgotten anything and catch sight of myself in the mirror. I look like I've lost a fight. If I show up at Jessamyn Jacobs's house like this, she will probably run away screaming. In my closet, I find a knit winter hat that covers my forehead perfectly. It's a little warm for the season, but maybe I can pull it off as a new fashion trend.

I open the window and stretch a leg out. I swear the tree has moved. Like, three feet away.

Taking a deep breath, I jump from the windowsill, and to my great shock wind up hugging the trunk tightly. I shimmy down, thinking of Oliver, who has to climb a cliff wall every day.

With a thumb I hit the ground and tiptoe down the block, to the cul-de-sac where Jules is parked and waiting, just like we'd arranged. She looks weird sitting behind the steering wheel of a car. When she sees me, she grins and lowers the power window. "You owe me big-time," she says.

I never would have guessed it based on her personality, but Jules drives like an old lady. She putts along ten

miles *below* the speed limit and puts on her turn signal miles before she actually veers off the exit. "So," she says, when we have been driving for ten minutes on the highway, "when are you going to tell me where we're going?"

"Wellfleet," I say. "On Cape Cod."

Jules nods, flexing her hands on the steering wheel. "Okay," she says. "*Why* are we going?"

I take a deep breath. "What I'm about to tell you isn't going to make a lot of sense," I say. "But I need you to listen to the whole story and not judge me, okay?"

Wordlessly, Jules holds up her right hand for a pinkie swear.

I start, well, at the very beginning. I tell her how I got a shock the first time I touched the spine of the fairy tale, and how even though it was a kids' book, I couldn't manage to put it down. I tell her about Oliver, the prince who grew up without a dad, like me. I explain how, one day, the illustrations changed before my eyes, and how without even trying, I could hear Oliver speaking to me—words that weren't written for him but that came from the heart.

I tell her about the spider and how the book caught fire and how I wound up getting sucked into it and then ejected.

I tell her that I might just be in love with Oliver.

When I'm done, Jules keeps staring straight at the road, completely silent.

"So?" I say.

Jules doesn't respond.

"You think I'm crazy."

Jules shrugs. "No."

"That's it?" I ask, incredulous. "You believe me?"

"Well," she responds, "I believe *you* believe it. And I'm your best friend. So that's good enough."

For the next few hours, everything seems almost normal. My best friend is my friend again; I don't have to pretend that this book means nothing to me. It's like old times. Jules and I play I Spy and eat a whole bag of Cheetos that she's brought along from home. Finally, the GPS tells us we have arrived at our destination. Jules pulls over on the side of the main street of Wellfleet, Massachusetts, hitting the curb with her tires.

"You just failed your driver's test," I joke.

"But think of how many hours of practice driving I've got under my belt now," Jules says. She looks into the rearview mirror. "So where are we going?"

Well. I haven't quite figured that part out yet. I don't have a street address for Jessamyn Jacobs, just the town in which she lives. But this much I know—I have to go by myself. Jules has already done enough for me; I'm not going to drag her into this mess. "Not we," I say. "Me."

"I'm not leaving you down here by yourself."

I shake my head. "Jules, your parents are already going to kill you for stealing your father's car."

She laughs. "That's my master plan. I'd rather be in reform school over the summer than with Aunt Agnes."

She unhooks her seat belt and gets out of the car as I grab my backpack. "Are you okay driving home by yourself?" I ask. "It'll be dark soon."

"Piece of cake," Jules says.

I give her a tight hug. "Thank you," I whisper, and I watch her get into the car and put on her signal in preparation for pulling out of the parking spot.

Before she does, though, she unrolls her window. "I hope you find him," Jules says with a smile. "Your prince."

There's a tiny coffee shop in the center of town. A bell rings when I walk through the door, and a waitress looks up at me. "Is there a restroom I could use?" I ask.

"Sure." She points down the hall, and I lock myself into the small room and pull the book out of my backpack. I suppose I could have talked to Oliver in the car, but it was nice to spend some time with just Jules. I've missed that.

As soon as I open to page 43, Oliver starts yelling. "Where have you been? You left me hanging in the middle of a very important conversation. This Jessamyn Jacobs woman—"

"Lives here," I interrupt.

I see Oliver peeking over my shoulder, taking in the scenery behind me. "Where *are* you?"

"Well, in a bathroom. She doesn't live *here*. But I'm in her town, and I'm going to figure out how to get to her house. If anyone knows how to get you out of the story, it's going to be the woman who wrote it."

Oliver scowls. "You can't very well walk up to her and say, 'I've fallen head over heels for one of your characters.'"

I smile. "Oh yes, that Socks is a sexy beast."

He laughs. "I'll tell him you said so."

"I don't know when I'll be back," I tell him. "And I don't really have a plan yet."

"And that's supposed to inspire confidence?" Oliver says.

"No," I tell him. "It's supposed to inspire trust."

I start to close the book, but I'm stopped by the sound of Oliver's voice. "Delilah?" he says. "I never really got a chance to say thank you. For everything you're doing to help me."

I look at the hope written across his face, as clear as any of the words on the page. "Don't thank me yet," I answer.

After I return the book to my backpack, I flush the toilet and wash my hands, so as not to seem too suspicious. The waitress is still wiping off the counter when I walk back into the coffee shop. "Party of one?" she asks.

"Actually, I'm just looking for directions," I say. "This is totally embarrassing, but I'm here to surprise my aunt for her birthday—I came in on the bus—and I can't remember how to get to her house." I offer my brightest I'm-not-a-psychopath smile. "Jessamyn Jacobs? Do you know her?"

The waitress looks at me uneasily. "She doesn't much like visitors."

"Visitors!" I say. "I'm *family.*"

The girl frowns. "Well, she's the last house on Wilson Street. It's the purple Cape that overlooks a cliff."

"Right!" I slap my hand against my forehead. "Duh. Wilson Street."

The waitress goes back to work.

"Can I ask just one more question?" I say, and I wait till she looks up. "How do I get to Wilson Street?"

Jessamyn Jacobs's house perches on the edge of a cliff overlooking the water, like a swimmer afraid to jump in. It's painted the color of a plum, and all the windows have curtains drawn down to their black trim. For a long moment I stand on the porch, running through possible introduction scenarios in my head.

Hi! I'm selling Girl Scout cookies—

No, too eager.

I'm doing a voter survey . . .

Nope. I don't look old enough to work for a political action committee.

I've lost my pet cat. Have you seen him?

No. What are the odds it would be hiding in her house?

Well. Maybe there's something to be said for brilliance under pressure. Before I can stop myself, I ring the doorbell.

But there's no answer.

I ring it again, as if that might change the outcome. No one is home. Never in my wildest imagination did I picture finally reaching Jessamyn Jacobs's house only to find her absent.

All of a sudden the garage door beside me magically opens, making me jump a foot. A moment later, a car comes around the corner and pulls into the driveway. It is a red minivan, like the kind we had when I was younger. A woman gets out of the driver's seat, carrying a bag of groceries. "Hi," she says. "Can I help you?"

I know it's Jessamyn Jacobs because I recognize the red hair and the features from her author photo on the book. Except this version of Jessamyn Jacobs doesn't look nearly as glamorous. She's dressed, well, like a mom.

"I, um, I'm Delilah McPhee. I'm a student," I stammer. "I'm doing an author project, and I was wondering if I could interview you."

She smiles a little sadly. "I haven't been an author in a very long time," she says. "You probably want to talk to someone else."

"No!" I cry. "It has to be you!"

She looks at me, a little alarmed by my outburst. "I'm afraid I can't help you, Delilah. That part of my life is over." Careful to put a good amount of distance between us, she opens her front door and walks inside.

I can't let it end like this. Not when I'm so close.

"Please," I beg. "Your book meant a lot to me." I

reach into my backpack and pull out the fairy tale, and to my surprise, Jessamyn Jacobs stops in her tracks.

She reaches one hand toward the cover, stroking it the way you'd touch something precious. "It meant a lot to me too," she murmurs. Then she smiles at me. "Would you like to come inside?"

"Most people who still write me fan mail are much older than you, and collect chain saws and instruments of torture," Jessamyn says, setting down a plate of cookies. "If I'm remembered for anything, it's my murder mysteries. Very few of my readers even know I wrote a fairy tale."

She is staring at the book, which sits on the coffee table between us. "It's my favorite story," I tell her. "I've memorized every single word."

Jessamyn smiles. "It was a one-of-a-kind book," she says. "And it inadvertently got placed in a box of toys and clothes that were being donated to a charity's yard sale. I always wondered what had become of it."

Behind her are the bookshelves and the fireplace that Oliver saw in the vision of his future in Orville's cottage. It is strange, seeing them again—seeing them for *real*— and knowing Oliver still isn't here.

My gaze settles on the view from the big picture window that overlooks the ocean. I am almost 100 percent sure I have seen this view before, but that doesn't make sense—I've never been here in my life. Then it hits me— page 59. When Oliver fights with Rapscullio and pushes him out the tower window. This is the illustration we see as the villain falls to the rocks below.

Jessamyn follows my glance. "Page fifty-nine," she confirms. "When I was painting the illustrations, I used all sorts of familiar places. The castle dining room is an exact image of the estate where I got married. Everafter Beach looks like the island where I went on my honeymoon." She gazes down at her lap. "I wrote the story after my husband died of cancer. He fought so hard for a year, but ultimately, he lost the battle. The fairy tale was my way of getting through that. And helping my son get through it too."

Suddenly I feel uncomfortable. Whatever the book has meant to me, it's meant so much more to Jessamyn. "I'm really sorry," I say.

"Don't be. It was a long time ago. It's why, in a way, having the book out of my house was a relief. As if it meant that part of my life—the sad part—was finished." She reaches for the book. "It's been a while since I read this," she says, and opens to page 43.

Oliver looks up, expecting me as the Reader. But

then he notices Jessamyn. I see his eyes widen—he recognizes her as the woman in the vision.

Jessamyn touches her finger to the crown of Oliver's head. I feel an actual ache in my gut, remembering what his hair felt like—the texture, the thickness. "Amazing," she breathes. "He looks exactly the way I imagined he would."

This doesn't make sense to me—since she was the one who drew Oliver in the first place. *Obviously* he'd look the way she imagined.

Jessamyn glances up at me. "You're not really here to do an interview for school, are you." It is not a question, but a statement.

"No," I admit. I take a deep breath. "I came to ask you if you'd ever consider rewriting the ending."

She smiles faintly. "Are you a writer, Delilah?" she asks.

"I'm more of a reader."

"Ah," Jessamyn replies. "Then I can see why you wouldn't understand."

"Understand what?"

"That the story isn't mine to change anymore. Maybe it belonged to me at first, but now it belongs to you. And to everyone else who's ever read it. The act of reading is a partnership. The author builds a house, but the reader makes it a home."

"But if you created it, you have to be the one to change it."

"Why should it be changed?"

"Because," I say, "it's not a happy ending. I can't explain why."

"Try me."

"One of the characters told me." I shut my eyes, certain that Jessamyn Jacobs officially thinks I've gone crazy. But to my surprise, when I open my eyes again, she just nods.

"The characters used to talk to me too," Jessamyn agrees. "I think any writer would say the same thing. But Delilah, even if I changed the ending, the story already exists in the world in the memories of all of its readers. Once a story is told to someone, it can't be erased."

What she's telling me is that I've hit a dead end. And I can't let that be true. "But you *have* to try!" I burst out.

She hesitates. "How would *you* have ended the book?"

Embarrassed, I mumble, "Oliver gets to leave the story."

She raises her eyebrows. "Ah. I think I'm starting to understand. He *is* quite good-looking. I used to develop crushes on characters. There was one detective in my murder series who had the dreamiest smile—"

Tears fill my eyes. "It's not a crush," I tell her. "He's alive, to me."

"And he always will be," Jessamyn says kindly. "Every

time you open the book. That's the beauty of reading, isn't it?"

If I can't make the author understand, then surely I have run out of options. I'm certain she thinks I'm nuts—some delusional girl who shows up unannounced, talking about a fictional character as if he might be sitting in the room sipping tea.

But how will I break this news to Oliver?

Suddenly, it's just too much. I thought if anyone was ever going to understand the things I felt for this story, it would be the author herself, and yet here she is telling me—like everyone else—that I'm wrong. That what's between me and Oliver is impossible.

I start sobbing. I get to my feet, embarrassed, suddenly intent on leaving as quickly as possible. I've been an idiot to think that real life could have a happy ending.

"Delilah! Are you all right?" Concerned (and who *wouldn't* be if a crazy girl was hysterical in the living room?), Jessamyn puts her hand on my arm. "Is there someone I can call for you? Your mother, maybe?"

This makes me cry even harder, as I think about how frantic my mom must be by now. During our car ride I had checked the messages on my cell phone; I stopped listening at number twenty-three.

Jessamyn leads me to a couch. "I'm going to go get

a glass of water for you," she says. "And then we'll figure out what to do next."

She leaves the room, and I take deep breaths, trying to calm myself down enough to at least be capable of opening the book and telling Oliver it's over.

I hear footsteps and look up, but it's not Jessamyn returning from the kitchen. Instead, standing in the doorway that leads to the front hall, is Oliver.

At first I think I am hallucinating. But then he glances at me. I would know those eyes anywhere. "Hey," he says.

Leaping up, I throw my arms around him. "Oliver! How did you get here?"

He shoves me backward, looking at me as if he's never seen me in his life. "I walked downstairs," he says. "And the name's Edgar."

My jaw drops just as Jessamyn enters, carrying a tall glass of water. She glances from Oliver to me. "Delilah," she says, "I see you've met my son."

And at that moment, everything goes black.

I'm not a fainter. I'm unfazed by the sight of blood, and I can watch horror movies without wincing. And granted, I apparently took a massive conk to my head when I fell yesterday—and then traveled 230 miles without eating anything but Cheetos. But all the same, I'm pretty embarrassed to find myself lying on a stranger's couch with a cold, wet washcloth on my head and a boy who looks just like Oliver but isn't, staring down at me with absolute revulsion. "You're drooling," he says.

Mortified, I wipe my hand across my mouth.

"She's awake," Not-Oliver says. "Can I go now?"

He is speaking to Jessamyn, who carries a bowl of soup from the kitchen. Why does everyone keep feeding me soup?

"Thanks for watching her, Edgar," Jessamyn says.

"Whatever," Edgar replies. He rolls his eyes and trudges out of the room.

"All right." Jessamyn sits on the edge of the couch. "It's time to tell me the truth. Are you in trouble, Delilah? Did you run away from home?"

"No!" I answer. "I mean, I *did* run away, but only temporarily. Only to find *you.*" I take the bowl she offers me. Broccoli cheddar. It smells delicious.

"And I'm guessing you have a mother somewhere who has no idea where you are right now?"

I can feel my cell phone vibrate in my pocket with yet another message. "Um," I say. "Yeah."

Jessamyn hands me the phone. "Call her."

Reluctantly, I dial the numbers. It hasn't even rung once when my mother picks up.

"Hi, Mom!" I say, as cheerful as possible.

I have to hold the phone away from my ear as she shouts at me in reply. Wincing, I wait till there's a break in the wall of sound and speak again. "I'm really sorry—"

"Delilah Eve, do you have any idea how worried I've been? Where *are* you? What were you *thinking*?!"

"I just had to do something and I knew you wouldn't let me leave if I asked first."

"Tell me where you are. I'm going to come get you. And then I'm going to ground you for life."

"I'm kind of in Massachusetts. On Cape Cod."

There is another torrent of angry sound as my mother yells her response. Again, I hold the phone away from my ear.

"Maybe I can help," Jessamyn says, and she reaches out her hand for the phone. "Hello? Is this Delilah's mother? I'm Jessamyn Jacobs." She hesitates. "Yes. Well, I used to be an author, anyway. Oh, that's very kind. I'm so glad you were a fan." Another pause. "Believe me, it was quite a surprise for me too. . . . No, no. It's far too late for you to make that kind of trip. Why don't you just let me host Delilah overnight, and you can be here bright and early in the morning. She can stay in our guest room."

I hear the buzzy warble of my mother's voice in return, and then Jessamyn gives her an address. She holds the phone out to me when she's through. "She'd like to speak to you again."

"Just so we're on the same page, you are still grounded until you hit menopause," my mother repeats. "But at least I know you're not wandering around on a street somewhere at night. You've caused this woman a great deal of disruption, so you'd better be the best guest she's ever had in her home. Am I clear?"

"Yes, Mom," I mutter. "I'll see you tomorrow."

"Delilah?" my mother says.

"Yeah?"

"I love you, you know."

I look down into my lap. I've created so much trouble—for my mother and for Jessamyn Jacobs, all in the hope that I can make the impossible possible and turn a fictional character real. Suddenly, I'm ashamed for being so selfish. "I love you too," I whisper.

I hang up the phone and hand it back to Jessamyn. "Thank you. For letting me stay here."

"It's no problem. It's nice for Edgar to have someone his age around. He doesn't make friends very easily."

I sit up. "Can I ask you a question? How come Oliver looks just like your son?"

"Because he *is* my son." Jessamyn looks up at me. "After Edgar's father died, he was so afraid of everything. I wanted to create a role model for him—someone who maybe wasn't the bravest or strongest boy in the king-dom but who managed to always triumph by using his brain. Edgar was younger then—I had to imagine the boy I thought he'd grow up to look like—and that was how I painted Oliver."

"Well, they're identical."

"Not really," Jessamyn says. "Edgar never became the Oliver I hoped he would." She smiles, a little sadly. "I wasn't very good at helping Edgar with his grief. I didn't know how to do that, but I knew how to write books. So I figured I'd try to help him, through what I do best. But when that wasn't enough, I stopped writing. Instead, I concentrated on learning how to be a better mother." She shakes her head, as if she's clearing it, and then pats my shoulder. "Why don't we get you settled upstairs?"

The guest room is painted the color of a sunset. There is a small wooden bureau and a double bed. Jessamyn leaves me with a stack of fresh towels and a promise to check in on me after I've rested for a while.

It's weird, having no luggage to unpack. I sit on the edge of the bed and look around the room. There are framed photos on the walls of a baby who keeps get-ting progressively older. This, I realize, is Edgar—but I find myself drawn to the walls, touching the glass on the pho-tos, thinking that this is what Oliver would have looked like when he was two, when he was four, when he rode his first horse, when he learned how to swim.

Suddenly, I really miss Oliver. I unzip my backpack and pull out the book. It falls open to page 43.

"It's her, it's really her! Delilah, you amazing girl, you did it!" He is so happy that it hurts me to look at him.

"Oliver," I whisper. "She won't change the ending."

His face falls. "Maybe there's a way for me to talk to her."

"Even if she could hear you, she wouldn't do it. She wrote this book for her son. She's not going to make any changes. It means too much to her personally."

"She has a son?" Oliver says. "Have you met him? Maybe *he* can convince her."

"Yeah, I've met him."

"Well, what's he like?"

"He could be your twin," I say.

For a moment, Oliver gets very quiet. "So you're in a house," he sums up, "with a guy who looks just like me, but who's real?"

I think of what Jessamyn said about Edgar. "He's not you," I state simply.

Whatever Oliver says in reply is drowned out by the strangest sounds coming from the room next door to mine. There are high-pitched screams and whistles and weird sirens.

"Well?" Oliver says. "What do you think?"

"I didn't hear what you said. . . ." Now, in addition to all the crazy noises, I hear a voice: *"I'm going to get you, you bloodsucking, boneheaded monster!"*

"What the—?" I look down at the book, careful this time not to slam it shut. "Wait here," I tell Oliver. I get up and walk into the hall, then knock on the door beside mine.

There's no answer. This isn't a surprise, because who could hear with that racket going on? So I turn the doorknob and peek inside.

Edgar is sitting in a strange reclining chair at floor level, holding a game controller in his hand. On a computer screen in front of him, there's an asteroid explosion in a galaxy. "Take that, Zorg!" Edgar hollers, and he punches a fist in the air. Letters roll over the screen:

HIGH SCORES

EDGAR 349,880

EDGAR 310,900

EDGAR 298,700

EDGAR 233,100

I wonder if Edgar's ever even played his video game against another person.

I remember what Jessamyn said about him being a loner. "Hey," I say. "You want company?"

He whirls in his seat. "Who told you I was in here?"

"I could pretty much hear everything through the wall. . . ."

Edgar narrows his eyes. "Have you ever played Battle Zorg 2000 before?"

"I can't say that I have."

He digs around in his desk for a second controller. "Then I suppose I'll have to teach you."

He fumbles through the opening screens of the game to set it up for two players instead of one. "I usually play solo," he says casually. "I'm actually sort of legendary, in terms of scoring."

I let Edgar explain to me about the Galactoids from Planet Zugon who are coming to take over Earth. "Our job," he says, "is to kill them before they plant a mind-control ozone bomb in the San Andreas Fault, or create a force field of incineration that burns everyone to ash the minute they come in contact with it."

It makes me think of the Pandemonium.

"If you can get past the foot soldier Galactoids," Edgar continues, "you can be admitted into the Astrochamber, where you have to complete fourteen tasks in order to face Zorg."

"Who's Zorg?" I ask.

He snorts. "Only the biggest, baddest robot-android hybrid in the Aphelion galaxy!"

I gingerly take the controller and press a button. "No!" he shouts. "Not until we've set up your avatar!"

With a few clicks, I become Aurora Axis, a geophysicist from Washington, DC. I follow Edgar's avatar through the levels of the game, getting knocked out almost immediately by a low-flying asteroid. "Shoot!" I say, angry at myself. "I should have been able to see that."

Edgar grins. "It takes a little bit of practice."

For three-quarters of an hour, we battle aliens with an array of weapons. I get killed more times than I can count. Finally, just when I think it's virtually impossible, Edgar and I double-team an Amazon made of starlight who is shooting electromagnetic radiation from her fingers, and we manage to drown her in a micrometeorite lake. Just like that, we are admitted into the Astrochamber.

"Yes!" we both scream as the door to Edgar's bedroom opens.

"Edgar!" Jessamyn cries, "have you seen— Oh!" She looks at me, and then at Edgar, and then back at me. "You're here."

Edgar pivots in his chair. "She wanted to learn how to play."

I grin. "Turns out I'm a natural with a neutrino ray."

Jessamyn seems surprised—by my comment, and maybe by the fact that her son has made a friend. "Good!" she says. "Can I get you two anything? Cookies? Milk?"

"Privacy?" Edgar suggests.

Jessamyn backs out of the room, and Edgar lifts his controller again. "Awkward," he says. "Now, where were we . . ."

"About to kick some Zorgian butt," I reply.

Edgar lifts his controller and points to the screen, but the computer blinks a steady neon green. "Shoot," he mutters. "Not *again.*"

"What's the matter?"

"Stupid old computer. It freezes up all the time. I just hope our game saved. . . ." He starts pushing buttons and rebooting the system. "My mom won't let me load my games on her new computer because she says they take up too much of the memory, so I have to work on this total dinosaur."

"It doesn't look that old to me—"

"That's because it was state-of-the-art when my mom was still using it to type her books. But believe me, I had to upgrade this puppy with major video cards and speakers just to get it compatible with Zorg 2000."

I sit up, alert. "This used to be your mom's computer?"

"Yeah. Why?"

"Do you know if her old files are still on it?"

"They're there," Edgar says. "She won't let me delete them." He rolls his eyes. "Every time I go to start a new game, I see that dumb fairy tale.

[299]

Between the Lines. It's listed right below *Battle Zorg 2000,* alphabetically."

I lean forward. "You don't like that story?"

"Hate it," Edgar says. "How would you feel if the whole world knew your mother thought you were a loser?"

"I'm sure she doesn't think—"

"She wrote that idiotic prince character wishing I could be more like him. But me, I'm not going to catch a dragon and talk it into getting its teeth cleaned. I'm not quite the fairy-tale type."

"The reason I came here is because your mom wrote that book," I tell Edgar. Taking a deep breath, I blurt out, "Can I ask you something that's going to sound a little strange?"

"Okay."

"When you play Battle Zorg 2000, does it sometimes feel like you're a part of it?"

Edgar nods. "Well, sure. Otherwise I couldn't score as high as I do."

"No. . . . I mean, do you ever wish you were *inside* the game?"

At first I am afraid to look him in the eye, but when I do, I find Edgar staring at me intently. "Sometimes," he admits quietly, "it's like I can hear the commanders talking to me, telling me what to do next."

I put my hand on his arm. "Edgar, can I show you something?"

I run to the room next door and crawl onto the guest bed. The book is still open to page 43, and Oliver is lying on his back, snoring. "Oliver," I whisper, leaning close to the binding, and then I shout, *"Get up!"*

He startles, smacking his head on a low branch jutting out of the cliff. Rubbing it, he winces and looks up at me. "Just for clarification, when you say you'll be right back, then you mean sometime in the next millennium?"

"I got distracted. But Oliver, listen, there's someone I want you to meet." I grab the book and carry it toward Edgar's bedroom.

"What? Do you really think this is a good idea? No one ever sees me, and it just makes you look even more insane."

"Thanks," I say sarcastically. I turn the corner and enter Edgar's room again. "I have a gut feeling about this."

"About what?" Edgar asks.

I set the book on the desk. "I wasn't talking to you," I explain. "I was talking to him." I point to Oliver, who smiles.

Edgar glances at the book, and then up at me. "Seriously? You think my mom's fairy tale is talking to you?"

"Just wait a second," I urge. "No one ever hears him talk—but that's because no one ever listens hard enough. But based on what you told me about your video game, I think you might be different. Please? Can't you try?"

"He's not very attractive," Oliver says, miffed.

"Oliver, he looks identical to you," I murmur.

Edgar folds his arms. "Look, pretty boy, my mother drew *you* based off of *me*—"

I gasp. "You heard him? You heard Oliver speak?"

Edgar's eyes widen, and he steps away from the book as if he doesn't want to get too close to it. He hits the side of his head with the flat of his hand, as if he's gotten water in his ear and is trying to shake it out. "No no no no *no*," he says, under his breath. "That didn't just happen."

"It *did*," I say, grasping his arm. "I know it seems crazy and impossible, but you have to believe me—it's real. *He's* real. And I promised I'd help him get out of this book."

This is huge. If I'm not the only person who can hear Oliver, then there's somebody else in this world who can help me save him. And yet, I feel the tiniest twinge in my chest, thinking that if I'm not the only person who hears Oliver, it makes the connection between us a little less special.

"What is *that*?" Oliver's eyes gleam. I follow his gaze off the edge of the page to the computer screen, which has rebooted and shows a massive army of aliens attacking Earth.

"Battle Zorg 2000," I reply. "It's a computer game."

"How did all those little people get inside the box?"

I'm not about to give Oliver a tutorial on electronics. "I'll explain it later. All you need to know is that that little box is the machine Jessamyn Jacobs used when she wrote *Between the Lines.* The original story is still in there."

"So what?" Edgar and Oliver speak simultaneously—and then look at each other.

"Oliver, *you* couldn't change the ending of the book. And Jessamyn Jacobs may not be *willing* to change the ending of the book." I wait for him to meet my gaze. "But I'm going to try."

PAGE 52

n the dungeon below Timble Tower, with rats running over his boots and bats screeching past his face in the dark, Oliver thought this was a rather ignominious way to end one's life story.

That is: failing in one's attempt to rescue a potential bride.

He felt sorry for Seraphima, but he felt even sorrier for himself.

He would never ride Socks again at breakneck speed across a meadow.

He'd never throw a stick for Frump to fetch.

He'd never rule a kingdom.

He'd never feel the rain on his face.

He'd never kiss his true love.

Think on the bright side, Oliver, he schooled himself. He'd never have to worry about going bald. He'd never have to suffer through another meal of liver and onions. He'd never get chicken pox.

He wouldn't have to feel that horrible little itch on the small of his back, which he couldn't reach because his hands were tied behind him.

Frustrated, he tried to inch his bound hands up toward the itch, but instead, he only managed to jostle his tunic.

Something clattered to the stone floor.

In the dim light, Oliver squinted. The shark's tooth that the mermaids had given him. He'd kept it, like a good-luck amulet, in his pocket. After all, it didn't have much use, unless you were a shark in need of dentures.

Or, perhaps, tied up in the dungeon of a tower.

Falling to his knees, Oliver fumbled for the tooth and managed to roll over it. With careful, small movements, he started to saw through the ropes that were binding him. It felt like it would take forever, and Seraphima didn't have forever. Any minute now, Rapscullio was going to take her as his own bride.

Oliver felt something scramble up his boot and then along his leg. One of the rats. The rodent, hearing some movement, had decided to get in on the action. Amazed, Oliver held still while the rat chewed through the rope enough for him to use his own strength to burst free.

The tower was too old to have formal cells, so Oliver only

had to hoist himself out of the dank, fetid pit where he'd been dumped. Silently, he climbed the circular stone stairs, listening for the sound of Rapscullio's voice. When he reached the tower room and poked his head inside, however, it was empty.

Or so he thought, until someone leaped onto his back from behind and started beating him around the ears.

In a cloud of tulle and taffeta, he wrestled Seraphima to the ground, pinning her by her wrists. "You're not Rapscullio!" she gasped.

He grinned. "Disappointed, are you?"

Seraphima shook her head and smiled. She was beautiful when she smiled. Then again, Oliver thought, she was beautiful when she didn't smile too. "I knew you'd come for me," she said.

Oliver stared down at her, suddenly convinced that he could slay a hundred men, if necessary. Was that all it took to be brave? Knowing that someone believed in you?

"I have a plan," Oliver whispered, pulling her to her feet. "But I need your dress to make it work."

OLIVER

I'M NOT SO SURE I AGREE WITH DELILAH.

In the first place, even if she manages to rewrite the story, that doesn't mean the fairy tale won't try to correct itself the way it's done a hundred times before.

Second, I feel a little uncomfortable watching Delilah sit at this computer box looking for the story in its contents. It's like sifting through someone's mind. Like stealing.

"I think this is a bad idea," I say out loud.

Delilah sighs. "Then tell me, Oliver—what are we supposed to do? We've tried everything else."

"I thought you told us that the author herself said you can't change a story once it's been told—"

JODI PICOULT & SAMANTHA VAN LEER

"Which is exactly why this makes sense," Delilah says. "We'll be the only ones with this edited version."

I can feel this Edgar character staring at me intently. Every now and then he jabs a finger up against my face, bending my world, still finding it hard to believe what's right before his eyes. *"Did you see that?"* he says. *"He moved, right?"*

Delilah swivels in her chair and, just like that, is out of my line of vision. "I can't see you," I holler, and she turns, exasperated.

"Edgar, can you prop up the book?" she asks.

I cling to the rock wall as Edgar tips me sideways, jabbing the points of a sagging letter *k* into my back before righting me again.

"Could we make this snappy?" he asks. "I kind of want to get back to my game."

I know Delilah has a computer too—she's mentioned this word to me before, and I've heard the faint clicking of her hands doing something computer-related, but I've never actually *seen* the instrument. There's a huge window with pictures floating on it, and it's attached by some sort of umbilical cord to what looks like an open book, with all the letters arranged in neat rows in a foreign language I cannot read.

Delilah's hands move over this odd book, and letters appear on the window, as if by magic. "That's amazing!" I cry out. "I must tell Orville about this!"

Delilah doesn't seem to hear me. "The file won't open. There's a password. It's five letters."

"E-D-G-A-R," I suggest.

Delilah types the word and hits another key. There is a high-pitched beep, but nothing changes on the big window in front of her.

"Can you think of anything else?" she asks Edgar. "Did you have a pet?"

"I'm allergic to everything but naked mole rats. . . ."

"How about your dad's name?" Delilah suggests.

Edgar looks down at the ground. "Isaac."

I watch Delilah's hands: I-S-A-A-C. Again, that high-pitched beep. Delilah bangs her fist on the computer table. "I can't believe we're this close," she murmurs. "Is there any other password you can think of, Edgar?"

He throws out suggestions: the street address of the house where his mother was born, the name of his mother's childhood pet, the title of her first published novel. But nothing works. With each failed attempt, I feel heavier and heavier, as if I am physically becoming part of the material of this book.

After a fruitless half hour, Delilah gets out of the chair and kneels down so that I can see her more clearly. "I'm sorry, Oliver," she whispers, her voice thick with disappointment. "I tried." She reaches her hand toward me, a five-fingered eclipse, and I raise my hand to hers.

But it's not like it was when she was inside the pages with me. Between our skin, once again, is the thinnest layer of paper.

Orville once told me that people never really touch. That's because we're all just a bunch of very tiny atoms surrounded by electromagnetic force. Even when we hold hands we're not holding hands. The only things coming into contact are the electrons caught between us.

It didn't make any sense to me at the time; it was more of Orville's scientific mumbo jumbo. But now . . . well, now I completely understand.

"So that's it?" Edgar interrupts my thoughts. "We just quit?"

"It was probably a stupid idea anyway," Delilah murmurs.

"But what about him?" Edgar jerks a thumb in my direction. "Everyone deserves a happy ending." He shakes his head. "I sound just like my mother. She used to say that to me every night before she tucked me in."

Delilah slowly turns, counting on her fingers. She slips into the chair again, and her hands fly over the letters in front of the computer. "Everyone," she repeats, and she types the letter E.

"Deserves." D.

"A Happy Ending." A-H-E.

And just like that, the window of the computer is

filled with hundreds of words—words I have lived a thousand times, every day of my life.

Delilah scrolls down and starts to speak. Before I can even realize what she is doing, Edgar flips through the pages of the book to find the part she is reading aloud.

Tumbling head over heels, I am slammed into the margins. A fairy crashes into me so quickly I cannot recognize her; just when I think I've caught a glimpse of her silver hair, all the breath is knocked out of me as Trogg the troll rolls like a cannonball and hits me square in the chest. "Places!" Frump shrieks, and Queen Maureen floats past me, the bell of her gown acting like a sail as we whip through a dozen pages to the final scene.

The sand is hot beneath my boots. Seraphima is wrapped in silk and lace and smug delight, clasping my hand. But for the first time, she's not looking at me. With a wistful expression, her gaze is following Frump as he waddles across the beach, the wedding ring tied to his collar. Socks waits and whinnies in the distance, with cans tied to his saddle and a big sash that reads JUST MARRIED fluttering out behind his hooves.

Delilah's voice narrates, as if on a loudspeaker, and like a puppet, I do as I'm told.

"On Everafter Beach, as far as the eye could see, the entire kingdom gathered to witness the wedding of Prince Oliver

and Princess Seraphima. Captain Crabbe and his mates had illuminated the beach with torches fueled by laughing gas and ignited with a gentle flame of Pyro's breath. The mermaids had crafted a long aisle of crushed pink shells; the trolls had built a gazebo of twisted willow fronds, which Orville had decorated with magical flowers that glowed from within, and that sang as the bride approached. The fairies carried Seraphima's silver train as she gazed up at the man she wanted to be with forever."

I can feel them bubbling up inside me, the same words I have said so many times before.

"Seraphima," I speak, my voice an echo of Delilah's, "everyone deserves a happy ending. Will you be mine?"

Hearing the sentence, I wonder why *I* didn't think of it as a password.

"Oh, Oliver," Seraphima replies. "Do you even have to ask?"

I may be the only one who notices the slight tremor in her voice. Could it be, finally, that she realizes there's more to us than just the story?

This is the part where she launches herself into my arms and slobbers all over me. I get the sense that perhaps for the first time, neither one of us wants to play the parts we must. I close my eyes and stiffen my spine, bracing myself for what's to come, but instead, I feel a magnetic pull on my foot, tugging me backward, as if I have absolutely no choice but to take a step away from Seraphima.

"Oliver," Delilah says aloud as she types, *"suddenly wrenches away from his would-be bride."* She glances over her shoulder at me. "How's that?" she asks.

My mouth fills with the sharp edges of words that poke into my tongue and force me to spit them out. "I can't marry you," I say, hearing Delilah speak the same sentence simultaneously. "I'm being sent to start my own story, in a different world, with Delilah Eve McPhee."

Seraphima blinks at me, her eyes bugging out. She looks hopeful, and scared, and confused, but she knows better than to question the plot when the book is wide open and there's a Reader involved. I can see, from the corner of my eye, everyone else shifting uncomfortably. After all, this isn't the fairy tale they know.

There is a tingle in my right hand. At first I think Seraphima has succeeded in cutting off my circulation, but then I realize my flesh is fading, flickering in and out like a flame, until in an instant, it's gone.

"Your arm!" Seraphima gasps, breaking the rules. Or so I think, until I realize that Delilah has said it too. I glance out of the book and see a disembodied wrist and hand floating in the space between Edgar and Delilah.

"I think it's working," Edgar whispers.

I'm feeling light-headed, and finding it hard to breathe. When I look down, there is a quivering in the fabric of my tunic, and suddenly, it begins to unravel and vanish before my eyes.

"Oliver," Delilah says, "your tunic. It's weaving itself together in front of us!"

My heart is pounding so hard I am certain that everyone on the beach can hear it, and possibly Delilah and Edgar too. Could this really be working? Could I be this close to being free?

I look at Frump, who stares at me with a mix of betrayal and fear on his furry little face. I can't speak to him—I haven't been given the words—but I silently mouth a message. *Goodbye, friend.* I close my eyes, and hope for the best.

"Edgar?" An unfamiliar voice floats over the beach. "What are you two reading?"

My world reels and then rights itself. Delilah's grabbed the book and has propped me against the computer screen. Now I can still peer into the room, but my perspective is from a different angle. Edgar has stepped forward so that the translucent phantom limbs that are knitting themselves together again are blocked by his own body—so that as Jessamyn Jacobs enters, she cannot see what's happening.

"That old fairy tale," Edgar says, his voice too high. How can she not guess that he's lying? "I forgot how it ends."

"Happily ever after, of course," Jessamyn says.

"Right." Delilah smiles brightly. "Of course."

All of sudden, I can feel the blood rushing back to my chest and my arm. It's like they are on fire, like I am about to burst out of my skin. Groaning, I fall to my knees on the sand, crippled by pain.

"I just came to say good night. Delilah, do you need anything?"

"I'm fine. . . ." She smiles. "Thanks. For everything."

Although I am kneeling now, I feel myself being dragged closer to Seraphima again. Yanked upward by some kind of reverse, perverse antigravity. My hand smacks against hers, glues itself tight in a clasp.

I know what's happening. Just like every other attempt to release me from the book, this one has failed. The story always wins.

Jessamyn comes closer, another Reader. I watch her peer down at the page. "I used to love this final scene. . . ."

Edgar grabs the book, making my head spin. "Whatever," he says, and he slams the cover shut, so that I collapse to the ground.

There is an immediate buzz as the other characters discuss the odd incident that has just unfolded before their eyes. Seraphima bursts into tears, covers her face with her hands, and runs off the beach. Orville rushes toward me, feeling the length of my arm. "My boy," he says, "what sort of black magic was that?"

"I'm fine," I tell him, and then I address the others. "It was a freak accident or something. Everything's back to normal."

At my reassurance, the little group begins to disband, still talking about what they've witnessed. Only Frump remains, sitting beside me. "Ollie," he says, "we've been friends too long for you to lie to me."

I scuff my boot in the sand. This is how it all began, with a chessboard we'd drawn between us. "I want out, Frump," I admit. "I don't belong here any more than you belong in the body of a hound."

"But that's not for us to decide," Frump says.

"How come I'm the only one who gets the happy ending?" I say. "Didn't that ever seem wrong to you?"

"I guess I just assumed you were the lucky one."

"We could all be lucky," I say. "We could all be who we want to be, instead of who someone else told us to be."

Frump shakes his head. "You're making things up, Ollie."

"Isn't that how we all got here in the first place?" I say gently.

Frump's eyes light up as he imagines the possibility of a future different from the one he expected. And then he remembers what happened to me minutes ago. "You were trying to leave," he states slowly, understanding.

"Yes. I can't stay here."

Frump sits a little taller. "Then I'll go with you."

I nod my chin toward the distance, where Seraphima is sitting on a rock near the edge of the sea, still delicately wiping away her tears. "That's not really what you want, is it?" I smile faintly at him. "If I get out of here, you have my word: I will do everything in my power to make sure you're a human again."

He scratches behind his ear, lost in thought. "Ollie? Could I ask you for something else? If you do get out of here . . . could you make . . . her . . . notice me?"

"I think she already *has*," I say, elbowing him gently. "Go on."

He shuffles down the beach to the rock where Seraphima is sitting. Absently, the princess begins to pat him on the head. Frump glances back at me, just once, his tail wagging.

I raise my right arm, a wave goodbye. My right arm, which is just where it always has been and always will be — drawn attached to me, on a page I may never escape.

Delilah

THE MINUTE HIS MOTHER LEAVES, EDGAR turns to me. "This," he says, wide-eyed, "is *wicked awesome*!"

I immediately sit down at the computer, furiously typing THE NEW END to the altered fairy tale that will allow Oliver out of the story—but the cursor leaps upward and begins to erase the words I've already written. The word NEW is the last to go, leaving THE END just the way it used to be.

"No." I gasp, and I turn around to confirm my suspicions: Oliver's body, which has been gradually appearing before our eyes, has vanished.

"Where did he go?" Edgar asks, looking underneath the bed and in the closet.

I don't know why I can't make the simple changes on the computer. Maybe it's a strange firewall the author installed for protection; maybe it's just some crazy virus. But this is a physical manifestation of what Jessamyn Jacobs told me: this particular story lives in the minds of its readers. It can't be altered, because it already exists in its original form.

It is just like the time Oliver tried to rewrite the ending of the book from within its confines, just like the time he summoned me into the pages. If something isn't part of the original version of the story, the change can't sustain itself. Once you call something a story, it's set in stone. It has a beginning, a middle, and an end that can't be transformed, because by definition, if you do that, it's not the same story anymore.

"It's happened before," I explain to Edgar. "It's like the story has a mind of its own."

He thinks for a moment. "How good a writer are you?"

"Why?"

"Because I have an idea." He sits down on the bed, placing his hand on the cover of the book. "You can't change a story once it's been told. But what if you create a new story?"

"I don't understand."

Edgar leans forward, excited. "Right now, Oliver is the only one who wants to change the plot. Imagine if all the characters inside that book are given a whole new play to perform. If they *all* buy into it, maybe the story will allow the change."

I grab the book and open it to page 43. Oliver—white-faced and exhausted—stares up at me from the rock ledge. "You're all right," I whisper.

"I'm what I always am," he mutters. "That's the problem."

"Edgar has an idea." I explain the concept to Oliver.

"I don't see why this is any different," he says when I finish. "I'm still a character in the story."

"But at the end of the new story, you leave," I tell him, "and all the characters are expecting it to happen."

Oliver sighs. "At this point, I suppose I'm willing to try anything."

I sit at the computer, because I'm the faster typist. I look at Edgar. "So," I say. "How does it start?"

We all get quiet. As it turns out, it's a lot harder than any of us imagined to create something from nothing.

"How about a dog that meets a cat and falls in love even though their families are against it?" Oliver suggests.

"Okay, Romeo," I reply. "Would you like to come out of the book as a poodle or a pit bull?"

Oliver shakes his head.

"No, I've got one." Edgar's eyes gleam. "It's a dark and stormy night, and a zombie ax murderer is on the loose—"

"You really *are* your mother's son," I murmur.

Edgar shrugs. "Well, I don't see *you* suggesting anything."

And then, all of a sudden, it comes to me. "There's this prince," I say. "And he's stuck in a fairy tale. Until a girl on the outside can hear him."

Bending toward the keyboard, I begin to type.

apscullio's footsteps thundered up the stone stairs of the tower. As he strode inside the room, a wind blew through the wide arched window. Beside it, Seraphima stood with her back to him, staring out at the ocean below.

"The pensive bride," Rapscullio said drily, coming closer. "If you're thinking of jumping . . . don't."

She didn't respond, just continued to stare at the crashing waves.

Rapscullio put his hands on her shoulders, squeezing. She shuddered. His breath was at her neck. "You *will* learn to love me," he commanded.

Seraphima turned in Rapscullio's embrace. He lifted the veil that obscured her features.

But it wasn't her face at all. "Don't count on it," Oliver said, and he rammed his head into Rapscullio's belly, knocking him backward.

The villain drew his sword. "What did you do with her?"

"She's safe," Oliver said. "And she's mine."

"That's where you're wrong, Your Highness. This is just payback, and it's been a long time coming."

Oliver stared at the pitted scars on Rapscullio's face. He had never met this man before; how could Rapscullio possibly hold a grudge against him?

"I won't let you get away with this," Oliver said.

Rapscullio's lips twisted in a mockery of a smile. "Why, that's exactly what Maurice said, just before I released the dragon on him. Like father, like son."

Oliver fell back a step. "You . . . you knew my father?"

"Correction," Rapscullio said. "I *killed* your father."

Suddenly Oliver's vision swam in a red tide. He couldn't think, he could only feel. He understood, in that crystalline instant, that courage wasn't something you were bequeathed at birth, and it wasn't a lack of fright. It was overcoming your fear, because the ones you love mattered more.

He drove forward, moving with pure adrenaline, and threw himself at the villain.

The skirts of Seraphima's gown were suddenly a hindrance to his speed and agility; what had seemed like a fantastic plan to trap Rapscullio suddenly wasn't so splendid anymore. Rapscullio swung his sword, cutting through the layers of tulle and nicking Oliver's shoulder. "Your father took from me the one I loved most in this world," he panted. "So now I'll return the favor."

Oliver dodged the next blow. The sword struck the wall, sending sparks flying. He rolled, tangling in this unfamiliar dress, and then tripped Rapscullio so that he fell facedown on the stone floor. Rapscullio grabbed Oliver's boot and pulled him down.

Oliver wrapped the veil around Rapscullio's wrist, trying to draw his sword arm back so that the weapon would fall. But in a match of sheer strength, Rapscullio had the upper hand. He slammed Oliver's elbow against the floor, forcing his release.

Free again, Rapscullio swung at Oliver, landing blows to his face and chest. Oliver rolled away, dazed and reeling, and staggered to his feet. It was enough of a pause for Rapscullio to leap up and point his sword at the prince's neck. "So, boy," he said, sneering. "Now what?"

Oliver took one tiny step back. The sword point bit into his neck, drawing blood. Rapscullio forced Oliver to take another step in retreat, and another, approaching the wall. In a moment, Oliver would have nowhere left to go.

Promise me you won't fight, his mother had said. *Anyone or anything.*

It was one thing to outsmart a dragon or trick a troll, to bargain with a pirate captain or compromise with mermaids . . . but how could he win a sword battle, when he didn't even carry a sword?

Rapscullio drew back his blade, his eyes wild. "Goodbye, Prince Oliver." He lunged forward, intent on driving his sword through Oliver's heart.

Call it coward's instinct, call it brilliant, call it whatever you like: Oliver ducked.

With no body to plunge his sword into, and an open window in front of him, Rapscullio fell forward, scrabbling for a moment on the slick granite of the sill before falling out.

Oliver sank to his knees, gasping. But before he could even feel relief, he sensed a tug on the skirt of Seraphima's wedding gown and realized that the last thing Rapscullio had grabbed on to for purchase was his clothing. Oliver found himself tumbling out the window too, hurtling down a sixty-foot drop to the jagged rocks below.

OLIVER

MY ARM IS ACHING. AS DELILAH HAS BEEN TYPING, I've written the entire story by hand with a small lump of coal on the rock wall, committing it to memory. Not that this is very difficult. After all, I've been living it.

When at last we're finished, Delilah leans in to the page. "Good luck," she whispers. "See you on the outside."

We've talked about it, and I know I'm on my own for this part: she has to stop reading the book and close it, so that I can gather all the characters together and tell them the new story. I see the sky spread and darken as Delilah shuts the cover. Then I take a deep breath and run a finger along the sentences I've scratched into the rock.

I climb down from the ledge on page 43 and start

hopping the gaps between the edges of the pages, crossing through the Enchanted Forest and the unicorn meadow. I will find Frump and ask him for his help. He's the only one who can rally the masses as quickly as I need it to be done, and I know I can count on him for his support.

But first, there's one more person I need to see. I find Queen Maureen in the rose garden behind the castle, pruning her beloved bushes. For a moment I hang back, watching the way she gently lifts the heavy head of a rose and strokes the petals. She was never really my mother, but she was the closest thing I had to one, and I'll miss that tenderness that comes so easily to her.

Taking a deep breath—it's now or never—I untuck my shirt, let it hang from beneath my tunic, and muss up my hair. Then I stumble into the queen's line of sight.

"Oliver?" she says. "What happened to you?"

I collapse in front of her, pretending to catch my breath. "The Creator," I gasp. "The one who made our world? She summoned me."

Her eyes widen. "She summoned you?"

"Yes."

"Goodness."

"I know."

She hesitates. "Is that why you started to disappear on the beach?"

"Exactly," I say. "She sent me back here with a message for everyone in the kingdom. Apparently the story we've been living—it's not the *real* story. Just part of a larger one."

"I'm not sure I understand," Queen Maureen says.

"I have to leave," I tell her.

"But you just got here!"

"No—I mean, I have to leave the *book*. It's the way the ending goes, in the bigger story."

She thinks about this. "But you'll come back again, every time the book is opened?"

God, I hope not. Did Delilah even *consider* that? "It's complicated. I'm going to explain it to everyone, on the beach. Frump is going to round them up for me."

"Then why did you come to talk to me privately?"

"Because," I confess, "you're one of the people I'm going to miss the most."

Her eyes shine with tears, and she opens her arms so that I can step into her embrace. I hold her tight, finding it hard to imagine that this might be the last time I ever do so.

Queen Maureen pulls back a little bit and looks me in the eye. "If I'd ever had a real son, Oliver," she says, "I would have wanted him to be just like you."

* * *

As we walk toward Everafter Beach, we are joined by others responding to Frump's call: the flitting fairies, who buzz in my ears, filling my head with questions; the trolls, stomping with each footstep. Rapscullio comes out of his lair with a piece of embroidery in hand; Seraphima is still wearing a robe and slippers.

The last to arrive are the mermaids, who swim up to the shore and lie in the shallows with their hair floating out behind them like colored capes. "Why the big rush, Frump?" Marina asks.

Beside the sailors, Pyro is blowing smoke rings that Orville waves away from his face.

"Ladies and gentlemen," Frump announces. "And mythical creatures. I've called you here at the request of Prince Oliver, who has a very important announcement to make." He wags his tail, turning the floor over to me. "Good luck, Ollie," he says quietly, for my ears alone.

I stand up, suddenly nervous. "Perhaps you all were a bit confused by what happened the last time the book was opened," I begin.

"Ye started disappearin'!" Captain Crabbe says. "We all noticed!"

"Yes, well, it was sort of a surprise to me too," I lie. "I was being pulled into the Otherworld."

A collective gasp rises from the crowd. "You mean," Sparks says, "the *audience*?"

"Even more important," I reply. "The Creator. The person who dreamed up the world we live in."

"Is it a man or a woman?" Ondine asks.

"A woman," I reply.

She smirks at her sisters. "Told you so."

"Is she beautiful? I bet she's beautiful," Ember says with a sigh.

I think of Jessamyn Jacobs. "I didn't really notice. I was too busy memorizing the new script." I pause for dramatic effect. "The one I'm supposed to tell to all of you."

"I don't understand," Biggle mutters. "We have new lines to memorize?"

"Well, only to some extent." I look over the crowd. "It turns out that our whole story has been a piece of a larger one. The *real* story is about a prince in a fairy tale—"

"That's you!" Seraphima gasps.

I force a smile. "Good guess! As I was saying—a prince in a fairy tale who is trying to escape."

"From the kingdom?" Scuttle says, scratching his head. "I'm not sure I understand. . . ."

"No, from the book. Into the Otherworld."

"But that's impossible," Orville insists. "*This* is the only world that was given to us."

"Yet we all agree that someone, somewhere else,

was living in a totally different place and time when she wrote this world for us to inhabit, right?" I say. "After all, we've never met her, and yet we're all here. That proves that there *always* has been a second world. It's where everyone who reads the book is, while they're reading."

I watch the crowd as they process this theory. Frump, assessing their reactions, interrupts the uneasy quiet. "I say that we let Oliver tell us the new story!"

Others nod. Even those who are still reluctant to believe that they haven't known the whole truth all along are drawn in by the power of words, by the thought that there's a new tale to be told. "I second the motion," Queen Maureen says.

With everyone's eyes upon me, waiting to hear their future, I start to speak. "Just so you know," I begin, "when they say 'Once upon a time' . . . they're lying. It's not once upon a time. It's not even twice upon a time. It's hundreds of times, over and over, every time someone opens up the pages of this dusty old book."

When I am done, there is absolute silence.

And then, everyone starts clapping. "Bravo!" Frump howls. *"Bravo!"*

Even the mermaids look a bit teary. "I guess not *all* men are squids," Kyrie murmurs.

Seraphima stares down at the sand between her

feet, puzzled. "So, the whole time, I've actually been fall-ing for Frump?"

I nod. "But you were too afraid to show it, because you didn't want to hurt Prince Oliver's feelings."

Seraphima smiles brightly and reaches out to pull Frump onto her lap. "I think I knew it all along," she says shyly.

"Are there any other questions?" I ask.

Socks paws at the ground with his hoof to get my attention.

"Yes, Socks?"

"Oliver, when you said I was a mighty steed in this new version—does that mean I'm maybe a little thinner?"

"You're the best-looking horse in the kingdom," I say. "You're the horse all other horses aspire to become."

He whinnies and tosses his mane, delighted.

Pyro raises one stubby arm. "I'm just not clear. . . . What's my *motivation?*"

"You want to channel all the pain and rage you've felt from being misunderstood as a destructive beast, and pour that into your performance," I suggest.

The dragon hiccups. "I can work with that."

"Great!" I clap my hands together. "So if we're all set, why don't we go off and practice so that we're ready the minute the book opens again—"

"Just a moment." Rapscullio stands up, tall and foreboding, his black hair falling over his forehead and casting a shadow on his scar. "What happens to *you*, Oliver?"

I grin. "Well, I guess I leave the book, and live happily ever after."

"But are you only the same size in the Otherworld that you are in this one?" Ember asks. "Then you'd be as tiny as a fairy."

"Are you going to look like they do, or are you going to be flat?" Walleye chimes in.

My stomach turns. Actually, I don't know the answers. I won't until we see whether or not this works. "I suppose it's all a mystery," I reply. "I'll let you know when I get there."

There's a soft whine, and I turn to see Frump clearing his throat. "Can we visit?" he asks quietly.

I meet my best friend's gaze. I can't imagine not seeing him again. "I'm not sure," I say honestly. He ducks his snout, disappointed, and I step forward to rub him between the ears and comfort him, but before I do, Seraphima reaches out and strokes his back. This much I know: Frump will be in good hands.

Suddenly the sand begins to spit and swirl as the edges of the beach curl upward. "Places!" Frump barks. "Everybody!"

I fall page after page, coming to an abrupt halt against the stone floor of the castle. I lift my head in time to see Queen Maureen smack into her throne so hard her crown goes flying. Frump catches it in his teeth like a Frisbee. "Your Majesty," he says, returning it.

The story starts like it always does, with me telling my mother I am headed off to find my true love. The difference is that this time, my true love isn't waiting for me on Everafter Beach. She's much farther away. "Wish me luck," I murmur under my breath, hoping that Delilah is listening, and I speak my lines.

For the next hour, I go through the pages: being attacked by the fairies, falling into the ocean to be captured by the mermaids, tricking the trolls. I get kidnapped by Captain Crabbe, battle Pyro, and visit Orville to find Seraphima's location. The other characters do their part as well. I am particularly impressed by Socks, who suddenly presents himself as a stamping, snorting white stallion. It's as if confidence alone has made him grow a foot in height. From the corner of my eye, I watch Seraphima giving longing looks to Frump after every one of our scenes together.

At one point, just like always, I scale the rock wall— but here, I pause and give a speech.

While she was writing the new story, Delilah realized she still needed a spot where I was alone, so that she could always find me on a certain page if necessary.

But now, instead of climbing the rock wall on page 43, I talk about Delilah. About this girl who, against all odds, noticed that I am real.

And then, before I know it, we are all gathered again for the final illustration on Everafter Beach. Here I am with Frump by my side, a wedding ring tied to his collar. Here's Seraphima, walking down the crushed shell aisle. But this time, I don't kiss the bride.

"I object," I say, my new line.

Captain Crabbe, who is officiating at the wedding, looks up. "I don't think you can object to your own wedding, son."

"But you can if it's not true love," I reply.

"I object too," Seraphima announces. "I'm in love with someone else." She looks down at Frump. "Some-*thing* else."

She leans down and plants a kiss on Frump's slightly damp snout.

There is a shower of sparks, and before our eyes, Frump transforms into a human again. A clothed one, this time. When Delilah wrote the scene, I made sure of it.

Frump feels his arms and his legs, and tosses me the widest of smiles. "True love," he says, "can break the most powerful curse."

The fact that Frump has morphed means that the

book is allowing some of the changes we've made. I can only hope it's a sign of what's left to come. This is our loophole: we're not changing the story, we're adding to it. There's nothing to be fixed, only more to be done by its characters.

I take Seraphima's hand and carefully place it in Frump's. "I wouldn't want you to miss out on a lifetime of love any more than you'd want me to miss out on the same," I tell her. "Everyone deserves a happy ending . . . and mine is somewhere outside these pages."

I've read Delilah's final paragraph a dozen times; I know it by heart. So I start moving. One foot in front of the other, down the beach, along the edge of the water. The mermaids wave, but I don't look back at them. I'm afraid if I do, I'll already start missing everyone I have to leave behind.

I am approaching the edge of the illustration, the part where the colors bleed to white space. Taking a deep breath, I jump.

And smack my face into something hard, stiff, unyielding.

For a moment, all I can see are silver stars, and white space.

I feel something licking my face and look up to find Frump, reverted once again to dog form. Then

Seraphima's voice floats over me. "Oliver?" she says. "Maybe this book doesn't want to let you go."

We are on page 43. Well, we're on different sides of it, anyway. Delilah has propped the book up against her pillow, and we are speaking through the darkness.

Once it became clear that our latest plan wasn't going to work either, Delilah politely said good night to Edgar and carried the book into the guest room. She managed to keep herself from crying until we were alone, but she hasn't stopped since.

"It's okay," I try to tell her, lying. "It's not so bad."

"You hate it there," she sobs. "And I can't stand it here without you."

I reach up to her, trying to remember what it felt like when I was holding her hand, walking down the roads of this kingdom. "I'm here whenever you need me," I say. "I think it's pretty clear I'm not going anywhere."

It turns out that there's something even harder than not being able to be with the person you love when you're happy: not being able to comfort her when she's sad. "Delilah Eve McPhee," I say, "even if I never leave these pages . . . I would do this a thousand times over again, just to have the chance to meet you."

"Oh, Oliver," she whispers. "I love you too."

* * *

Delilah falls asleep with the book open, which means I can watch her. You may think there's nothing very interesting about seeing someone sleep, but that probably means you've never found the girl of your dreams. With each breath, she stirs a lock of hair that's fallen in front of her face. Sometimes she clutches the pillow and sighs.

Now that I know I can't be with her forever, I don't want to waste the minutes I've got. For this reason, I haven't closed my own eyes to get a good night's rest. I'm afraid that if I do, she might disappear.

That's why I'm awake when the door to the bedroom where Delilah is staying creaks open. Immediately I leap upright, clinging to the rock wall the way I'm supposed to on page 43 when the book is wide open. But the face that peers down at me is one I recognize. "Shhh," Edgar says, and he carefully lifts the fairy tale from Delilah's loose grasp.

I start to panic. What if he's come to destroy the story? He never really liked it, by his own admission. What if he's jealous and wants Delilah to himself? What if he's sleepwalking and throws me out with the rubbish?

But instead, Edgar brings me into his own bedroom and closes the door. He sits down on the bed and bends his knees, resting the book along the slope of his legs so that I can see him while he speaks to me. "I know why it didn't work," he says. "You can't take a character out of a story. Every time the book gets opened again, he's right back where he started. What you need—what the *story* needs—isn't an escape but a twist at the end."

I shake my head. "I don't see the point, if it means I'm still stuck here—"

"But what if it wasn't you?" Edgar says. "What if you told the *wrong* story? What if, at the end, everyone finds out that you were an impostor all along?"

"Not a prince?" I ask.

"Not even Oliver," he says. "Just someone who looks, well, remarkably similar."

I am stunned into silence for a moment. "You would do that? For us?"

"No, but I'd do it for me," Edgar says. "You don't realize how much alike we actually are. We're both stuck in worlds we don't really fit into. We both lost our dads. We both wish we could be someone we're not. I'd trade places with you in a heartbeat."

But if I have learned anything, it's that saying goodbye to the people you love isn't easy. And when I wrote Delilah into the book, she was desperate to come home to her mother. I haven't had one myself, but if I did, I can't imagine leaving her behind forever. "What about your mom?" I ask him.

"She created everyone in there. She'd be all around me. Besides, she always wanted a son like you.

And after all, if I can hear *you* in there, you'll most likely be able to hear *me.* If I want out, I'll find a way to let you know." He shrugs. "What have you got to lose, Oliver? For once, you get the right girl, and for once, I get to be a hero."

He lifts a stack of papers I haven't noticed before. Only now do I see how red his eyes are, how tired Edgar seems to be. Whatever he's been doing, he's been up all night. "I'm not much of a writer," he says, "but this is a story I could live with."

I wish I could shake his hand. I wish I could thank him properly. This may not work, but it's certainly worth a try. Lifting my face, I nod at Edgar. "Well then," I say. "Let's hear it."

Delilah

WHEN I WAKE UP, I HAVE NO IDEA WHERE I AM.

The sheets aren't the ones on my bed at home; the walls of this room are painted a different color. I can't hear my mother singing off-key as she fries bacon downstairs in the kitchen.

Then it all comes rushing back to me.

Running away from home.

Being grounded till I die.

Jessamyn Jacobs.

Edgar.

The revised story.

Failure feels like a punch. All I have to look forward to today is four hours of *What the heck were you thinking?*

from my mother during a long, painful car ride back home, and the knowledge that I finally found someone who understands who I am and likes me for it—only to realize that he's a figment of my imagination.

I pull the covers over my head, wishing I didn't have to wake up. At least in my dreams I can be with Oliver.

Oliver.

I feel around under the pillows, but the book is missing. Jumping out of bed, I look beneath its frame, and on the dresser. I rip the blankets and sheets off. I know I fell asleep with the fairy tale in my arms last night. I just know it.

"Where *is* it?" I mutter, and at that moment there is a knock at the door.

It swings open, and Edgar is standing on the threshold, book in hand. "Looking for this?" he asks, grinning.

"Yes!" I grab it out of his hands, angry. "You shouldn't steal other people's property."

"Well, it's not technically yours, is it? You stole it from your school library."

"I'm the only person who ever checked this book out of—" I break off, my eyes narrowing. "How do *you* know that?"

"Because I listen," Edgar says, coming closer. He takes the book from me and sets it on the bed, then holds my hands. "I listen to everything you say, Delilah."

He's staring at me as if he can see right inside me,

and that's creepy, because this is Edgar, after all—Edgar, who locks himself in his room to play video games all day. Except his eyes are different. I can't really describe it, but they look softer around the edges. Wiser. And maybe, a little amazed.

"Delilah," he whispers. "It's *me.*"

"Of course it's you, Edgar. Who else would it be?"

"Oliver. It *worked*, Delilah. It actually worked." He smiles, and for a moment, I almost believe him. The way his mouth tips up on one side. The way his voice has the gentlest hint of a British accent.

But it *didn't* work. I saw that with my own eyes. I take a step backward, shaking my head.

"I can prove it," Edgar says, and he picks up the book. Pinching one page with two fingers, he slides his palm across the sharp edge, giving himself an inch-long paper cut.

"Stop that!" I grab his hand, but it's too late. The book drops to the bed again, closed, as I turn his palm over to see how deep the cut is.

He's bleeding, but the blood isn't red.

It's black as ink.

urtling toward the churning seas, Prince Oliver closed his eyes and prepared to die. The wind and the spray lashed his cheeks; the shreds of Seraphima's gown flew behind him like a banner. He heard Rapscullio's scream, and knew that his own moment of impact was seconds away.

As he fell, the chain around his neck worked its way free, floating delicately upward, over his head. His father's compass. Oliver reached out, wrapping his fingers tightly around the small disk, hoping for just an ounce or two of his father's legendary bravery at this moment.

The brass hinge popped open, and the needle of the compass spun wildly. With his last breath on Earth, Oliver thought of home.

The world was suddenly blindingly white. Oliver winced as his vision slowly came back.

He was not falling anymore. He was not broken into pieces across the jagged rocks in the pounding surf. Instead, he was whole and safe and wrapped in Seraphima's arms.

At that moment Oliver realized that home is not a place, but rather, the people who love you.

Which means, of course, that Prince Oliver and the girl he adored lived happily ever after.

OLIVER

I CAN TELL THE MOMENT SHE BELIEVES ME. HER whole face changes, like the sky after a storm, open to possibility. "But Edgar . . . ?" she says.

"It was his idea," I tell her. This time, *I'm* the one opening the book. It feels odd, as if I've suddenly been granted a phenomenal amount of power.

The story falls open to the illustration on the final page. All the characters are gathered on Everafter Beach, but there are some significant changes. For example, Seraphima is wearing a form-fitting suit of galactic armor. Frump—now human—is wielding a laser beam. And standing in the middle of the fray is someone who looks a great deal like Prince Oliver, holding a sword in one hand and the severed head of the mighty Zorg in the other.

"How fortunate they were to have learned that the intruder in their midst had never really been a royal prince at all—but actually, a seasoned soldier from the future," Delilah reads out loud. *"Once the last Galactoid from Planet Zugon was dispatched by the guerrilla fighters of the kingdom, Edgar swung his blade and with one mighty blow brought down the monstrous Zorg. 'Victory!' he cried."*

I am pretty sure that both Delilah and I see Edgar wink at us.

Gently, I close the book, imagining Frump yelling "Cut!" and everyone grinning and congratulating each other on a job well done.

"Funny," she says, "that's not quite how I remember the story."

"Oh really?" I clasp my hands behind her back and draw her closer. "How *do* you remember it?"

"Something like this," Delilah says, and she reaches up on her tiptoes and kisses me.

She's right. This is exactly the way the fairy tale was supposed to go. Except this time, when I glance up, I don't see the words THE END written above my head.

I guess that's because it's just the beginning.

Acknowledgments

Just like it takes a cast of characters behind the scenes to bring a fairy tale to life every time a reader opens a book, there are a vast number of people who helped us create our story as well. We'd like to thank all the people at Emily Bestler Books and Simon Pulse who got just as excited about *Between the Lines* as we were: Kate Cetrulo, Caroline Porter, Judith Curr, Carolyn Reidy, David Brown, Ariele Fredman, Mellony Torres, Jon Anderson, Bethany Buck, Mara Anastas, Michael Strother, Lucille Rettino, Sooji Kim, Carolyn Swerdloff, Dawn Ryan, Lauren Forte, Jessica Handelman, Mike Rosamilia, Russell Gordon, Julie Doebler, Paul Crichton, Nicole Russo, Michelle Fadlalla, Laura Antonacci, and Venessa Williams. Thanks also to Camille McDuffie and Kathleen Carter Zrelak for their assistance in spreading the word!

Special thanks go to Emily Bestler and Jen Klonsky, for helping us define our imaginary world better, and for agreeing when we wanted to create a final product that was a little "out of the box" for a normal YA novel. In this ever-changing world of electronic books, we wanted to create a story that was a keepsake—one you'd pass down to your children because of its beauty and design—much like the fairy tale in the story is to Delilah. Just like those gorgeous picture books from the turn of the century with colored plates by Arthur Rackham, we wanted a novel that took one's breath away. Thanks to the spirited support of Emily and Jen, we got exactly that.

Which is why we also must thank Yvonne Gilbert, who

brought our handsome prince to life, and Scott M. Fischer, whose silhouettes still astound us. Quite simply, you blew us away with your vision and your passion for this project.

Thanks, too, to Laura Gross, who encouraged us to take Sammy's idea and run with it; and to Tim van Leer and Jane Picoult, who read the early drafts and laughed in all the right places.

Finally, thanks to all the readers of Jodi's books, who have asked her for years for a story they could use to introduce her writing to their children—some of whom were too young to address the issues in her adult novels. We hope they enjoy sharing this with their kids as much as we enjoyed working together to create it.